Buffalo

Mountain

The Urbana Free Library

To renew materials call
217-367-4057

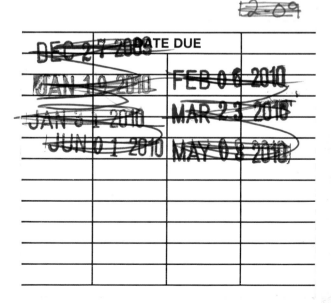

Books by Frederick Ramsay

Ike Schwartz Series
Artscape
Secrets
Buffalo Mountain
Stranger Room

Other Works
Impulse
Judas: The Gospel of Betrayal

PO-51

Buffalo
Mountain

Frederick Ramsay

Poisoned Pen Press

12-09
15-

Poisoned
Pen
Press

Copyright © 2007 by Frederick Ramsay

First Trade Paperback Edition 2008

10 9 8 7 6 5 4 3 2 1

Library of Congress Catalog Card Number: 2006934089

ISBN: 978-1-59058-537-5   Trade Paperback

Poisoned Pen Press
6962 E. First Ave., Ste. 103
Scottsdale, AZ 85251
www.poisonedpenpress.com
info@poisonedpenpress.com

Printed in the United States of America

To Q. D. Thompson,
who helped me through the sixth grade and
later, much later, introduced me to
Buffalo Mountain

Acknowledgments

First, an apology of sorts: To the people of Floyd County, Virginia, and the towns of Floyd and Willis. As you read this book, you may not recognize your surroundings at all. Put it down to a Damyankee invading your space and inventing things just to tell a story. You live in a singularly beautiful part of the Shenandoah Valley and everyone who visits it envies you.

Then, thanks to my colleagues at The Southern California Writers Conference for the constant encouragement this old man requires. To my critique group, David, John, Misty and Bridgett, who keep finding ways to improve my writing.

To my publisher, Robert Rosenwald, my editor, Barbara Peters, and all my friends at Poisoned Pen Press and the Poisoned Pen bookstore who permit this to go on. And last, but certainly not least, to my wife, Susan, my home editor, chief critic, and mainstay in this peculiar business.

Chapter One

The body lay face up, halfway in the town's corporate limits, halfway in the state park. Dead eyes stared heavenward at a wintry sky. Deputy Sheriff Whaite Billingsly studied it for a moment and called in.

"Ike, I can shove him six feet west and let the state boys have him, or we can keep him. What do you think?"

Thursday afternoon and a snowy weekend approaching, Ike Schwartz, Picketsville's chief law enforcement officer, sighed. "Lord knows, it's tempting. But no, I reckon it'd better be us. Where are you exactly?"

"Out on the Covington Road—west at the town line. Funny thing about this guy—"

"What's that?"

"He looks familiar."

◇◇◇

Ike peered through the park's barren trees and caught sight of Whaite twenty or thirty yards in. He shivered and looked skyward. Dull late November clouds piled up in the southwest and sent ragged streamers across the valley. The temperature had dropped five degrees since noon. His nose began to run but he could still smell snow on the way. He shivered again as a gust of cold air blustered down through tree limbs and made billows of brightly colored leaves swirl this way and that.

The shiver had less to do with the cold than with thoughts of automobiles skidding on roads and extra duty for his deputies. Picketsville did not handle snow well. Usually an inch or two fell, melted, and then the temperature would drop back below freezing, turning the roads into skating rinks. County trucks spreading a combination of salt and cinders provided the only relief. Picketsville didn't rank high enough on the County's priority list to get any attention until a half dozen cars, trucks, and, sometimes, farm tractors ended up in ditches, upside down or worse. A real snow—six inches or more—would create a major traffic disaster and shut down the town for days. And the Sheriff's Department, his department, would be the one to sort it all out.

He retrieved a roll of yellow crime scene tape from the trunk of his cruiser, wrapped one end around a sign post, and walked it toward the area he assumed held the body. His breath left a steamy trail as he struggled up the embankment.

"How do, Ike, bit frosty today. The body's over there." Whaite tilted his head toward a shallow swale at the foot of a tree stump. "I came up here on the rise so you'd be sure to see me."

"Appreciate that."

"Town line runs down to the sign there and over there's a survey marker." Whaite pointed toward a concrete marker. "So if I run a line between the two, I make it he's laying about half in Craddock's Woods and half in the park.

"Somebody cut it kind of fine if the idea was to give him to us and not the state."

"Or the other way around."

"Or the other way round."

A congregation of black birds, grackles, and starlings, flocked up for winter, rose like a plume of smoke from black, skeletal tree limbs, circled, and following some inherent aerial choreography, swooped, climbed, and drifted south in a cacophony of avian complaints.

"You're driving your Circus Wagon today? Where's the truck?" Whaite, when off-duty, usually drove a beat-up Ford 150 pickup.

Ike had pulled up behind Whaite's bright red, souped-up, 1967 Chevrolet Chevelle.

"Truck blew a head gasket. I got her in the garage. Be awhile 'fore she'll be back on the road, I'm afraid. This one's a show car, Ike, not a circus wagon, won a prize or two."

"Sorry, just kidding, it's a fine looking piece of machinery. So, what have we got so far?"

Ike rocked back on his heels and waited. Whaite, he knew, could pick through a crime scene and pull out the important bits. He rarely missed anything and Ike needed to hear him tell it as he saw it. They sidestepped down into the gully and stood shoulder to shoulder staring at the body. Its arms were folded as if in prayer. Autumn leaves nearly covered the legs, but some drag marks from the road were still discernable.

"Well, if you ask me, it looks like a robbery gone bad. His wallet is empty. Driver's license says he's Randall Harris."

"A license? I thought you said the wallet was empty."

"Was. The license was in a side jacket pocket. I reckon whoever did him didn't think to look for it or maybe didn't care. Probably in a hurry. Anyway, it appears whoever pulled this off drug him here after they shot him somewhere else. You can see the leaves are all pushed aside and the back of his shoe is scuffed up."

"Shoe?"

"Yep, just the one. Must have lost the other when they hauled him up here."

"If it's not between here and the road then it's probably where he was killed. Find the shoe, find the killer. By the way, how'd you find him?"

"I didn't. I was down to the junkyard looking for some parts for the truck. On my way home, I saw this kid coming out of the woods and acting funny, so I stopped to check him out. He parked his pickup in the middle of the road. Told me he stopped to relieve himself and found the body. He said he was about to call it in."

"You believe him?"

"I expect so. No way to know for sure. I had no probable cause to search him or his vehicle. He took off before I got the info from his driver's license but I did get a tag number so we can run him if we need to, wrote it on a piece of paper here." Whaite tapped his shirt pocket.

"He's not a suspect?"

"No. This body's been here a while. Probably dumped last night."

"Did he touch anything?"

"I don't know. Maybe. He must have come this way a bit, though—to make sure the guy was dead. You can see the leaves, where they're deep, how he came in and where he did his business. Now down in this swale, the wind whips around and moves the leaves all around so that would erase any footsteps. Like I said, I don't know for sure."

The wind, on cue, gusted through the trees and whirled leaves in noisy eddies around their ankles. The temperature seemed to drop another ten degrees. Ike stepped closer to the body. "You said the victim looked familiar. What did you mean?"

"He looks like a Harris."

"Well, he is, isn't he? I mean that's what his driver's—?"

"No, I mean like someone I know. There's lots of Harrises in the world, as you for sure know, but…well, I wasn't raised up in Picketsville. I come from down past Floyd, up on Buffalo Mountain. You know the mountain?"

"I heard some stories about it from my father. Used to be a rough place, they say."

"Before the war, World War II, that is, especially during the Depression, it was a hard place. Shootings and stabbings were as common as colds and one of the meanest families in the area back then was the Harrises—old Claude especially. They said he looked like President Wilson. Can't say as how I'd know about that, but that's what they said. Anyway, some of the later Harrises have that same chiseled look you see on this fella. That's what I mean about he looks familiar. He looks like a Buffalo Mountain

Harris. Like I said, driver's license says he's Randall Harris. Looks like maybe a Sutphin decided to even the score."

"You're losing me here, Whaite. You can fill me in on the folklore later."

"Yes sir, but I reckon all we need to do is slip on down to Floyd County and find us a descendent of a Sutphin and we'll have our killer."

Ike studied the face frozen in death and shuddered. "I don't think so, Whaite."

"No?" Whaite looked disappointed. "Why is that, boss?"

"In the first place, why would a…whoever…or anyone else for that matter, come all the way to Picketsville to dump the body? If it was a traditional Buffalo Mountain killing, wouldn't they want everyone down there to know about it?"

"Well, I guess they would but—"

"In the second place, whatever his ID says, this man is definitely not a Harris or anyone else from Buffalo Mountain. His name is Alexei Kamarov. He's supposed to be dead."

"Well, I reckon that part is for sure done. But who is Alexei…whoever?"

Ike studied the all too familiar face of an old enemy/colleague from another life and sighed. This was not good. The congregation of blackbirds evidently finished with its sortie south, returned, and settled back into the trees with a discordant chorus of squawks and chattering. Ike had to raise his voice to be overheard.

"I need to make a phone call. Wait here."

"Well sure, Ike, but—?"

"Be right back. This is not good."

Ike walked back toward the splash of red Whaite's Chevy made against the gray concrete and tree trunks by the road. He paused, his back to the woods, and punched in a number he had committed to memory. He waited while the number connected.

"Garland."

"Charlie, it's Ike. We have a problem."

"We have a problem? You mean you have a problem? What kind of problem are you talking about? Another big crime and you need me to give you advice or—"

"Listen to me, Charlie, Alexei Kamarov is dead."

"Well golly, we knew that. At least we supposed that when he disappeared after Eloise…after the shooting…after Zurich. He tried to find you, right? He couldn't and then he disappeared. Figured Moscow Central had him put away. That was a while back, though."

"Maybe they did and maybe they didn't. But right now his body is lying not twenty yards from me, in the town limits. My town limits."

"No."

"Yes. Why is he here, Charlie? You want to take a stab at that? Is somebody trying to send me a message?"

"Maybe to you or maybe to the Agency. It could be they wanted us to know, figured you'd be sure to send it. I'll get back to you. Rats…bad news. Why is it always you that brings me bad news, Ike?"

"Not my game anymore. You call me ASAP, Charlie. I'm getting really nervous down here." Ike zipped up his coat and slapped his sleeves against the cold, which now seemed much more intense. He walked back up the rise to Whaite.

"You know I used to work for the CIA?"

"I reckon everybody does by now, Ike."

"This man used to be on the other side. We had dealings. He was supposed to have been eliminated."

"You're sure it's what's-his-name?"

"No doubt about it. I just called an old friend in the Agency. They're on it and will make an absolute ID soon, but it's him. We need to secure this area as tight as a drum and Whaite…not a word of this to anyone, you hear? If anybody asks, we have a John Doe. No Harris, no Kamarov. For now, no one knows who he really is but you and me. You got it?"

"You're the boss."

Chapter Two

Samantha Ryder huddled against cold bricks hoping to avoid the worst of an icy wind that skittered the last of the leaves around the building's corner. She hugged herself for warmth and watched as a childhood memory rolled into the parking lot. A fresh blast made her eyes water and blurred her vision. She hunkered her six-foot-three-inch frame, blinked back the tears, and focused again on a bright red Chevy Chevelle, SS 396, all three hundred and seventy-five of its dealer-installed horses rumbling through dual glass pack mufflers, the deep throbbing that turned men's heads. Her father thumb-tacked pictures of that same car to his garage wall. She remembered seeing him staring at them, a faraway look in his eye. He'd dreamed of owning that muscle car. Some Sundays he'd pack Sam and her younger brothers into their dowdy family sedan and travel across town or out into the suburbs to look at a Chevelle—the Chevelle. Her father would circle the car and talk to the owner about carburetors, injection systems, and custom rear ends. Sam would stare at the machine and wonder. She never understood why that car so infatuated him. At the end of each meeting with a purchase price established, her father would frown, scuff his toe on the ground, and declare he'd have to think it over. He never bought any of the dozen or so he looked at. Years later Sam came to understand that he never intended to. He just liked the idea of owning one, of talking about it, but with four children to raise and educate, he could never justify spending the money to purchase it.

She watched as Whaite parked the Chevy carefully on a separation stripe, taking two parking spaces to discourage anyone from dinging his paint job with a carelessly opened door. The finish glittered in the morning sun, adding a dazzle of bright red to an otherwise dull day. She had not inherited her father's love for Chevelles—or any other car, for that matter. She drove an old Subaru Forester she'd bought used when she was trying to manage the transition between college and the world of work.

"Where's your truck?" she asked.

"Head gasket blew. I've got to replace it."

"You going to do them both?"

"Oh yeah. Once you get down to the heads on a V8 you might as well do them both."

"It's a beautiful car." Sam resisted the temptation to tell him about her father.

"A hobby, Sam. I always wanted a street rod so I bought this thing half restored and finished the job."

"Love the paint job."

"You think? Funny thing, that. When I got around to shopping for paint—I knew I wanted her red, that's all—I met this guy who restores motorcycles. He told me the Harley dealer over in Waynesboro over-bought red paint, Midnight Pearl Red, a special run for the ninety-fifth anniversary or something. The manager figured there'd be a big demand for it. He had gallons in his stock room and was practically giving it away. So, you are looking at the only Harley-Davidson red Chevy in the world—well, in the county, anyway."

They stood admiring the car.

"I thought we were getting some snow yesterday. Had the boss all worried, like," he said.

"Blew over. Lucky us. What will you do with the car when you've finished fixing it up?"

"I guess I'll sell her and start in on another one. I always wanted one of them pre-war cars, maybe a thirty-nine Ford coupe, one with a big flat head V8. I don't know for sure. Long-range planning isn't one of my strong suits. By the way, what're you doing standing out in the cold?"

"Ike called me in early. I thought I'd wait for you and find out why. Something go down yesterday?"

"We got us a corpse over at the ME's office. A John Doe from Floyd, we think. Ike says you and me are to partner up and work the case."

"You and me…work a homicide?"

"That's what the man said. He wants to see us this morning."

Another gust of icy wind rattled the office door and invited them in. Sam waved a good morning to Essie Falco behind the dispatcher's desk.

"He in yet?" Whaite asked.

Essie waved back. "Shut the door, you're letting in all the cold air. Yeah, he pulled in half an hour ago looking a little worse for wear. He said to send you right in, Whaite. And Sam, he wants you to check out some things on the internet, and then go see him. The list is on your desk. I guess it's about the dead guy."

"Your boyfriend, the FBI guy, comes to town this weekend?" Whaite said as he pulled mail from his box.

Sam had found someone in the fall who matched her in both stature and brains. FBI Special Agent Karl Hedrick stood an easy two inches over her six-three. He had arrived in Picketsville that summer in pursuit of a missing felon. The case had gone south for him, but Hedrick lingered in town for another month— presumably to keep his connection with Sam—and they had become an item. When he was finally recalled to Quantico, Ike feared she would follow and he would lose his newest deputy, but she had stayed on. She said it was too soon to make a commitment like that. Nevertheless, every other weekend she took off for Northern Virginia and on the alternate weekends, Hedrick traveled down to Picketsville.

"No, it's my weekend to go to Fairfax."

"You ever see that movie, *Sleeping with the Enemy?*"

Sam closed her eyes for a second and shook her head. "The FBI is not the enemy, Whaite. The trouble with you is you just assume that they're a problem for us locals. We need to learn to trust and work with them."

"I bet you believe in the Easter Bunny, too."

"Honestly. Until that attitude goes the way of the dodo, there'll never be any progress in, um…interagency cooperation. Besides, that movie was about a woman trying to escape an abusive husband—"

"And you aren't married yet."

"No, but…well…wait a minute."

Whaite perched a pair of out-of-kilter reading glasses on his nose and began sorting through his mail. He discarded half of it unopened and headed toward Ike's door. "Hey, I like Karl, but I'm telling you, Sam, he's one of them and would sell us all out in a heartbeat if he thought it served the Bureau's best interest."

"Karl would never do that. And, well, I'll just tell him that when I see him this weekend. Then we'll see what he has to say to you."

"Not this weekend, Sweetheart. You and me are working a homicide. You better call him up and cancel your romantic dinner on the Potomac."

"This weekend?"

"That's right. You wanted field duty. You got it."

"But the weekend? This weekend?"

"This one and all the ones to follow until we close the case with an arrest or it goes cold. Sorry."

Sam's heart dropped into her shoes. Her instincts told her that this was to have been an extremely important weekend, a turning point in their relationship. Maybe the big one. Now this.

"Couldn't we start on Monday?"

Whaite, eyebrows up, only looked at her over his half-rim reading glasses and pushed Ike's door open.

"Go clean up your desk and draw a parka, Deputy. It'll be cold down in Floyd."

◇◇◇

Ike looked up as Whaite entered. He seemed preoccupied. He chewed on the end of a pencil and swiveled back and forth in his desk chair, which in turn made a horrific squeal on each pass. The aroma of fresh and, Whaite guessed, very strong coffee filled the room, overlaying the scent of linoleum polish and wet boots.

"I want you to take Sam with you when you check out our friend from the park. Work it like a routine John Doe homicide, okay? Go on down to Floyd and start asking questions. I'll be on the phone to their chief first thing so you won't have any jurisdiction problems. He's a good guy and will help us if we need backup."

"But if you know we ain't looking for a Harris killer, what's the point?"

"Well, we don't know that, do we? Someone's our man and the name on his driver's license is Harris. He's from Floyd. For all they know down there, he's a Harris. It's just that you and I know better. Look, Whaite, it's important to see how Sam works out. She says she wants to be a real cop. Well, she has to learn sometime and this looks like as good a time as any. Whether we are looking for a descendent of...who did you say...that person you named yesterday?"

"Sutphin."

"Right, or someone else, it works the same way. Sam doesn't have to know about Kamarov to do a competent investigation. We still want to know who he hung around with, where he spent his time, and so on. You work it with Kamarov in mind, but at the same time, keep an eye on Sam. But be very careful. If we're looking for a Harris named Kamarov, it's pretty likely someone else is, too. Stay with John Doe as much as you can."

"That'll make it kinda hard, Ike. I mean, how'll we find who he was with without letting on he was a Harris?"

"Do what you have to do, but until we figure out why Kamarov called himself Harris, he's John Doe."

"You're the boss. Sam's pretty bright. She might figure out we're sending her out looking for the man who wasn't there."

"Whaite, the man is there. He just isn't your mountain man. He's someone darker, devious maybe, I don't know. Either way, we need to find him. Work the case straight. She's looking for someone who wanted to kill a Floyd man, you're looking for someone who wanted to kill an ex-Russian agent using Harris as an alias. Let's hope you both find the same guy."

Chapter Three

Sam retreated to her work space. She never thought of it as an office. A converted holding cell crammed with computer equipment linked to nearly every criminal investigative site in the country and smelling slightly of electronically created ozone did not qualify as an office. She'd been handed the job of taking Picketsville into the twenty-first century and she'd done it. She'd gone a few hundred steps beyond that. The Sheriff's Department did not have to call on Richmond or any other jurisdiction to tap into AFIS, FBI, or state databases. She didn't like to think of herself as a hacker, but she had the skills to work her way into many more as well, even if that was not a matter of general knowledge.

Whaite pounded on her door. "Ten minutes, Sam, then we roll."

"Okay, I just need to make a quick call and clear Ike's list."

She settled into her ergonomically correct chair and sighed. She'd need to call Karl and tell him the bad news. She riffled through the papers on her desk hoping to find a project needing her attention, and so important, she would have to be excused from this homicide thing. She really did want to learn police grunt work, but at the same time, her computer held her in thrall, and then there was Karl. Men like Karl came by once in a lifetime. She stared at the phone.

Whaite banged on her door again. "Let's go, Sam. We're wasting daylight."

"Yeah, yeah, I'm coming." The phone rang.

"Hey, it's me." Karl.

"Hi. What's up?" Be cheerful. Break the bad news later.

"I have to cancel this weekend, Sam. I'm sorry but we have an emergency and they sort of transferred me."

"Transferred? What happened?" Sam felt the relief tinged with the guilt that comes when someone else does your dirty work for you.

"Well, I can't really say. Same church, different pew, I guess."

"A witness missing again?"

"Can't say."

"Okay. Listen, I have kind of a problem at this end, too, so it's just as well. Next weekend?"

"We'll have to see."

She hung up. That was better. She'd miss the time together, but this way nobody got hurt. Whaite banged on the door again.

"All right, I'm coming." She stood and tucked in her shirt. Because of her height, a regulation size, standard issue blouse did not work. The distance from the nape of her neck to her waist measured at least three inches more than an average woman, leaving her very little shirttail to tuck. She buckled her duty belt, grabbed her hat, and headed out the door. "I'm coming."

◇◇◇

Essie Falco tried unsuccessfully to work the buttons on the new intercom and, failing, shouted at Ike, "Miz Harris on two."

"Which Miz Harris?"

"The Miz Harris that's president of the college. How many Harris women are you squiring around anyway?"

Ike wagged his hand in her direction. "Sorry, I got Harris on the brain today."

Someday, he thought, he would hold a training session on how to use the intercom. He'd get Sam to do it. She seemed to be the only one able to decipher the codes and buttons. For years, communications in the Sheriff's Office had been a matter of shouting from one room to another, unless there were visitors in the building. Then they would walk across the room to the desk or office of the person they wanted to contact and speak in a normal tone. The office rarely had visitors.

"Schwartz," Ruth Harris barked, "I could kill you."

"Not today, Ruth, I'm pretty busy. You can kill me tomorrow. What's up?"

"You know those new 'tenants' you got for me?"

Ike had managed to find someone to lease the abandoned art storage facility behind her main building. It had not been easy. A gigantic late nineteen fifties, four-level, mostly underground, reinforced concrete bomb shelter did not make for an easy rental, but he had friends in a certain governmental agency and they were ecstatic about it.

"Nice people, aren't they?"

"Do you have any idea what they're up to?"

"No clue. Hanging curtains, faux painting the walls—"

"This isn't funny. They're in there wearing guns and hauling in boxes of electronic crap that looks really suspicious and black paint and...did I mention guns?"

"You did. And black paint."

"What are they doing to my building?"

"It sounds like they're painting and installing their computers."

"Black paint?"

"So it would seem. Not the usual color recommended by interior decorators, but who knows, maybe black is this year's mauve."

"Don't get smart with me, Bubba. They're packing heat."

"They are carrying, not packing. How many times do I have to tell you? And why is all of this a reason for you to want me dead?"

"My faculty is up in arms. They want to know why they weren't consulted on the lease."

"I hope you told them it was none of their bleeping business. That letting the faculty of a college meddle in its management is like putting the inmates in charge of the asylum."

"You know I can't do that."

"I would."

"Yes, you would. And putting you in charge of a college would be like putting…oh hell, I can't think of anything."

"Sugar in the gas tank, fox in the hen house, salt in the wounds, square peg in a round—"

"Enough already. Ike, if I put together a small group of faculty…wait, don't interrupt me. Hear me out…a small group of reasonable men and women who will listen, would you come out here and talk to them about the Agency and how they are not…um—"

"Toxic?"

"Well, yes…sort of."

"On one condition."

"Here it comes."

"I just want a level playing field. Every time I meet up with your people I get the impression they think I'm either some mentally challenged rube cop or part of some great police state conspiracy. They seem oblivious to the whole concept that police are here to protect and serve. To protect and serve *them*, I might add. I'm tired of being stereotyped by that bunch of—"

"I said I'd get reasonable ones, Ike. They are not all your enemies. I promise."

"Okay, what time?"

"This evening work? Say seven o'clock?"

"You in that kind of a hurry? Okay, I guess I can manage that. By the way, you don't have relatives living down south of here, do you?"

"Yes, I am in a hurry. I need to make this problem go away. What kind of relatives? You mean like uncles and aunts, cousins, that kind of relatives?"

"Yep. We have a murder on our hands and his last name is Harris. Any kin?"

"Ike, if his name was Nixon, would you be calling Whittier, California?"

"Guess not. Just a thought. Lots of men named Harris down on Buffalo Mountain and one of them got himself shot. In the old days there'd be another killing pretty soon, and then any Harris would be fair game."

"Never heard of the place."

"You have a local historian on that faculty of yours?"

"Yes."

"Ask him to the meeting. It's my compensation for coming. I need to talk to someone who knows the history of Buffalo Mountain."

"You'll come, then?"

"And stay over."

"Well…"

"And nobody at the meeting will be packing heat."

"Yes to the first, I can't guarantee the second. Better wear your cop belt."

"Duty belt…I think I'd make a very good college administrator."

"Right. And Don Knotts would have made a very good linebacker for the Oakland Raiders."

◇◇◇

"Will somebody please explain to me how Kamarov managed to slip away from his minders and disappear?"

Andover Crisp sat behind his recently assigned large government-issue mahogany desk and glared at the half-dozen men standing across from him. Tom Phillips stood in the back of the hastily assembled group of men. From that vantage point he could just make out, in the reflected image made by the desk's glass top, that Crisp had missed a spot on one of his chins when he shaved that morning. Tom blinked and suppressed a smile. He was not a stake holder in this one. His head would not be one to roll if things turned out badly. He just handled logistics, the HR guy, so to speak. As soon as this crowd developed their plan, he'd find the manpower to staff it. He only needed to hear the problem, listen to some likely responses, and he could begin his own planning.

"We go to enormous expense to get the guy and now he's lost—Lost!"

Crisp's voice gained a few decibels as the silence on the other side of the desk continued. "You boys have forty-eight hours to find him and get him back or there'll be one hell of a shuffling of assignments around here."

"Sir," Palmer said. Palmer was senior and at less risk than the others in the room. "The problem we have, as you no doubt know, is the nature of Kamarov's situation. If we bring in the wrong people, some of what he's up to will invariably leak and…" He swept the room with a worried look. He didn't have to say anything else.

Tom frowned. What in the devil was going on here? "Ah, sir, Mr. Crisp, perhaps I had better step out. This sounds like a NTK and I don't need, or, for that matter, want to know," he said.

"Yes, you're right. Thank you, Phillips. You will be called in later. The rest of you, except Palmer and Kevin, step out. We'll call you when we need you."

The last words Tom heard as the door swished shut sounded like…*the Agency*.

Chapter Four

"It's no business of mine," Sam said, "but why are we heading south in your Chevelle instead of a cruiser?"

Whaite smiled and glanced at her out of the corner of his eye. "She needs a good run. Clear out all the carbon. A show car like this one doesn't get any real road time and it tends to gum up. Besides, we are moving into a different jurisdiction and I thought it might be a good idea not to attract attention to ourselves."

"And you think this candy-apple red car with the gutted muffler won't attract attention?"

"Hey, we're going to Floyd, NASCAR heaven, we'll fit right in."

"You think?"

"I grew up in that part of the world. I still have relatives all over the area. Trust me."

Floyd County, Virginia, lies south and east of Roanoke, and, if you can find the right plot of land, offers a wonderful view of Buffalo Mountain. The surrounding community is rural, green, forested, and populated with the usual mix of young and old, professionals and tradesmen, and a somewhat higher percentage of retirees, particularly former government workers.

Whaite said he figured to make a quiet survey of the area, and perhaps establish how their John Doe was connected. It would be the best place to start, he thought. Sam wondered how that would even be possible—two out-of-town deputies in a noisy street rod—but it was Whaite's backyard and he ought to know. Besides, he also said he knew a place where they served killer ribs. It would be time for lunch soon and then she could look forward to several hours of chat with the local police, residents, and folks Whaite said "knew things."

◇◇◇

Ike had expected worse. His previous brushes with the faculty at Callend College had ended in verbal chaos. Except for a brief attempt at cop baiting by Everitt Barstow, a chemist and, as far as Ike was concerned, a twit, the meeting went well. Most of the attendees understood the difficulty of replacing the lost revenues subsequent to removal to New York of the renowned Dillon Art collection from the storage facility. They also understood that the facility was essentially useless for anything short of what Ike had arranged. He had been somewhat less successful in persuading them of the relatively benign nature of the agency now installed in the building. When the conversation turned to town planning, Ike decided to dummy up. He had no desire to engage in the conversation that he felt sure would follow. He found the coffee pot in the corner of the library's conference room and poured a cup of the slightly burnt brew.

The school's amateur architect began to extol the potential of a renovated downtown. "Antebellum," he'd announced as if he'd just discovered a cure for herpes. "Imagine Main Street lined on either side by building and storefronts circa 1860. Of course some of the current structures would have to be removed, but for the benefit of the concept, it would be worth it."

In spite of his earlier decision to sit this one out, Ike could not resist and interrupted. "The Crossroads Diner wouldn't be one of those structures, would it?"

"Oh heavens, yes, absolutely. The building is hideous—all forties-fifties art deco. No place for it."

"You believe that you can make Picketsville into a Civil War Williamsburg?"

"Yes, that's the concept."

"But Picketsville never was a major center in the war. Cavalry from both sides galloped through and there are a dozen or so chips in some of the brick buildings that we like to think are bullet holes from one or more skirmishes. But that's questionable and even if true, hardly warrants the sort of treatment you all are suggesting."

"Nevertheless, it could be an economic boon to the town."

Ike only shook his head. He had learned not to engage in arguments with Ruth's faculty. He never won, and it always made her angry with him when he tried.

◇◇◇

Later, sitting in front of a fire, drinks in hand in Ruth's high-ceilinged front parlor, Ike turned to Dr. Leon Weitz, the local historian.

"You heard the talk about reinventing the town, Doctor. You have an opinion?"

"In my view, it's nonsensical. As you pointed out, the town played a relatively minor role in the War Between the States. Moreover, most of the buildings that now line Main Street were built in the 1890s. The original structures were, for the most part, clapboard, some even log. When the town had a surge of prosperity, they were all torn down and replaced with what passed for modern then. I have photographs—not Matthew Brady's, but maybe Gardner's, of Main Street in 1860. The road was mud and served as a wallow for a dozen or so pigs. The only building still standing from that time now houses the bookstore. The rest are long gone. Civilization, such as it existed, centered in Bolton, two miles to the west."

"It annoys me when people with limited knowledge and no emotional investment in a community move in and begin to lecture the locals on what's best for them." Ike was winding up for a small polemic.

"Don't start, Ike," Ruth said, "or I'll cancel our deal. Leon, don't listen to him."

"I will resist," Weitz said. "Perhaps when the sheriff is free for lunch we will continue this conversation. I will say the Crossroads Diner is probably the most authentic piece of architecture in the town. If I were going to make over Picketsville, I would restore it to what it was in the late thirties and forties. Now, that would be different and attractive to tourists. Picketsville does have a history in the migration of rural men and women out of the mountains and valleys north to the cities along old Route Eleven and before that, the Brownsburg Pike. Something along the lines of the Route Sixty-six restoration out West would be more appropriate, I should think. The South is loaded to capacity with ersatz Civil War ambience."

"You have a friend for life," Ike said. "I take it all back, Ruth, at least one of your faculty members has his head screwed on right."

"Thank you for that, I think," Weitz said. "Dr. Harris said you wanted to ask me some questions."

"Right. I almost forgot. What can you tell me about the history of Buffalo Mountain?"

Weitz sat back and stared at the fire for a moment. He smiled. Ike swirled his drink and listened as his ice cubes played counterpoint to the crackle and hiss of the fire.

"Ah, speaking of the history of migrations out of the mountains…there's a place worth studying. How much time do you have? Or perhaps I should ask you, how much do you want to know? Is there a context in which you have framed your question?"

"Context? Yes, as a matter of fact, I have a body in the morgue that has been identified as a Randall Harris. That's just between us, by the way. He's from Floyd. At least that's what we're working with at the moment. My deputy grew up there and started to fill me in on the culture, at least what he'd heard as a child—shootings, moonshiners, feuds…all that sort of stuff."

"It sounds like another lunch to me. But in the meantime, I suggest you read Richard Davids' book *The Man Who Moved a Mountain*. It's out of print but you can order it in any decent independent bookstore or I can lend you a copy. When you've had a chance to go through it and if you need more information, call me."

"Rough place? The mountain folk like the Hatfields and McCoys?"

"No, not like them. Most of the folks up on the mountain and back in the coves were related somehow. The people who lived there were almost in a time warp. It seems odd to us at the remove of seventy and more years to think about people actually looking and living that way—"

"What way?" Ruth had leaned forward. This was an area her Ph.D. in history never covered.

"Fifteen or more packed into a one-room cabin and moonshine and Johnny ashcake for breakfast. Boys became men about twelve when they bought or stole their first pistol. Most folks settled their differences without the benefit of the law. Anyway, it was that way, not anymore."

"Now?"

"It's all cleaned up, as you will read, and is becoming a place for retreats, tourists, rental cabins tricked out to look primitive but complete with cable TV and Jacuzzis. Do you suppose the would-be renovators of Picketsville have something like that in mind?"

"I wouldn't put it past them."

"Well, on that happy note, I will leave the two of you alone. Good night." Weitz disappeared into an icy night.

Ike stretched out his legs and drained his glass. Outside, the wind gusted and he heard the rattle of leaves swirling about on the lawn, the creak of protesting tree limbs. A night to stay indoors by a fire, to read or... Ruth closed the door after Weitz and returned. She stood over him and smiled.

"You get a star for tonight," she said. "Another drink?"

"A small one. Why a star?"

"Because you behaved like a normal human being. I'm amazed. Usually my faculty acts like a red cape and you're the bull. Are you feeling all right? You're not coming down with something, are you?"

"Very funny. I'm fine. It's just that I have more important things on my mind right now than listening to elitist nonsense."

"You liked Weitz?"

"Good guy. I think I will have lunch…or is it do lunch…I can never remember the correct figure of speech to use."

"Just be yourself. Down here don't y'all say 'grab a bite'?"

"Don't start."

"Do you know what constitutes a seven-course meal for a redneck?"

"No, but you're going to tell me."

"A possum and a six pack."

"Have you been saving that up for me?"

"Oh yeah."

"Do you know how many Ph.D.s it takes to change a light bulb?"

"Four, five? I don't know."

"Two, one to mix the martinis and one to call the electric company."

"Do you want to quit while we're even?"

"Absolutely. It's been a worrisome day and—"

"Say no more. Drink up and come upstairs. I'll go slip into something—"

"Comfortable? Slinky?"

"Flannel. It's cold and you and I are way past slinky."

◇◇◇

Donnie Oldham needed money. The last few dollars from his sawmill pay were gone. He had a truck payment due. He had food to buy and he owed Wick Goad almost a thousand dollars. He was sure Goad cheated at poker, but he never could catch him. And cheater or not, he held Donnie's paper and would come looking for him soon. The wallet only had thirty bucks and the credit cards.

It had felt weird picking through some dead guy's wallet, but shoot, he wouldn't need the money anymore and Donnie sure did. He would use the credit cards for a while—maybe over the county line down in North Carolina, though it could become risky after a couple of days.

He wished he had a way of figuring out their PIN numbers. Then he could use them and the bank card at ATMs. He thought of Hollis. Hollis' dad used to be a spook or something and Hollis said he knew all about how to do stuff like that. He'd ask Hollis. Then he'd, quick as a rabbit, milk the bank account for as much cash as he could and sell the cards. He could pay off Goad, the finance company, and nobody would be the wiser. Of course, Hollis might want a cut. Son-of-a-bitch-greedy-bastard. He'd take care of him later if he did, but first he had to get the PIN number.

He cracked open another Miller Lite and watched *Saturday Night Live*. Those guys were, like, super funny. He'd someday go up there to New York and see them make that show. He could do it. All he needed was one lousy break. It wasn't his fault his old man couldn't make a go of the gas station. Stupid old man. The fire had been an accident, everybody knew that. He should have collected on the insurance. But did he? No, he'd listened to those pussy investigators and then they all looked at Donnie and the next thing you know, the money, the gas station, and finally, even the old man went away. A pussy, that's what the old man was.

"Well, I'm not," he shouted at the TV. "I'm getting mine, you wait and see."

Chapter Five

Sunday seemed to have mislaid its dawn. The night's black simply paled into progressively lighter shades of gray until daybreak could be confirmed. The threat of snow menaced the mountains to the west. Sooty clouds scudded across a gritty sky. Cars pulling out of the church's parking lot made crunching sounds, as if their frozen tires were battling the macadam to see which would crack first. The Reverend Blake Fisher stood shivering just inside the double doors, seeing his eight o'clock congregation on their way home.

Robert Twelvetrees, Colonel, United States Army (ret.), first attended Stonewall Jackson Memorial Episcopal Church the day after he officially became a civilian thirty-five or forty years previously. Except for a rare bout of flu, he never missed a Sunday. He sat at attention in the third pew from the rear on the left side.

"The gospel side," he corrected those who did not know that churches did not have rights and lefts. Not in his world, they did not. They had an east and a west, a north and a south. The altar was always east, even if a compass indicated otherwise. The entrance and narthex, if one existed, were west and then the left and right side of the nave as you faced the altar were north and south respectively. It was a simple system and he could not understand how anyone could miss it.

"If the left side is north," they asked in obvious confusion, "why do you say you sit on the gospel side?"

Colonel Bob would shake his head sadly and wonder at the ignorance of the generation that would soon be in charge of the world.

"Because that is the side they read the gospel from," he'd snap. "Any fool can see that."

"But the vicar always reads the gospel in the aisle about halfway down in the...ah—"

"Nave. Yes, but that is new. The gospel used to be read from over there." He gestured left. "So they call it the gospel side."

"I thought you said it was north."

"It is. The gospel side is north."

For Colonel Bob, that was all he would say. He mentioned to Blake the problems he saw with these young people who were turning up in droves and who did not know anything about church. He hoped he would straighten them out—pronto. He envisioned an ecclesiastical boot camp for these young folks.

"Do them good," he barked and turned on his heel and left.

Boot camp? Blake liked Colonel Bob. He was a relic of two wars and another age. Actually, it might have been three wars. Blake had the impression that the Colonel had served as a raw Second Lieutenant in the Second World War, at its very end, and then Korea, Viet Nam, and skirmishes in Granada and Lebanon.

He didn't talk very much about his time in the army. Blake found that those who survived combat rarely did. The support troops, the stateside wonders, and those who commanded LMDs—large mahogany desks—talked endlessly about their army days. But old soldiers knew better than to pretend that war was anything more than pain, fear, blood, and death.

Colonel Bob met with his old Armored unit every two years and kept in contact with a dozen or so throughout the year as well. But he confessed to Blake he did not know how much longer he could go on. The number of his old comrades in arms dwindled yearly as age and illness took them one by one. Except for failing eyesight, Colonel Bob soldiered on, back ramrod straight, head erect, as if he were on the parade ground and his hero, General George S. Patton, was reviewing the troops. He even knew what the S stood for. "Smith," he would bark. "Any fool knows that." There were other military types in the congregation, of course, but Colonel Bob stood out as one of a kind. Blake crossed his arms and shivered. Cold air rolled in the door and caused the furnace to kick on. The grass on the lawn seemed to crackle from the hard frost still on the blades. He could smell snow and wondered if it would be a big one.

He watched Colonel Bob maneuver his battered Buick around the parking lot. He narrowly missed a minivan, clipped a yew bush, and rolled uncertainly out onto Main Street. Blake flinched as he weaved across the yellow line, corrected course, and disappeared, moving at a brisk fifteen miles an hour.

◇◇◇

By ten twenty-seven, Blake was back at the narthex door greeting the few last minute arrivals. Rose Garroway, her sister Minnie, and a young man with eyes set wide and a thatch of unruly blond hair puffed up the gentle wheelchair ramp to the church.

"This is my nephew T.J.," Rose announced. The young man smiled uncertainly and stuck out his hand.

"T.J., nice to meet you. What does T.J. stand for?"

"Thomas Harkins," the young man replied, brow furrowed in concentration.

Rose, seeing Blake's confusion, added, "Tommy is named after his father. He's a junior—Thomas Junior—T.J."

The young man nodded his head vigorously. "T.J." he repeated, as he stared hard at Blake and shoved his hands deep in his pockets.

"Good to have you here, T.J."

"Yes," T.J. said, and bent forward to peer around the doorframe and into the church. Blake caught Rose's eye. She smiled sadly and glanced at the back of her nephew's head. T.J. was one of God's gentle gifts—a young man of limited intelligence, and a reminder that shortcomings can be overcome, that what we wish for is not always God's plan for us, and in his eyes, a cheerful spirit is valued more highly than worldly accomplishments.

"He will be staying with us for a while," Rose said. "He's going to run errands and drive the car—he's a very good driver—and just help out two old women."

"I can drive real good," T.J. added, eyes bright, still nodding.

Blake watched the trio move down the aisle and slip into a pew. He turned in time to see Samantha Ryder sprint up the steps.

"Good Morning, Sam. Karl not with you this weekend?"

"No, not today, Vicar—"

"Blake…"

"Blake, yes, actually, Karl's been called out and then I've been assigned to a homicide investigation so neither of us…well, no." She worked her way around the choir that stood in a close huddle just inside the church's glass doors.

At ten thirty-five Mary Miller, at a nod from Blake, switched from playing a prelude and launched into "Onward Christian Soldiers"—a little political incorrectness on a cold Sunday morning. The choir started its stately, if somewhat disorganized, procession to the front of the church. Blake followed, his hymnal at the ready but his eyes surveying his congregation. He let his mind slip into the clergy person's Sunday litany—how many here this morning? Who is here, who is missing? Are there any faces I do not recognize? Are the candles lighted? What did I do with my sermon notes? What was the point I wanted to make in the sermon? He could not remember. He fought the twinge of doubt he always felt when the service started—would he get it right?

Blake knew the first and last verses of most of the hymns in the book. He knew many in their entirety as well, Christmas and Easter hymns in particular. But the exigencies of his calling made it particularly useful to know at least the first and last. They were sung when he and most clergy were out of position or without a book at hand.

He paused and waited at the head of the aisle for the hymn-ending Amen to fade. It would be called a transept in a large church, Blake mused, thinking of Colonel Bob and his annoyance at "those young people"—a transept running north and south.

Blake did not think his sermon met his standard, but he figured it would do, might even be a hit. He'd discovered years before that he could never judge how sermons would be received. The ones he worked on the hardest often evoked the fewest comments, the least praise, and ones he threw together at the last minute seemed to have the greatest impact on the most people. He learned to accept it, convinced it was how God amused himself, but he knew the phenomenon still rankled many of his colleagues. Some even denied it completely and remained convinced that their painstakingly researched and carefully crafted sermons were moving mountains.

The service ended with a closing hymn. Blake positioned himself again at the narthex door ready to shake hands, respond to comments, and listen for signals that he needed to call on someone or to commiserate. He never knew if he got it right. He sometimes wished his congregation would stop thinking of him as a mind reader and just come out and tell him what they, or their children, husband, or neighbor needed. Rose, Minnie, T.J., and Sam arrived at the exit at the same time.

"Rose, do you know Samantha Ryder?" he asked.

"I've seen you, dear, but never really met you." She held out her hand. "This is my sister, Minnie, and our nephew, T.J."

"Sam is a deputy sheriff," Blake added.

"You're a policeman?" T.J. asked, eyes wide.

"A deputy sheriff, yes. Are you interested in police work?"

Rose looked nonplussed. T.J. was hardly police academy material.

"Yes, I am. I would like to ride in a police car."

"Well, T.J., I'll tell you what," Sam said. "Some afternoon when I'm off duty, maybe we can fix it so you can do just that."

◇◇◇

Whaite told Sam to take the rest of Sunday morning off but said he wanted to be back in Floyd by early afternoon.

"I got a call last night on my answering machine. Some guy said it was urgent and I should get down there right away."

Some guy?

Chapter Six

Sam and Whaite failed to find the caller. The contact had been traced to a payphone on the wall at a fire station. In an age of ubiquitous cell phones, it may have been the only payphone for miles. No one in the fire station could remember anyone using it.

"Hey, it's cold outside. It's not like we was sitting and rocking out there like it was summer, Whaite." Clint Kemp and Whaite grew up together. Clint gave Sam the once over as he spoke. "Well, well, now, ain't you a tall drink of water." Sam could feel the heat rising up her neck—half blush, half anger. She started to say something but Whaite cut her off.

"Careful there, Clint. Your woman finds out you been making moon-eyes at this here deputy and I might pretty soon be investigating another homicide. 'Sides which she has got herself a black belt or two and might just save the little woman the trouble. Ain't that right, Sam?"

Sam hitched herself up to her full height and nodded. She was struck at the ease with which Whaite lapsed into the local dialect's soft drawl. He'd told her he came from the area and she supposed it was a natural thing to do. She hoped the speech pattern wasn't contagious. She had a tendency—she deemed it a bad habit—to acquire the cadence and idiom of any area where she lived. She never managed to sound like a native and frequently received odd looks from perfect strangers who wondered if she were mocking them. She didn't have a black belt in anything.

"Maybe you can help us anyway," she said. "What do you know about this here Randall Harris?" It had started. She bit her tongue.

"Stranger to me," Clint said, and gave her a look.

"Never heard of him? Never came to no spaghetti dinner at the fire house? Seems like everybody does...ouch."

"Something the matter, Sam?" Whaite seemed concerned.

"Bit my tongue. Bad habit."

"I'll tell you who might know," Clint said, eyes still on Sam. "Steve Bolt. He hangs around with that Oldham kid. That's the little creep that starts fires. I'd like it if he's the fella you're after. Burned his old man's garage down for the insurance money only the company didn't pay because they weren't as stupid as he figured. So the old man went bust and left town. His wife always was a drinker but when he lit out she hit the bottle big time. Oldham had her put away."

"So which one? Bolt or Oldham?"

"Bolt. Oldham ain't got the brains of a toad frog."

"Where'll we meet up with Bolt?"

"He moved down in the Hollow back a while."

"He still there?"

"Can't say for sure. He got himself a job of some sort over in Floyd. He don't say much and I don't ask."

Whaite thought a moment. "He wouldn't be kin to the Freeda Bolt that was in that song about being killed and left up on the mountain, would he?"

"Can't say. That murder were a long time ago and that fellow, Harmon, the one who did her, is long dead by now, too. But Bolt comes from that part of the county, so could be."

"Well, much obliged, Clint. We'll be leaving."

"Good talking to ya," Sam said and winced. They walked to Whaite's car. "Who's Freeda Bolt?" she asked.

"Local story. Freeda lived in Willis and got herself pregnant. This guy Buren Harmon took her up to Bent Mountain, tied her up, strangled her, and put her in a shallow grave. A day later he went back to check and she was still alive so he strangled her again. Dimwitted, they said he was. That's how they talked about slow folks then. Come out as a song some local boys wrote and recorded." He looked at the sky. "I reckon we'll have to pick this up tomorrow. That's if it doesn't snow."

◇◇◇

Rose Garroway had volunteered to serve as the church's secretary when Millicent Bass became the second murder victim in the church's one hundred forty-year history. That is, as far as anyone knew for certain, she was the second and not the third. There were rumors of a duel fought between the Reverend Philip Burwell and a drummer from Pittsburg a century and a half ago. Burwell was related to Robert E. Lee in some way, but when the War Between the States broke out, folks had more engaging things on their minds. How the family of the deceased man from Pittsburg felt they never knew. He might very well have been the first casualty of that great conflict, John Brown notwithstanding. The residents of Picketsville believed so and derived a certain civic pride from the notion.

Since another killing preceded Millicent's by less than two weeks, the congregation had nearly fallen apart. Murder is not something that visits a church often.

Rose had served Blake and the congregation well. She knew everybody, had been a member of the church for decades, and had the serene disposition necessary to calm everyone. Unfortunately, she could not type, file, or function in the job. Blake was extremely fond of her and dreaded the day he would have to ask her to step down. There had been so many changes, he was not sure he wanted another, so it was with some trepidation that he returned the call posted on his caller ID.

"Vicar," she said. "I've been thinking about the secretary's job. You know, I am past eighty and even though you only need me four hours a day, it's wearing me out. Now that the bad weather is here, I'm not even sure I can get to the office. You know if it snows, the plow won't get down here for days."

"That's not a problem, Rose. I can manage. There won't be much to do, anyway."

"No, that is not what I meant. I want to give up the job. The only reason I haven't done it sooner is, well, I know how much at loose ends you've been and without a replacement, I'd feel bad leaving you in the lurch. But now I have a solution." Blake did not know whether to be pleased or sorry. "Do you have a minute to talk?"

"As it happens, I do."

"You met T.J. this morning. Well, his mother is my niece. I told you T.J. is a junior. His father was one of those charming but ineffectual men you meet now and then—always dreaming up some get-rich-quick scheme. He tried this and then that—multilevel marketing, payphones, those hidden dog fences, gumball machines. He had a website and sold worthless junk to gullible bargain hunters. The government closed that down and…you get the picture. It was one failure after another."

Blake shuffled papers and wondered where all this was going.

"When T.J. was born, his father seemed to straighten out. He had a son, after all. He talked about sending him to Harvard, of his becoming a doctor, that sort of thing. But when T.J. was diagnosed as retarded—I know, I'm not supposed to use that word, but I'm eighty and I don't feel like learning all that new soft jargon—a spade is a spade as far as I'm concerned.

"When Big Tommy found out that his son would never be rich, famous, or even average, he took it personally. His son became one more failure in a long string of failures. He took to drink and then to taking all those years of frustration out on my niece. She got a restraining order and he disappeared, but not before he cleaned out the bank accounts, mortgaged the house to the hilt, and if that weren't bad enough, didn't bother to pay his income taxes. My niece—her name is Gloria, by the way—is stuck with the lot, the debts, the back taxes, and is about to lose her house."

Blake started to say something, he wasn't sure what, but Rose kept talking.

"She supported her family off and on during those years by doing secretarial work. You said last month you wanted a full-time secretary. I hear the money is in the budget, and she needs the work. We will have the little apartment fixed up over the garage soon and she and T.J. will live there. It will be a blessing. Minnie and I are both getting to the point where having someone around will be a real godsend. So, it works for everyone. What do you say?"

Blake did not know what to say. The usual drill would be to advertise the position, involve the Mission Board in the decision, and then hire. On the other hand, one of the church's obligations was to reach out to those in trouble and help them if it could.

"I'll tell you what, Rose. Have your niece come to see me. If she is all you say she is, I will take her on temporarily, like on probation. If she works out, and I am sure she will, there should be no objection to making the job permanent. And if she does not like us, well, she'll have time to look around. Fair enough?"

"Perfect. I'll bring her to the church as soon as I can—unless we're snowbound. It's beginning to look bad."

Chapter Seven

The snow the television weatherman had been predicting for days, and everyone else anticipated or dreaded, arrived before dawn. Thick heavy flakes began to fall, lightly at first, and then heavier and faster. In an hour the ground disappeared. By six, the trees and roads, lawns and forests, were blanketed in white. Automobiles were no longer on the roads. Snowplows, salt trucks, and a few brave souls in four-wheel-drive SUVs or pickups were the only vehicles able to move, and none of them were in sight in Picketsville.

Sam surveyed her six loaves of whole wheat bread, two gallons of milk, and twenty-four rolls of toilet paper. She had succeeded in beating several dozen shoppers to the milk the night before and felt very satisfied with herself. The fact that she never ate that much bread, drank that much milk, or used that much toilet paper in a month did not deter her from joining with her neighbors in a pre-storm, late-night sortie to the supermarket. Even though snowfalls in this part of the country rarely lasted more than a day or kept folks at home more than two at the most, the threat of snow and isolation brought out hibernating instincts in even the most rational.

She wasn't sure if she would be able to get out later in the afternoon for her meeting with Whaite and, in the meantime, she would catch up on her reading. She actually looked forward to a day, or at least part of a day, shut in by the weather. As long as the power stayed on and the furnace worked, she felt content. She grabbed G. K. Sentez's latest Scott Sledge thriller, *Cat's Eye*, from the bedside table, flopped into her favorite chair, and settled into a three-hour stint of comfort reading. She felt guilty about not working—for about five minutes.

◇◇◇

"Ike?" Charlie's voice sounded far away and tinny, as if he were speaking from the bottom of a garbage can.

"I'm here, Charlie. What do you have for me?"

Ike and Charlie Garland went back many years, back to the time when Ike had been a field operative for the CIA and Charlie served as a PR flack. It turned out that Charlie attended to much more than an occasional press conference, but no one knew that, or if they did, they kept it to themselves.

"I can't talk much. I've been looking into our little problem and I think we should get together—not here. Can you meet me somewhere?"

"Charlie, it's snowing like we're in Reykjavik. This town is going to be a driving disaster for the next forty-eight hours. We'll have ice and—"

"I'll send a helicopter."

"You'll send a what?"

"We have to talk and you don't have a secure phone. I need to change that—"

"Whoa. Slow down, Charlie. This is about you-know-who, right?"

"It's a little complicated, Ike. I can't...you know the drill."

"Well, if you want to keep this low key, sending in a Blackhawk with no markings is hardly the way to go about it."

"News Channel 4. It's their chopper. We're going to borrow it for a while. They're doing a story on the big storm in the valley. Where's a good place to set it down?"

"Not a good idea, Charlie. I don't need to be a public figure. No, delete that. I refuse to be a public figure until I know what's going on. Since we found Alexei, I feel like I'm in somebody's crosshairs. Here's what we'll do. I'll get my Jeep out of the garage and, if it will start, I'll drive up to Weyer's Cave. There's an airport there, Shenandoah Valley Regional. The FBO is an Avitat. Your pilot will know what that means. Fly whatever you want there and we can talk without forty-teen people looking on."

◇◇◇

Sledge dropped to the ground and rolled to his right, jerking the Kimber Executive II from his waistband in one smooth easy movement. He snapped on its custom Belgian chrome alloy noise suppressor and squeezed off two quick shots at the dark man wearing what looked like a fur yarmulke. The heavy-load "cop killers" splashed a large hole in the guy's chest. The surprised look on his face disappeared in a puddle of Macon Blanc-Villages '97 as he pitched forward on Sledge's table. The fur yarmulke sailed past him like a kosher Frisbee. Its former wearer gurgled a curse in Thai and lay still.

Scot surveyed the mess he had made of his lunch. The wine bottle had shattered on the sidewalk and its contents were now puddled up around the creep with the hole in his chest. "Good year, bad vintage," he thought. The chicken paprika had bounced off the table and skittered six feet to the wall.

"Too bad about that—Serbs really know how to do chicken."

He recognized two Manchurians in ski masks who bore down on him riding a pair of champagne Honda Goldwing Air Rides, their muffled motors huffing so quietly Sledge nearly missed their coming. He pivoted his pistol fractionally and sent another parabellum bullet into a critical half inch of the first bike's racing Michelins. The tire blew, the front wheel twisted sideways, and the bike flipped its rider over the handlebars, arms flailing, only to land face down on the cobbled street at seventy miles an hour. He left a bloody streak for twenty meters and disappeared into a pile of African watermelons, which tumbled over him, effectively blocking the street.

"That will keep the cops out," Sledge muttered satisfiedly.
The Manchurian's Uzi skittered toward a woman in a Versace pink halter and Capri pants. She ignored it.

The second rider hit the first bike and soared, Evel Knievil-like, high into the air, barely missing four men in Armani suits at the next table. If they hadn't been leaning forward over their lentil soup, they would have been decapitated as the bike and its rider vanished over the low wall of the café and fell a thousand feet into the Orinoco.

"He said something in Thai," Scot said, knowingly. Now he knew where to look for the Prime Minister's daughter.

Sam threw the book cleanly across the room at the trash can next to her desk. She missed and the book sat, propped like a pup-tent, against the wall. She was not in the habit of cursing but she could not contain herself. Some pungent phrases followed the book to its resting place. She felt cheated. She'd bought the book because it promised a good read, an international thriller. Instead, she got Scot Sledge, a man described as the new James Bond. Sledge had, according to the jacket, no fewer than three black belts in as many varieties of martial arts, a Ph.D. in Ancient Near Eastern Philosophy, spoke six languages fluently, and served in the Navy SEALS. By page one hundred forty-seven, she'd had enough of the mindless plotting and idiotic actions by the equally moronic hero. Ph.D. or not, Scot Sledge had the intellectual capacity of a Pop Tart. He careened around Europe eating gourmet meals, which were described in mind-numbing detail, drinking expensive gin, and making inane remarks to his female counterpart. He left broken furniture, limbs, and hearts in his wake. He had been shot, stabbed, run over by a Mini Cooper, and changed his appearance and identity four times. It was ridiculous.

"Can't anyone write a decent thriller anymore?" she said to the trashcan. "Is it too much to ask for the plot to be at least plausible and the characters realistic?" She realized that this was the eighth in the Sledge series and by now the author didn't have to work at his craft. His books were all marked, *By Best Selling Author*...and that was sufficient to move them briskly off the shelves. She was about to search for another book—something uplifting or maybe technical—when the cell phone rang.

"Hey, Sam, where you at?"

"Home alone in the snowstorm, Whaite."

"Well, you're supposed to be at the office."

"I figured with the storm we wouldn't be going south today. You said you'd call if we were."

"Yeah, but there's still work that can be done. You still driving that Subaru?"

"Yes."

"It's got four-wheel drive?"

"Yes."

"Then get on down here. I expect there's stuff you can do on the computer."

"Like look up Randall Harris?"

"Ike's been called out of town and this little homicide is getting sticky."

"I'm on my way."

"Hey, Sam?"

"Yeah?"

"Can you pick me up? I don't want to risk the Chevelle on these roads and the truck's engine is in pieces in my garage."

"Twenty minutes."

Sticky?

Chapter Eight

Donnie talked to Hollis and as he'd guessed, Hollis wanted a cut of anything the PIN number produced. They argued about the amount over a couple of beers—then a couple more. At one point, Hollis took a swing at Donnie, who went to get his gun. By that time, neither of them could see, much less shoot straight. Hollis ran out into the snow only to slip on the shallow steps that led from Donnie's back porch. He landed face down in the snow next to the truck. It was not clear how in doing so he broke his leg, but he did, and that ended the argument.

Donnie took him to the hospital in Christiansburg, no mean feat under the circumstances. The roads out of Willis were nearly impassible and Donnie was drunk. He turned west at Floyd. The road between Floyd and Christiansburg is a challenge on a dry, calm, summer day, winding and twisting through the valley. Luckily, Donnie had had the presence of mind to toss four fifty-pound sacks of sand into the truck bed and that helped keep the rear end on the road. Somehow he found the ER in spite of the weather and avoided killing them both. Hollis received a shot of Demerol in the ER, which seemed to mellow him a bit, and, before the local anesthetic wore off, he agreed to a thirty percent cut, which Donnie figured would amount to less than ten because he had no intention of telling Hollis about all the transactions he would make. Leg set, Donnie loaded Hollis back into his truck and skidding and slewing on the same road, took him back home, where the two of them proceeded to polish off the remainder of the beer.

"How am I going to explain this to my old man?" Hollis was supposed to be at his house, keeping an eye on his little brother, Dermont.

"Tell him you busted your leg on your back steps."

"We don't have steps—back or otherwise."

"Well, then, how about your driveway?"

"Won't work. My brother will rat me out."

"Tell him you'll break *his* leg if he tells."

"He won't believe me."

"Then tell him I will."

"That'll work."

◇◇◇

Snow in the valley was a problem off the main roads, in the developments, and out on the farms. Since heavy snow came only rarely, small towns were hard put to justify the expenditure of large sums on plows, salt, and all the logistical problems ice and snow created. The trip from Picketsville across the Covington Road to I-81 had been a challenge. First, it took Ike nearly half an hour to get the old Jeep CJ started. Even with the four-wheel drive, he'd slipped to the shoulder frequently. Jeeps are great for all kinds of adverse weather, but his did not have the weight and, therefore, the traction to overcome ice. He did better than people in sedans and a few of the big rigs. Once on I-81, Ike managed to move along with minimal trouble. One lane on either side of the divided highway had been cleared and he followed an eighteen wheeler most of the way north. Even so, it took him nearly two hours to cover the fifty or so miles to the turnoff outside of Winchester and another twenty minutes to work his way to Weyer's Cave and the airport. He found Shenandoah Valley Airport and pulled onto its parking lot just as an unmarked helicopter settled on the ramp in a flurry of relocated snow. Ike made his way to the café and had a cappuccino and biscotti in hand when Charlie Garland burst through the door. Without looking at Ike, he led the way across the lobby to the Jack Martin Conference Room. "We have this room reserved," he said.

"Good to see you, too, Charlie…No, not much trouble getting here…Just two and a half hours of eyestrain and acid indigestion…So how was your trip?…Glad to hear it."

"What?" Charlie's glasses had fogged up, not the disability it might have been for anyone else, as Charlie rarely cleaned, much less polished, his glasses.

"I said hello."

"Close the door, Ike, we don't have much time. I have to be back at Langley in two hours. Here, this is for you." He shoved a leather case across the table at Ike.

The room could be interchanged for any of a hundred like it across the country. It had a table that looked vaguely like a surfboard on steroids and a dozen black leather swivel chairs arranged around it. A white board adorned one wall and a large aeronautical chart of the valley another. Ike sat and stared at the case. "What is it?"

"Cell phone."

"I already have a cell phone."

"Not like this one."

"What does this one do that mine can't?"

"It's secure."

"How?"

"I don't know. The guys in tech say it is. There're complete instructions in the case. The short course is, you call me…I have a new number, by the way, and when I answer, you push this button, and count to four or something, and then talk normally. It's satellite and so there's a delay sometimes. The electronics encrypt your transmission and then decode it at my end."

"This is like those James Bond movies. You don't have a Rolex watch with a steel-cutting laser in it for me, too? How is Q, by the way?"

"Not a joke, Ike. Now, I need to fill you in on what we've uncovered so far about Kamarov."

Ike opened the case and lifted out the phone. "This thing must weigh five pounds."

"Just over one. It's the electronics and the battery, they tell me. Oh, and don't hold it up to your ear. Use the hands-free gizmo."

"Because?"

"It's a little...no, make that a lot, more powerful than the usual thing you get at the phone store. Use it too much and it could fry your brain."

"I won't use it at all."

"And don't leave it in your lap either. Bad for the...you know."

"All the more reason not to use it. I won't even turn it on."

"You've got to."

"Can't. New town ordinance. I can't use a cell phone while operating a motor vehicle. Amazing. I never thought I'd be happy about that. Irony, that's what that is."

"Can't use it while operating a...not even with the hands free?"

"Well that would put it next to my heart—not good—or in my lap—worse."

"Ike, can we move along here? It's just for emergencies and I hope we won't need it. But you are conducting an investigation in the field and you are more likely to turn up something needing an urgent response than we are."

"You'll have yours on all the time?"

"All the time."

"But not in your lap. I would hate to think of Baltimore society being deprived of another generation of Garlands."

Charlie sighed and leaned forward in his chair and fiddled with an unused glass ashtray. "This is as far as we have gone. It's delicate, Ike. You know we are in another round of reorganization talks to make the country's intelligence community cooperate, blah, blah, blah."

"Yes, and good luck with that."

"Don't be cynical. You're probably right, but it's best to stay hopeful."

"Absolutely."

"Anyway, that means another round of jockeying for position and power. Before the final configuration is set, everybody in all the agencies and the Bureau is anxious to get an edge."

"They want to find out your weak spots so they can pull you down."

"Yes. And that leads us to Kamarov." Ike unwrapped his biscotti. The rattle of cellophane drowned out Charlie's words. "Do you mind, Ike?"

"Sorry." Ike slid the biscuit from its wrapper and tentatively dipped it in his coffee. "Go on."

"Okay, to Kamarov. He was not eliminated as we believed. He went to some place in Siberia called Novosibirsk and then disappeared from there. It looks like someone over here spent some serious money and committed their Russian assets to get him and squirrel him away. You know black programs?"

"A black program…funding not logged in on anyone's budget. Strictly *ad hoc* and not accountable to Congress, the Administration, or even God. Whose?"

"We don't know. We're guessing FBI, but it could be anybody, Defense Intelligence Agency, White House, or one of the really deep units that we know for a certainty exists only by the footprints they occasionally leave behind."

"Kamarov could hardly tell them anything about the old Soviet intelligence that we don't already know, and it's all dated anyway."

Charlie did not seem to be his usual composed self today and Ike wondered why. Not a good sign. Charlie never seemed to worry about anything. "He came here, I'm guessing, at great expense because they think, or he convinced them, he could tell them secrets about us."

"Not us—you, the Agency. I don't work there anymore, remember? Look, surely whoever is running the black program can find that stuff without him. I know half a dozen senators on the Intelligence Committee that would happily leak it."

"What if he had knowledge of 9-11?"

"He couldn't know anything about the Agency or 9-11. He'd already taken up residency in the frozen tundra by then."

"Suppose they didn't know that. Let's say he's approached by whoever is behind this and let's say all they want is some information about CIA operational failures in the past. They promise to send him to some place warm. But Alexei wants more—a lot more—so he increases his value by hinting he knows things about 9-11, never says he does or doesn't, just intimates and..."

Ike scratched his head and watched as the end of his biscotti detached and sank to the bottom of his cup. "Okay, he bargains his way into their program. The testimony from a spy of his caliber, whether true or false, would kill you. But what happens when they finally figure out he doesn't know anything?"

"They get rid of him and dump him on you—a little joke."

"Or, he goes snooping around and actually finds something that is, if not as valuable as 9-11, worth keeping him around for."

"Like what?"

Ike tried soaking the biscotti again. Timing seemed to be everything. "I don't know. By the way, what are your people doing up at Callend College?" Charlie's normally ruddy face faded to off-white. "Uh oh, do we have a problem? And here's another thought. One of your people recognized him. He's living down near Floyd, for God's sake. What knucklehead put him there, I wonder? And the suits in DC are told and they order him terminated. End of story."

"Or, going back to your first thought, his new employers discover he's useless and drop him themselves."

"It would be easier to just retire him to Miami Beach." This time the biscotti end fell into Ike's lap on its transit from cup to lips.

"...or Rio de Janeiro, Ike. Until we know for sure, we have a serious problem. He's dead. He's in your jurisdiction. Why is that? Did someone find out about...Peter? Is someone sending you a message?"

"Are you absolutely sure the Agency didn't put him there?"

Charlie looked down at the table's surface. "Ike, I honestly don't know."

"They left his driver's license like they wanted whoever found him to believe he was Harris. Well, maybe not…you don't think it's just a coincidence he's dumped in Picketsville?"

Charlie only closed his eyes and shook his head. "No, I don't guess it could be."

Ike dropped the remainder of his biscotti into the cup and shoved it aside.

Chapter Nine

Sam could only stare at Whaite. She'd driven across town in the snow. She nearly hit a minivan with Michigan plates whose owner had decided the middle of Main Street was the safest place to drive. All that effort spent to pick him up assuming that she would be asked to start tracking down Randall Harris on her computer. When they reached the office, she'd planned to access state, federal, and other databases that might have something to offer. Instead, Whaite told her to wait.

Finally, regaining her voice, she said, "You don't want me to find Harris on the computer."

"Not now, no. Don't put his name, fingerprints…anything into your queries. Stay away from the feds especially."

"This is not making any sense. Where's Ike?"

"He had a meeting."

"A meeting? In this weather he's at a meeting? Where?"

"I don't know."

"I'll call him."

"He won't answer. He can't use the phone in the car."

"I'll get him on the radio."

"He isn't in a cruiser. He's driving that Jeep of his."

Sam exploded. "I've spent the last six months building the information technology capacity of this department so that it is the match of any in the state—no, in the country. We can tap into Richmond, Washington, anywhere. We have software that will let me into places even the President of the United States can't access and you say, don't use it? Why am I here?"

"Wait 'til Ike gets back. Then maybe he'll tell you why."

"This is deep stuff, isn't it?" Sam swiveled around in her chair and stared through the rime-encrusted window. There wasn't much to see. The snow had lightened and would probably stop in a few hours. If the temperature rose, tomorrow would be a normal day. If it dropped, there would be trouble—ice. She drummed her fingers and tried not to show her annoyance.

"So what *do* you want me to do?"

"Ike wants you to tap the state's motor vehicle database and track Harris' driver's license number."

"We already know that. Why look for him there?"

"Not by name—by number."

"Just the number?"

"That's it. See if it really belongs to him. Then, if it does, and remember, stay in the motor vehicle database—don't go anywhere else—see if he has any violations, outstanding citations, stuff like that."

"Suppose, for the sake of argument, I come up blank on the first."

"Then run license issues for the month before and after the issue date on his. See what you find."

"That's it?"

"For now—that's it."

◇◇◇

Andover Crisp was having a bad day. He watched helplessly as Operation Cutthroat went into the toilet. His man had skipped and all the assets he could bring into play had failed to find him. Every hospital in the area had been checked for accident victims, illness, heart attacks, you name it. No DOAs, no John Does, nothing. No one even remotely answering to Kamarov's description had boarded a plane, train, or rented a car. He did not enter Mexico or Canada. Where was he? Crisp picked up the phone.

"I want you to do it again." He waited for the silence at the other end to break. He shuffled his papers.

"Again? You mean everything?"

"Everything—hospitals, airlines, cars, all of it."

"Okay—"

"Any hits on his credit cards?"

"No sir, not yet."

"Bank account still intact?"

"No activity there either."

"Keep it open. He's going to need money eventually. When he does, I don't want him to think we're on to him. Let him get the money. With any luck he'll leave a trail."

"Okay. Sir?"

"What?"

"Have you considered the possibility that the Agency found out about him and took him out?"

"I have. Look, they're not stupid. If they tumbled to him, they'd hold him and try to turn him. He has friends over there, to hear him tell it. He'd probably soak them for more cash and sell us out. No, I don't think they did anything to him, but if we get close and it looks like they are on to him…well, you know what to do."

"Sir?"

"I shouldn't have to say it, should I?"

"No, sir."

"Now, go over the ground again and again until we find the gap he slipped through. If he's out there, he's on tape somewhere and he's findable."

◇◇◇

Sam stared at her screen for a full minute. Something had to be wrong. "Whaite, can you possibly get Ike on the phone? Maybe he's not driving or maybe he'll answer if he sees you on his caller ID. He's just contrary enough to ignore the ordinance."

"You have something?"

"I don't know. Look here." She pointed at the screen in front of her. "Harris' driver's license number is listed but without a name. It just says 'assigned.' What does that mean?"

"Beats me. I'm out of my depth here, Sam, but I think you need to back out of that database right now. Can you do that without anybody knowing you were there?"

"I can try. I don't know what kind of monitoring program they run up there. What with all the phony driver's license scams and attempts at identity theft they've had lately, they may be running a tracking program and be on to us already. If they trace us, I'll make sure they know we are a police department. That should satisfy them."

"Could you make it some department other than this one?"

"Who?"

"Someplace far away, like Kansas."

Sam typed furiously for several minutes. She sat back and looked at the screen in front of her. Then she quickly shut the whole bank down. One by one the flat panels flickered and went black.

"Why'd you shut down? Now nobody can contact us and—"

"Two reasons. One, I am not doing another blessed thing unless and until you or Ike tells me what this is all about. I know I do not have much experience in the investigations department and I do not know the routines. I have never worked a homicide, but I know that what we are doing here is not normal and I won't go any further until I know."

"What's the other reason?"

"Someone was trying to trace us. I hope I shut down before they confirmed."

"Whew. That gadgetry blows my mind. You could tell if someone was trying to find us? So they know it's us?"

"Not if I shut down in time. They may not accept the Kansas address, but it's all they have. They'll assume it was just another hacker."

"You're sure about that?"

"We live in hope."

◇◇◇

Donnie's head buzzed a little, but not enough to keep him from seeing what needed to be done. "If your old man is gone for the day, why don't we just go get that PIN right now?" Hollis, his mind awash in painkillers, did not answer.

"Hollis," Donnie shouted, "wake up. Let's go do the PIN now before your old man gets home."

"Donnie, I can't today, man. I busted my leg, my little brother has probably trashed the house, and all those pills are making me feel weird. Hand me the bottle."

"You done took them all. The doc said one every four hours and you've took the whole two days' worth already."

"Weird, really weird."

"Let's go. I'll take you home. Tomorrow we go for the PIN, you got it? Tomorrow."

"Tomorrow, tomorrow, I love ya tomorrow, you're only a day away…Tooo…morrow—"

"Shut up and get in the truck."

"It's stopped snowing."

"Whoopee. Get in the truck."

Hollis frowned and looked owlishly at him. "Someday you're going to be in real trouble, Donald."

"Maybe, and maybe you're my ticket outta this burg."

"What did you do to the dude?"

"Do? I didn't do nothing."

"You got his credit cards."

"Finders keepers."

"I ain't seen him around lately."

"It's the weather. Maybe he's a pussy when it comes to cold."

"Take me home, James."

"Shut up."

◇◇◇

Ike found a Denny's open along I-81 and pulled off for a break. He needed time to think. He carried Charlie's secure cell phone in with him and placed it on the table. Denny's did breakfast.

He knew they also served lunches, platters, dinners, and a great variety of menu items, but the only thing worth eating at a Denny's, Ike believed, was breakfast. While he waited he pulled the phone from its case and read the instructions printed on the inside. The phone appeared to have been borrowed from a SEAL team. Or perhaps it had been issued to them and returned. Either way it was undoubtedly government issue.

"Well now, it's been a long time since I seen one of them old timey cell phones," his waitress said as she placed silverware and a glass of water in front of him. "You get that at a yard sale?"

"No yard sales in this weather, darlin'."

"Well, my daddy had one like that back in the day. Like, he was the first man in our town to have one. It didn't work so good though. No towers out where we lived. Be right back with your coffee."

Ike pushed the phone back into its case and stared out the window. The sun hovered low in the west just above the mountains. The snow had stopped and tomorrow would be cold. He had no idea what he would do with the phone. Give it to Whaite? He, more than Ike, would likely turn up something useful. But it had been issued to him, to Charlie, actually, and was signed for. If it went missing, Charlie would be held responsible.

Ike did not like the possibilities Kamarov's death created. Someone killed him and that someone could be one of Charlie's colleagues, from the presumed black program, or…it occurred to him, even a Russian sent to shut Kamarov down for certain. Where do you begin to sort that out?

"Say, you're that sheriff from down to Picketsville. I thought I recognized you. Here's your coffee. I hope it ain't too hot. You done had that big robbery with all them pictures and stuff, didn't you?"

"Yes, we did. You remembered."

"Well shoot, yes. It was on the TV and in the papers—even *USA Today* had you. I seen you on one of their pages. I get to read the papers the customers leave behind all the time. Never have to buy one. It's like a perk or something."

"Yes, well…" Ike sipped his coffee. It was too hot.

"So, how'd you catch the bad guys anyway?"

"Routine police work. You ask questions, poke around, ask more questions, and get lucky."

"You don't have to check their DNA and stuff like that? I watch the TV and that's how they do it. They never, you know, bang into rooms and such. They sit in this lab-like place and do tests and then go arrest bad guys. And they're always right. You don't do that?"

"Only when we don't have any other choices. Mostly we ask questions and put people in the right place at the right time. Give me a Grand Slam, bacon crisp, please."

"Okay, coming right up. Well, it's been nice talking to you. The manager's giving me a look. He don't like us fraternizing too much with the customers, but seeing as how you are a police, I guess it don't matter."

Routine police work. He'd send Whaite and Sam out again. Starting tomorrow, they'd just have to grind it out.

Chapter Ten

Colonel Robert Twelvetrees stared at the predicament he had created with his car. It hung halfway in the driveway and halfway in the street, its rear end buried in a low snowbank that he had not seen, a snowbank created by a well-meaning neighbor plowing the street. Successive melting and thawing during the previous day had turned it into nearly solid ice. Now he could go neither forward nor backward and he needed to get to the store. He stood alone in the cold, squinting at the sunlight reflected off the car's windshield. He'd mislaid his gloves somewhere. Luckily, his neighbors had all left for work or were warm and safe indoors. Had they been outside and nearby, they would have heard some United States Army Cavalry language that would have made a sailor blush.

He stood with his back to the street and told his battered Buick what he thought of snow, snowplows, and the weather in general. He did not notice the car that stopped a few yards from him. Rose Garroway called out, "Colonel, can we give you a lift anywhere?"

He spun and squinted in the direction of the voice.

"Who's that?" he barked.

"It's Rose Garroway from church," she replied. "Do you need any help?"

"My car's stuck in this dad-burned snowbank. I can't get her loose and I need to get to the store."

"Come with us and when we get back, T.J. will help dig you out."

"Who's T.J.?"

"My nephew. Hop in."

The colonel hesitated. He did not like being helped and he especially did not like being helped by women. But he had no choice. He made his way to the car and climbed in next to a woman he took to be Minnie.

"Buckle up," T.J. directed. "Can't move until everyone's buckled up."

Colonel Bob struggled with the rear seat belt. Grunting and mumbling under his breath, he finally got himself secure and the car moved on. T.J. sounded like an old master sergeant he had in Korea. He could only see the back of his head and that only dimly. He rubbed his eyes to clear them. It did not help. He was having a particularly bad eye day.

They stopped at a grocery store just off the Covington Road, not the one he usually patronized. He preferred the market a bit closer to the highway. He knew his way around that one, and the clerks knew him and what he liked. If he wanted an inch-thick filet mignon—filly mig-nons he called them—they would cut it for him specially.

In this store, he did not know where to find anything. He bumped into a cart and made his way tentatively down a side aisle, nearly knocking several cans of pumpkin pie filling on the floor before he got himself centered. He knew he needed a plan. This new store would not give up its secrets easily. Coffee, steak and potatoes, and a few cans of vegetables would hold him, he figured. His eyes should be better tomorrow and then he'd unstick the car and get the rest.

He picked up a can and peered at the label. He held it close to his face. He knew it was green, but peas, beans, or spinach? He moved uncertainly down the aisle searching for familiar labels and boxes, dropping likely candidates into the cart. When his nose told him he had reached coffee, he grabbed a bag and peered intently at it. He covered one eye with his left hand. The brand name swam into view. It was not one he recognized.

Rose Garroway wheeled her cart up beside him.

"Colonel, are you all right?" the concern in her voice evident.

"It's these glasses of mine," he grumbled. "I must need a new prescription. Can't see a thing today." He held the bag of coffee near his nose and studied the label.

"T.J.," Rose called, "see if you can give the Colonel a hand here. His glasses aren't working."

"I can help," T.J. said and took the handle of the cart. "What do you need, Mister Colonel Bob?"

"Just tell me what this label says."

"Fol…ger's High Mountain de…caffeine…ated coffee, thirteen oh zee…"

Bob turned to look more closely at the boy. Blurred as his vision was, he saw the broad forehead and wide-set eyes.

"You can read okay, T.J.?"

"Oh, yes, I am the best reader in my class."

"You are, are you? Well, if this don't beat the witches. The Halt and the Blind. All we need now is the Lame and we'll have a complete set."

"A complete set of what?"

"It's from the Bible, boy. Never mind."

"Okay. What else do we need there, Mister Colonel Bob?"

"Well, son, you can take us to the bananas. Do you like bananas?"

"Yes, sir, I do."

They finished shopping. Colonel Bob explained to T.J. that oh zee meant ounces and el bee ess meant pounds. For reasons he could not understand but he guessed some fancy-pants psychologist could, he had taken a liking to the boy. By the time they met Rose and her sister at the front of the store they were as chummy as two ice fishermen in a small hut on a frozen lake in Minnesota.

"So, T.J., you think we can get this buggy dug out?" Colonel Bob asked. His vision had cleared up a bit. He knew it would not last, that the blurriness would return soon. The doctor had said macular degeneration. He knew enough about that to know he would be blind in a matter of months, a year at the outside. He looked at his stranded car and wondered if it made any sense to dig it out. He could barely drive it now. And without the car, he would be alone, isolated, unable to get to the store, or anywhere. His heart sank.

"Yes sir, Mister Colonel Bob, we can get her out."

"T.J., drop one or the other of those titles, will you? Either no colonel or no mister."

"Okay, which one?"

"Drop the mister. Now, how about I back up a little—see if it can move."

"No, don't back up."

"Why not? The front is on solid ice. Back is the only way she'll go."

"No back up, Colonel Bob. Let me dig out the front."

Colonel Bob walked to the rear of the car to explain to T.J. why backwards was preferable to forwards. The blurred image of his mailbox swam into view. It hung at a thirty-degree angle off dead center, snug against his rear bumper. Back would have flattened it.

"Oh, I see," he said. "Listen, T.J., I'm going to get my mail out of that box and go inside. Here are the car keys. You dig it out and park it in the driveway. Then come in. We'll figure out what I owe you. Oh, and if you see my gloves anywhere, bring them in, too."

"Okay, Colonel Bob," T.J. said and slid the shovel under a pile of ice and snow.

Inside, the colonel could make out the fire flickering on the grate. Its warmth cheered him a bit. He always left the television on when he went out. He had an idea that anyone thinking about breaking in would assume that there must be someone home if the TV was on. He did not watch much television anymore except the news. He mostly listened. News programs were talking heads and he could hear them. If he turned his head sideways and looked at a spot a few feet to the left of the screen he could make out faces on it. Occasionally he managed to watch an old movie, one he had seen many times before so that the images were familiar and he did not miss the focus.

Colonel Bob snapped off the television and turned his attention to the fistful of mail. It consisted of a stack of Christmas cards the senders of which he probably would not be able to identify, bills with sums he could not read without his magnifying glass, and a letter from the Department of Motor Vehicles. He retrieved his glass. This would not be good news. He read and reread the letter. Then, a decision made, picked up the phone, and carefully punched in the number on its oversized buttons.

◇◇◇

Nearly an hour had passed when T.J. pushed through the kitchen door. Colonel Bob waved in the general direction of a packet of cocoa mix on the table and the steaming tea kettle. T.J. blew on his hands and sat momentarily unsure what Colonel Bob wanted him to do.

"Colonel Bob, I found these gloves in the snow. They must be yours because mine are not this color."

"Thank you. They're mine. T.J., I want to make you a proposition."

"Make me a proposition?"

"A deal, an offer. I just talked to Miz Garroway, and she said it would be fine. She said you are one heck of a driver and handy. She hopes you will be living over her garage in a month or so, and helping her and your great aunt Minnie. But she can't pay you anything. I need a driver and a helping hand right now. This is a letter I received from the Department of Motor Vehicles. It says I have to take a retest to renew my driver's license. I'll never pass. I can't see any better'n a bat. I want to hire you to drive me around, help around the house and so on. What do you say?"

"Aunt Rose said it's okay?"

"Yep, starting right now. She said I should pay you half and the rest is to go into an account she will set up for you at the bank. That suit you?"

"Yes, sir, Colonel Bob."

T.J. let his considerable forehead fall into a frown.

"Aunt Rose is who she is. You are Colonel Bob, and I'm just T.J. Shouldn't I be something T.J.?"

Colonel Robert Twelvetrees, once a very young soldier in the ranks with George S. Patton himself, a graduate of the Citadel, and decorated combat veteran of several wars, gazed at a boy who would never be any of those things and saluted.

"Thomas Harkins," he announced solemnly, "by the power invested in me as a colonel in the United States Army, I hereby promote you to the rank of master sergeant. From now on you will be Sergeant T.J. This is a field promotion, you understand, and subject to subsequent approval by CICUSA, that's commander in chief of the United States Army. The paperwork may take some time. I've got some old stripes around here somewhere."

"Sergeant T.J." the new non-com said, his face beaming. "Yes, sir, Colonel Bob."

Chapter Eleven

Sam swallowed her irritation at being left out of the loop or whatever Whaite and Ike had going. She felt like a fool. Something big had happened and she was being treated like some airhead prom queen instead of a colleague. When Whaite arrived she gave him a grunt for a greeting. He smiled, waved to everybody else in the office, and took her by the elbow. "Boss' office. He wants to see us. Actually he wants to see you."

"This had better be good."

"Oh, it will. You're going to love it. At least at first, then when you see the work ahead, you may want to change your mind."

◇◇◇

Ike sat with his back to the glass panels that formed most of the wall that separated him from the world. His mind wandered over possibilities. He stared at Charlie's secure cell phone and drummed his fingers. He jumped when Whaite rapped on his door, setting the glass panels rattling.

"You ready for us, Ike?"

He waved his two deputies in and asked them to sit. Whaite knew the general outline of the problem. What he had to say primarily concerned Sam. He spent the next fifteen minutes filling her in on the details. Sam listened at first with a frown on her face, then a look of amazement.

"I still don't see how this…Kamarov is connected to you. I know you were CIA but what has that got to do with this man?"

"It's enough to know that I left the Agency because my wife's death was part of a cover-up in the Agency. Kamerov apparently found out the general outlines and tried to tell me, I think. He disappeared and we supposed he'd been eliminated. We were wrong."

"So now he's part of a...what did you call it...a black program?"

"He *was* part of a black program. The question is whose?"

The three sat quietly, each absorbed in his or her thoughts. Sam shifted around in her chair. "So what do we do now?"

"That's the question, isn't it? There's an enormous amount of work ahead of us but I'm not sure we can do it."

"Why not?"

"Sam, I have to ask you something and it's personal."

"This is about Karl, isn't it?"

"More or less. Where is he now?"

"Oh my God. He's been reassigned. I thought he'd been assigned to another witness protection program dropout, but this could be Kamarov, couldn't it?"

"He's part of a group looking for someone?"

"I'm not sure now. I thought so. I mean, that's what I heard."

Essie Falco at her desk and some clerk from the Town Council were the only occupants of the adjoining room. Whaite stood and closed Ike's door, anyway. "Better safe than sorry. If it's our man, it means the program is FBI."

"Back to Karl. Sam, what happens if we confirm the black operation is the Bureau's? You will be working against them and not in a nice way. Can you do that?"

"You mean could I pursue whatever measures I'm called on to do even if it means compromising or putting Karl at risk?"

"In a nutshell—yes."

"Oh my. I've only known him for a couple of months but I thought this weekend he would..."

Ike waited. His heart went out to her. She was bright and quick and loyal. He had a feeling that her relationship with Karl Hedrick could be the first really serious one she'd ever had. At the same time her dream of becoming a law enforcement officer was at stake as well. Ike sighed, afraid he would be the one to break her heart. She swallowed. "If it's about murder and my job is to find that out, then Karl will have to understand. If he doesn't, I guess he's not the person I think he is."

"You don't have to do this, Sam. I can take you off this case and find something else."

"I'm in."

"Okay. Here's what we do next."

◇◇◇

An hour later the three separated. Whaite headed to Floyd County to track down Donnie Oldham and Steve Bolt. Somewhere in the county someone knew what had happened to Kamarov/Harris. The smart odds were not on Bolt or Oldham, but you had to start somewhere. Ike explained how the secure phone worked. Whaite looked at its bulk and declined.

"Look, I'll just use the normal one to call you, Ike. The town ordinance probably doesn't carry down there and even if it does, who's going to know?" Ike nodded and Whaite slipped out the door.

"Okay, Sam, now you understand why I didn't want you on the internet or poking around in law enforcement databases. The minute you started, whoever is behind this would disappear into thin air. We'd never find out what happened."

"We're good. The only possible hit is with the driver's licensing people and, worst case, they think they were hit by a hacker."

"Sam, what can you do with that system of yours?"

"It depends on what you have in mind. But if you're asking, can I go deep into programs and sites—yes, I can."

"How deep?"

"Pretty nearly anywhere. I have the latest and the best software. In a way, we are a black program ourselves."

"How's that?"

"Like your former colleagues in the government, we are almost completely off-budget and we don't have to take low bid.

Most of this software came to me from friends and acquaintances in the field. Some of it isn't even registered anywhere."

"You can out-do the CIA, FBI, DIA, and NSA?"

"I didn't say that. To do that, we'd need a quantum computer. You don't want to know the price tag on one of those. What I said is, we have the capacity to get in anywhere. I presume they do, too."

"I see, I guess…okay, see if you can track down the black program…but be careful."

◇◇◇

Hollis settled in front of his father's computer. He turned and looked at Donnie. "You don't have his driver's license?"

"It wasn't in the wallet."

"Man, I can't do anything without someplace to start."

"You're stalling. You have a name. Don't you just swipe that thing and read the PIN off the back?"

"It isn't that easy."

"How often have you done this, Hollis? I mean, you know what you're doing, right?"

"I watched the old man a couple of times."

"You watched. That's it?"

Hollis gazed at the blue-green screen and tried to remember what he had to do next. He opened his father's files and began to look for one that had a name that might tell him what it was. His father had not left a pathway. He knew his father's password—period. He felt Donnie's anger building. Donnie was crazy. You didn't want him angry at you. He had some notion he really was a throwback to the old mountain men that used to live in the area and he was as likely to shoot you as look at you. At least that's what Hollis believed.

"Whatcha doin' at Dad's computer, dork?" Dermont asked.

"Looking for something, stupid."

"Yeah? What?"

"None of your business."

"We want the thing that can read PIN numbers," Donnie said.

"What'll you give me if I tell you?"

"You know?" Donnie and Hollis said in unison.

"Yep."

"Ten bucks."

"For a PIN number. You got to be kidding."

"Okay," Donnie thought for a moment. "You know Dolores over at The Pub?"

"The one with the big boobs?"

"Yeah. I'll fix you up with her."

Dermont's hormones had kicked in the previous summer and the thought of an hour or two with Dolores was more than he could resist. The fact he was only thirteen, skinny, and barely five-six, while Dolores went five-eleven and one hundred sixty-five pounds and might overwhelm him, so to speak, did not deflect his ambition. He'd fantasized enough erotic behavior in the last six months to persuade himself he'd be the match for any and all.

"Get out of the way, Hollis." He slid into the chair and in ten minutes had the PIN numbers for all of the cards, Randall Harris' social security number, and his zip code as well. He turned to Donnie. "When?"

"When what?"

"When to I get to do Dolores?"

"I'll let you know. She's in Richmond visiting her sister this week."

"I seen her this morning."

"She left this afternoon."

Chapter Twelve

Blake Fisher climbed the stairs to the double offices wedged into the rear of the church building. Voices and footsteps on the stairs announced the arrival of Rose Garroway and her niece, Gloria. Blake spent the next hour showing Gloria the routine he hoped to adopt. He was delighted at how quickly she assumed charge of the files and equipment. Obviously, she knew her way around a computer and soon sorted and disposed of the piles of papers and correspondence her aunt had created on the desk. She needed no instruction in the mechanics of the answering machine—a fact that impressed him enormously, as he usually had to make two or three stabs at recording a message before getting it right. With a sigh of relief, he gave her the times and dates of the Christmas services and listened as she recorded the new message flawlessly on the first try.

Marge Burk thumped up the stairs just as she finished.

"Vicar," she grumped. Marge had not yet warmed to Blake. She still pined for his predecessor, even though the latter had been dead nearly a year. Marge, as church treasurer, handled the books, deposits, and bill paying, including cutting Blake's paycheck, a fact that always made him a little nervous. If Marge had been an ally, he probably would not have worried.

"I need your signature on these checks." She dumped the checks out in an untidy pile. He spread them out and inspected each as he signed.

"No need to read 'em," Marge said. "They're all legit. Nobody's skimming the till."

"Never believed they were," he said, trying to keep the annoyance out of his voice. "I just like to see what I sign. There ought to be an easier way to do this."

"You don't bank over the internet?" Gloria asked.

"Can't figure computers out—hate 'em, in fact," Marge said. "What's to keep the whatchacallems…hacks, from getting in and taking our money?"

"Hackers. Well, you have password protection and a PIN and the fact is, if they wanted our money and were really that good, they'd have had it years ago. The money is in the bank and the bank's computer is the one they would attack, not ours."

"Still, I'd have to learn to use that thing there and I don't want to. How come you know so much about it, anyway?"

Blake interrupted before the winter's chill outside was replicated by the one developing inside.

"Marge, you haven't met our new secretary. Gloria Harkins, this is Marge Burk, our treasurer." Gloria smiled. Marge grunted.

"I used to work at a bank, Mrs. Burk, and there is no reason for you to have to work the computer at all. If you leave me a list of the bills and the amounts you want transferred, I can do that for you."

"You can do that? See, that's what I mean. If you can do that, what's to prevent someone else from signing on and—?"

"I would have to set the system up with the bank. Only authorized persons could log on and access the system. All you would need to do is deposit the money and designate what bills were to be paid and when. I would set it up for only the signatories, which includes you, and when you have a moment I could show you how to use the system, just in case I wasn't available or you preferred to do it yourself."

"Um, you do that, honey…how long would it take?"

"I can have it up by tomorrow."

"Good, we'll hold these bills and do them then." Marge scooped up the stack of checks and thumped down the stairs without a thank you or a goodbye. Rose, who had been uncharacteristically quiet, said, "She's just like her mother—rude as a Russian." Blake was not sure how rude Russians were, but he guessed in Rose's octogenarian world, they must be very rude, indeed.

"Gloria, there is nothing I can teach you, and Rose can show you where she's hidden all the things she did not want me to see. I have a luncheon appointment and will be out the rest of the day. My calendar is on my desk. Feel free to fill it if necessary."

◇◇◇

Donnie decided to milk ATM machines before he tried credit cards, but his gas gauge read empty. The garage where he stopped to fill up had a sale on tires and his were looking bad, so he bought a set of four and had them mounted. He almost went for four custom chrome wheels as well, which would have set him back another two grand. He didn't know if the card would take that much or not. He settled for a tank of gas and four tires. The bill came to nearly seven hundred and fifty dollars. He swiped the card and waited while the processing program ran. He put the card away. The clerk looked at him and asked for some identification. He showed him his driver's license. Fortunately, the clerk hadn't thought to ask for the card back. There was no way he'd ever pass for Randall Harris. Flushed with this minor triumph, he ditched his plan to do the ATMs first and headed for the ABC store. Using a second card, he stocked up on vodka—the big gallons. To complete the transaction all he had to do was enter a zip code. The beer he picked up with a second card and then some groceries, again with the first. He'd be fixed for a week at least. Overall, he'd managed to charge over a thousand dollars.

He drove to Roanoke and hit two ATMs, extracting three hundred dollars from each. From Roanoke he drove south to Rocky Mount, Martinsville, and then across the state line into North Carolina. The ATMs continued to spill out money. Since he'd never had an ATM card, it didn't strike him as odd that the

ATMs kept paying the minimum instead of shutting him off. He glanced at the remaining balance line and whistled. The dude had nearly one hundred thousand dollars in his account. What kind of person had that kind of money in a bank account? He headed west to Mount Airy, hit two more machines, and then caught I-77 to the parkway and drove home. He tried to calculate how many ATMs he'd have to hit, at three hundred dollars a pop, to pull out the whole one hundred thousand. He quit after the third three in a row appeared in his mental arithmetic and the prospect for yet a fourth seemed likely.

◇◇◇

Sam stared at her computer. As long as its use had stayed within ethical parameters, she had no problem, but she could be breaching those boundaries and moving into areas she'd only flirted with before. In the past, entering into her personnel file or doing a favor or two for a friend had constituted her only brushes with serious hacking. But probing into the dark recesses of the intelligence world…She could only imagine what the consequences might be were she caught. She shivered. Ike said she didn't have to do it, but the challenge was irresistible. She'd never done anything on such a grand scale.

She took a deep breath and typed in the characters that would activate her genie program, her first-level search engine. Once started, she would stay at the task for the next fifteen hours. She would not want to back out and try to reenter. If she'd inadvertently left a footprint, there could be a tracer program waiting for her when she logged back in. By staying online she could see one coming and shut down before it found her, as she had with the Department of Motor Vehicles.

After an hour she hit on a program that seemed to be paralleling hers. Someone else asking the same or similar questions. She followed it—a lion stalking a water buffalo—risky for both. She ran her program invisibly on top of the other. A series of numbers scrolled down the screen—apparently dollar amounts—and she guessed location codes. She actuated a save program and grabbed the file as it grew, as well as all of the previous entries. The scrolling stopped and she backed out.

"Ike," she called, "you need to see this."

◇◇◇

Andover Crisp's phone rang. "This had better be good news or heads will roll."

"It's a start, Mr. Crisp. He's on the move. We have hits on credit cards and ATMs. He left Roanoke and headed south. Then he veered west. His next stop should be Bristol, Tennessee, or somewhere down I-77."

"What's he doing?"

"It looks like he's cashing out his bank account and buying things."

"What kind of things?"

"We won't know that for a while. We have to wait for the transactions to be posted or send someone in. And he's drawing out the maximum three hundred at every ATM."

"Keep the accounts open. I want to follow him wherever he goes. Put everyone on it. I want that man."

Chapter Thirteen

T.J. stared over the fence as Donald pulled his truck into the yard. He watched him park and unload bags and bottles, carry them into the house, and carefully cover his vehicle with its tarpaulin. T.J. knew Donald always kept his truck covered because it was a special truck. Donald told him so. Everybody knew Donald. He had money and lots of friends at The Pub. T.J. didn't go to The Pub, but he knew about it. Donald had told him—about the girls and the fun they had there. He said T.J. should come with him some time. He said the girls asked about him. T.J. thought that would be a fine idea. He didn't know much about girls—only what Donald told him and he wasn't too sure about most of that. Some of the things he said happened between men and women didn't make much sense and he thought Donald must be fibbing. Still, there were times when…he wanted to know for sure. He lifted up on his toe tips to see better.

"Hey, Donald, what're you doing?"

"What's it look like I'm doing? I'm putting the tarp on the truck like I always do."

"Are you going to The Pub, too?"

"Probably. Going to look in on some of the girls. I think they missed me. I had a payday today and I think I'm going to make a night of it." He waved a stack of bills at T.J. "What do you think of these babies?"

"That looks like a lot of money, all right."

"Those girls are going to be hot for me tonight."

"I bet they will be. Why don't you take them for a ride in your special truck? They would probably like that and maybe they would do those things with you."

"Forget the truck, T.J. No bimbos ride in it with me. You got that?"

"Is it because you don't want them to see the dented fender?"

"What are you talking about? There ain't no dented fender on this truck."

"I saw a dent in there."

"You didn't see nothing, dummy. You got that? Say anything else and I'll tell them girls you're a idiot. Now beat it."

"I'm not a dummy. I'm the best reader in my class."

Donald scooped up a handful of snow, packed it, and threw it at T.J., who barely ducked in time.

"Beat it, you hear me? I don't have time for you, dummy."

"I'm not a dummy," T.J. repeated as he turned away. "You'll see." His mother stood in the kitchen door and waved to him.

"T.J., it's cold out there. Come in and help me put these groceries away. It's getting late."

"I'm coming."

"You look upset, T.J. What happened?"

"I'm not a dummy, am I?"

"Who said you were a dummy?"

"Well, Donald did…and Dad. He said it a lot."

"Your father is not the one to judge anyone. You are a wonderful person and I depend on you, T.J. I could never depend on your father for anything but I can with you. So, does that make you a dummy? Of course not, and you can forget Donald Oldham. He's a lazy bum who lives on disability checks he doesn't deserve."

"No, he has lots of money. I saw it."

"He also called you a name. So, if he does that, do you believe everything he says?"

"No, I guess not. He told me about girls, too. He said…"

Gloria Harkins blushed and said, quite quickly, "Well, I don't know, T.J., but some time we'll talk about all of that…not now, though."

"I think I should call Miss Deputy Ryder and ask if she can take me for that ride she said she would."

"Not today, T.J. I think the roads are still a little slick."

Chapter Fourteen

"You owe me thirty bucks." Hollis hobbled up the steps to Donnie's door.

"What makes you think I owe you thirty?" By his calculation Donnie figured it would be closer to two hundred. But thirty suited him just fine.

"Them machines have a limit of three hundred a day. Ten percent of three hundred is thirty. You used it yesterday so that's thirty bucks you owe me. "

It was doubtful Donnie had ever heard the expression "honor among thieves." If he had, he felt no compunction to correct either Hollis' assertions or his math. He peeled off a ten and a twenty and handed them over.

"Another thing, I need to use the card myself."

"No way, man. This card don't leave my sight for a minute."

"Yeah? What happens to that card if I tell certain people you have it?"

"And you'd go down with me for giving me the PIN."

"Well, as to that, actually it was Dermont who did it, so I'm in the clear. He wants to know when you're going to fix him up with Dolores, by the way."

"The runt would suffocate if he got near her. She's over a hundred fifty pounds of skin pillows. Besides, what's he going to do if he got there? I'll string him along and then…who knows, maybe old Dolores might just give him a go."

"I still need that card."

"You ain't getting it."

The two glared at each other. Hollis figured with a broken leg, he didn't stand a chance if he tried to wrest it away. Finally he pleaded.

"Donnie, please. It's only for a couple of days. My folks are taking us to Charlotte and I thought I could, like, pick up the max on each of the days. When I get back, you'll have it again."

"There's no way. Not ever."

Hollis clenched his jaw. "I could make trouble for you, you know."

"And I could shut you up forever." They glared at one another for a few seconds. Hollis almost backed down.

"Okay, I got something better," Donnie capitulated.

"How better?"

He pulled the three credit cards from his pocket and selected one—the one that seemed to require a picture ID. "I'll rent you this one. It's better because you can not only charge stuff, but you can get a cash advance at most of the ATMs, as well."

"What kind of cash advance? Do they have a maximum on them?"

"Not on these, no sir. This guy must have been rolling and the credit line is really big. So you charge some stuff, hit an ATM, and you're good to go."

"Sooner or later they'll get suspicious."

"You said you wanted the card for a couple of days. What can happen in a couple of days? If they start looking at you funny or anything, say it's your uncle's or something and you don't know squat."

"How much you want for it?"

"Fifty bucks."

"Fifty? All I got is this thirty you just gave me."

"I'll take the thirty, you can owe me twenty."

Hollis handed the money back and Donnie gave him the card. "When do you leave?"

"Tomorrow."

"So, you start getting rich tomorrow."

◇◇◇

Ike rubbed his eyes and leaned back in his chair. He'd spent an hour staring at the computer screen trying to understand what Sam had turned up. They'd guessed they were watching someone track credit or cash card transactions. He couldn't imagine what that might have to do with Kamarov. Sam had copied the whole operation on a disc and returned to her probing. She called it "flying a stealth bomber." There did not seem to be anything more for him to do and that made him frustrated.

He went back to his office and dialed Ruth. He drummed a pencil on the desktop while Ruth's disapproving secretary made a point of putting him on hold. Tappity-tap-tap. He didn't expect a simple hello and he didn't get one.

"What's up, Sheriff? Nothing important to do so you call your sweetie?"

"My sweetie? Who is this? Agnes must have connected me to the sophomore dorm."

"How's this, then? Whatcha want?"

"Better. Lunch with my sweetie, and a little…I think the expression is, face time."

"In the cafeteria and public eye and I can't give you more than half an hour."

Ike drove through town and up the hill that led to Callend College. The driveway into the campus had been plowed and cindered. Apparently Callend College had a better street maintenance capacity than Picketsville. He parked in a No Parking area, locked his duty belt and gun in the trunk, and climbed the four steps to the broad porch that ran the length of the building. Winter had reduced the college's signature wisteria to a leafless snarl of ancient branches clinging to sagging trellises set in the porch eaves.

The cafeteria was located in the basement of Lowell Callend Hall—Lo Cal to the students. He entered and was assailed by a cacophony of female voices, clinking plates, and a gust of unexpected heat. Ruth waved to him as he entered and pointed to a tray in front of an empty chair. Unless he'd gone through the line with someone with a Callend College ID, he would not have been able to buy anything. Apparently Ruth did not want to wait and had chosen lunch for him.

"What's this?" he asked and inspected something that looked vaguely like an egg salad sandwich on white bread. It had two toothpicks with frilly ends sticking through a pickle slice in the middle of each half. Someone had thoughtfully removed the crusts, thereby rendering the bread visually as well as nutritionally neutral. Next to it was a squarish lump, the dark brown color of which suggested it might be chocolate, and a shallow cup filled with canned corn.

"Out of respect for you and the approaching season of Chanukah, I chose the closest things I could find that were kosher."

"Very thoughtful. The next time I buy for you I will remember that. How do Connecticut's aristocrat wannabes eat at Christmastime, anyway?"

"Out."

"What this place needs is a New York deli—real kosher dills, rye bread, hot pastrami, and no mayonnaise on anything."

"Sit and eat. You're wasting time."

"You behind in your payments again, or is the faculty still up in arms over the residents of the old storage building?"

"That's the irony. As you predicted, the residents, as you so delicately put it, have solved my financial problems, but at a cost. The faculty union is meeting this afternoon to call for a vote of no confidence."

"And that vote carries weight?"

"No, it's just a positioning thing. Let people know how upset they are at me. It's your fault, Ike."

"Exactly how many of your highbrows actually take this deal seriously…I mean, what's the extent of the damage, really?"

"Less than a dozen."

"So your worry is…?"

"I have to take it seriously."

"You have to pretend to take it seriously. But I know you, Madam President—you're not even a little bit worried."

"Don't talk so loudly, someone might hear. And what are you up to?"

"I have a problem."

"Serious?"

"Very."

"Tell me."

"I can't. Well, I don't know. Can you keep this under your hat?"

"Never wear hats, but the soul of discretion, that's me."

"Do you remember what I told you about my wife Eloise's death? There was a Russian agent who got involved after I bolted the Agency. Apparently he figured out what happened, but not all of it. He came looking for me to tell what he knew. He never found me. He disappeared and we supposed the powers that be in Moscow had him put down."

Ruth raised her eyebrows and spooned some soup. Ike had told her the story before. Now he filled her in on what Sam was up to and what he hoped Whaite would find, and most importantly, what the Agency believed. Ruth made him repeat the part about black programs.

"You don't suppose the black paint they're splashing on the walls in my storage building is because it's a black program?" She was joking but when she realized Ike wasn't smiling, she leaned forward and studied him. "It is, isn't it?"

"Not because of the paint, but it could be. I don't know."

"Woof. Maybe I should vote for no confidence myself."

"Nuts. Help me think this through. Wheel out your Ph.D. brains and give me a different take, one that won't keep me up all night."

"Well, two thoughts occur right away, maybe three. One is, perhaps this killing had nothing to do with anything at all. Somebody just mugged him and dumped him and he happened to fall on your turf."

"Would you like to calculate the probabilities of that happening? What are the odds?"

"Not very good, but still a possibility. Okay, my second thought is, I don't think you've considered all the other possibilities."

"Like what?"

"It's not Kamarov, just a look-alike."

"Been there, done that, have to pass. It was Alexei."

"Okay, here's the third, but you are not going to like it."

"Try me."

"Are you sure all the bad guys that set you up in Zurich were rooted out? Like, how do you know the guy, what's his name—the sleeper you said your friend, Charlie, took care of was really, um, taken care of? You didn't see him do it, did you? So maybe this guy was trying to tell you that and they got to him first."

Ike's jaw snapped shut. Had he? He'd spent years blotting out the memories, even the end game. He remembered hearing elevator doors open. Did he see them open? Yes, but only the tops, but what then? He couldn't be sure, and there was no way to find out. Maybe Sam could. He'd ask.

"I don't know. Thanks a lot. Now I won't sleep at all."

"You asked for the Ph.D. brains—you got them. And I can help out in the sleep department."

"No, you can't. If what you've just supposed is true—as a hypothetical, mind you—then I am not the only target. You know the whole story, and Charlie knows you know."

Ruth turned pale and pushed her soup away. "I had to hook up with an ex-spook with a history and now I'm a target."

"Could be worse."

"How?"

"I could be short, ugly, and dull."

"Schwartz, I want you in my house with your gun and whatever else you need tonight and every night until we eliminate the possibility."

"Well, as the soap salesman once told me, in every adversity lay the seeds of an equal and opposite benefit."

"Yeah, consider it a perk."

"You didn't come up with that scenario just to lure me into your boudoir?"

"Take a hike, Schwartz, and call me when you're on your way over tonight so I'll know it's you at the door. And don't forget your cop belt."

"Duty belt."

"Whatever."

Chapter Fifteen

Whaite eased the Chevelle to a stop. It had taken him several days to track down Steve Bolt. Nobody would admit knowing him. The community around the mountain may have been civilized in the early 1940s, but the part of the culture that remained suspicious of outsiders endured. Whaite knew people from the area, but closer in on the mountain—it had been a while since he moved among them, and they hesitated.

Bolt owned a cabin set back a hundred yards or so off a gravel road. Whaite sat in the car, its motor and heater running while he studied the still snow-covered driveway glistening in the sun. He focused binoculars on the cabin's roof. No smoke arose from the chimney. He left the car's warmth and picked his way across the icy road to its junction with the driveway. A single set of tire tracks either coming in or going out marked its length. He held the binoculars to his eyes again and studied the entire area. No garage but a carport of sorts. A rusted De Soto, up on blocks, rested under its sagging tin roof. The tire tracks began eight or ten yards from the house. He focused in on the steps. One set of footprints. He adjusted the focus and looked again. He couldn't be absolutely sure, but the footprints seemed to be heading away from the house. He swung his vision to the beginning of the tire tracks. There were small piles of snow on either side. It appeared Bolt had walked around the vehicle at least once.

Whaite shivered and returned to his car. Bolt had come out of his house, brushed the snow off his vehicle, and driven away.

No smoke meant he'd been gone for a while. Whaite knew he could not stake out the house in a bright red street rod, so he did a careful three-point turn and headed down the road to a filling station at the bottom of the hill where he would be less noticeable.

He pulled the car around the leeward side of the building. From there he could see the road leading to Bolt's cabin, but not be seen. He cut the engine and stepped out into the cold. The wind had picked up. A general merchandise store was attached to the gas station. He jogged to the building and an old-fashioned bell over the door tinkled as he let himself in. Coffee and something to eat. He didn't hold out much hope for the food but he knew these country stores generally brewed a decent pot of coffee. He bought a hot dog. The coffee was only passable. The clerk behind the counter looked familiar.

"Say, aren't you Wick Goad?"

The clerk looked up and smiled. "That's me. Who might you be? Hold on, I got you. It's old 'Wait-a-minute Whaite.' You had that hesitation step—wait a minute—when you played football. Where you been?"

"Well, I'm deputying up in Picketsville."

"Well, I'll be. You're a police. Who'd a thought? Why I remember one time you and Randy Swank took that car and—"

"We can let that'un go if it's all the same to you, Wick."

"Well, I reckon. You here on official business? You're a little out of your jurisdiction, ain't you?"

"Just poking around. We got us a dead fella up to Picketsville with a Floyd County address and I figured the place to start is down here."

"Don't know of anybody gone missing."

"Listen, I can't stay in here too long. Does this road connect with any other? Can someone get in to, say, Bolt's place from up the mountain?"

"Maybe in the good weather but not today. There's a dinky little road that runs over the mountain but it ain't much more than a foot path. You after Steve?"

"Just to ask some questions. He knows somebody we're interested in for the shooting and I want to hear what he has to say."

"Well, Steve came through here two days ago. He said he had to go north for a while. I ain't seen him since. But look here. You can sit in the window and see him coming. He's going to stop here anyway. His house'll be colder than a tax man's heart and he'll stop by for kerosene and grub. He's been fixing up that old place but there's a wait to get a propane tank so he's still using one of them old space heaters. Lots of folks back up the mountain do."

"What's he driving?"

"Old VW Beetle. I reckon he's swapped the engine out of that buggy four, five times by now."

Whaite drank his coffee and several more cups. He waited until dark and gave up. Bolt might come back in the dark, but he doubted it.

Something was wrong.

Chapter Sixteen

As a rule, breakfast was the only meal Ike ate at the Crossroads Diner. He believed it nearly impossible for anyone to ruin breakfast. A succession of Flora Blevins' short-order cooks-of-the-week proved the exception. Yet, he kept going back, hoping each new spatula wielder would turn out better than the last. The latest teetered precariously on a stepladder that qualified as an OSHA "what not to do." Swaying dangerously on the top rung, he attempted to hang an antique string of large-bulb Christmas lights across the top of the mirror behind the counter.

Ike, resigned to bad weather and closed businesses, had to eat dinner in the diner. He regretted it almost immediately. The plate of fried chicken, mashed potatoes swimming in beige canned gravy, and a side of suspiciously green coleslaw curled up in his stomach like an overweight cat. He longed for a real restaurant within striking distance of town. The new French restaurant, Chez François, hadn't really mastered anything more complicated in French cuisine than baguette rolls and *boeuf rôti*, which to Ike's mind was lunch. Even so, had it been open, he might have given it a dinner try. Now, he wished he'd saved the dreary sandwich he'd been offered at the cafeteria. He wished he knew how to cook. He speed dialed Ruth's number, watched the ladder begin to splay at its base, and wondered if this cook would end his employment with a workman's compensation suit.

"Change of plan," he said.

"What plan?"

"Me protecting you from the bad guys all night."

"Oh…about that…"

"Change your mind?" Ike winced as the ladder collapsed and the cook sprawled, unhurt, on the floor.

"How will it look if your car sits outside my house all night, every night for who knows how long?"

"Exactly. That's the change."

"Same problem, if you're suggesting I come to your place, which, by the way, I have never seen…why is that?"

"I'm afraid you won't approve of my collection of kama sutra wall posters. No, the plan now is my folks' place. No hint of scandal. Abe and my mother will be there and everything will be very proper."

"But what will my people say?"

"Tell them the truth, sort of. You received some threats and the sheriff has asked you to stay out of sight temporarily."

"What happened to your equal and opposite benefit?"

"Bad seeds—never sprouted, although—"

"Although what? You'd better tell me now, Schwartz. If you sneak into my room at three a.m. to surprise me, you might get a knitting needle between the ribs."

"I didn't know you knit."

"I do now—big number ten needles. Those are the big ones, aren't they? Never mind, you know what I mean."

"I'll pick you up in an hour."

"Do you really have kama sutra wall posters?"

"Would you like me to?"

"Some other day. You know this move isn't going to fool anybody."

"It's not supposed to fool anyone, it's intended to put a face of propriety on the whole business and, if you are right, the bad guys will know what's up and know that we know, and will have to revise their plans as well."

"Why don't I feel reassured?"

Ike disconnected and started toward the door. Flora Blevins, the diner's ancient proprietor, skewered him with a look that would sober up a drunk. Eyes narrowed and chin set, she railed into him about the citified people who came into her establishment, didn't order anything, but said they thought the diner ought to be torn down or moved.

"They think the diner is ugly."

"They have no taste, Flora."

"They want to build a Holiday Inn in its place."

"Hardly a move upward."

"You tell them for me, Ike, if they come around here fixing to touch the Crossroads, I'll get out my old scattergun and show them what I think of a motel here or anywhere else."

"I'll tell them."

◇◇◇

Sam was still at her desk, eyes glued to the screen, and watching as another set of numbers in columns flickered downward. Ike started to tell her to go home and try again tomorrow, but she held up her hand and then motioned for him to come and see. He watched for a moment. The numbers looked like the ones he'd seen before.

"They at it again?"

"It's a different group looking for the same thing. That's two separate probes after the same information."

"You're sure this has something to do with our guy." Not a question, Ike already knew what she would say. Sam was good.

"While you were out, I backtracked the first group and I got something."

"What?"

"Does the word or term 'cutthroat' mean anything to you?"

"Not since I gave up reading pirate books in the fourth grade."

"I'm serious, Ike. I caught just a piece of the address before it blanked out. They had a sensor looking for hackers. Anyway, cutthroat is what I got. It doesn't ring any bells?"

"Sorry, no. The problem with a name like that is, it could be anything or anybody. It could be another hacker like you, who uses it as a—whatever you call them—moniker, nom."

"It could be. I ran it through a little program I have that stores names as I run across them and it isn't in there. Of course, that doesn't mean—"

"Sam, enough already." Ike was beginning to sound like his father, a sure sign he was tired. "We've all had a long day. Shut this down and tackle it in the morning. If you want to work on it, give it some thought time. Find out what your instinct is trying to tell you."

"I don't do instinct, Ike."

"Time to start. Good night. I'm on my cell phone tonight if anything comes up."

The door whooshed shut as she left and an inch of cold air spread across the floor to cover Ike's feet. He checked his watch. He still had a half hour before Ruth would expect him. He retreated to his office to think through the past week. He was no closer to finding out how Kamarov ended up in the woods than when he'd started. All he knew for certain, he wasn't the only one looking. That did not make him feel better. And Ruth's suggestion that Charlie, or more likely Charlie's superiors, might be involved worried him more than he'd guessed it would—scared him, in fact. He and Charlie had a history. He didn't relish even the possibility that Charlie might...He shook his head. He needed some answers—now. And why hadn't he heard from him, anyway? Unless...The phone rang.

"Why isn't your new phone on?"

"I don't like it."

"Turn it on." Charlie hung up. Ike retrieved the phone and turned it on. It vibrated almost immediately.

"Tango blue leader, this is foxtrot, over."

"Stop horsing around, Ike, and listen. This is what we know so far. Whoever had Mr. K. on their payroll does not know he's dead." Charlie sounded tired, edgy.

"We figured that." He'd pretty much come to the conclusion that the columns of figures Sam had been watching must belong to Kamarov. They were tracking his credit cards or bank transactions.

"You know? How?"

"Someone has been tracking his credit or bank cards and they're active. Here's something else for you. There are two other groups following those accounts. One yesterday and another joined in today. That's not counting us, of course."

"Two...just two?"

"Two, besides us, right."

"Good. You're tracking and you found that out how?"

"You have the power of the Agency's super computer, I have Sam the hacker. It appears, on balance, I have the edge."

"I'm impressed. Sam, you say?"

"You try to recruit her away from me and I'll—"

"No, you won't, but I'll resist stealing your guy—"

"Woman."

"Woman...at least for the time being. I'm afraid to ask, but have you turned up anything else?"

"Maybe. Who or what is Cutthroat?"

"Sam again?"

"Charlie, I'm waiting. Please don't tell me you don't have Cutthroat on your radar screen."

"Thanks for the lead. How about out in the field. Anything there?"

Ike thought a moment and then told him what Whaite had been doing. The Steve Bolt lead had gone cold and that seemed odd. Charlie said he'd do an all-points search for Bolt—hotels, airports, buses, the works—and call back in the morning. Ike told Charlie he would not be reachable—would be incommunicado. He told him why. He owed him that. After a silence that seemed to last minutes, Charlie said he understood—sort of. He sounded hurt but did not protest. He did insist that the mole definitely went down but beyond that, whether there might be more people involved, he could not confirm or deny. The answer died with their man.

"Okay, Ike, you keep your lady safe from us, and anyone else for that matter. I won't try to find you."

"Thank you for that. You know what I want to believe."

"You didn't last long in the field by being stupid. Who knows, Ruth might be right, at least in principle."

Ike thought he ought to feel better. He didn't.

Chapter Seventeen

Picketsville hung its Christmas decorations a week after Halloween. In years past, they would have gone up later, but a warehouse fire that destroyed the town's surplus office equipment and its only working snowplow had also consumed the array of plastic pilgrims, turkeys, and autumnal icons that formed the nucleus of the Thanksgiving display. Rather than replace them, the Town Council moved the Christmas setup forward a month.

The Jeep's wipers flicked erratically across its windshield. Squinting through its slush-smeared surface, Ike noticed that one of the candlesticks and two of the stars set in the center of wreathes festooned at irregular intervals across Main Street were dark, their bulbs already burned out. Along the sidewalk, lights twinkled, flickered, or raced in mad circles around display windows. Rudolph in several guises flashed his red nose at passersby. Bing Crosby and a dozen imitators moaning "White Christmas," competed with an equal number of jolly voices narrating the unlikely itinerary of "Frosty the Snowman."

Christmas was not Ike's holiday, but he did enjoy the season. True, the crime rate, suicides, and fatal accidents always escalated in the weeks between Thanksgiving and New Year's—The Month of Heavy Eating, his mother called it—but for most people it was a time of good cheer and remarkable generosity.

Ruth sat huddled, grim faced and shivering, in the Jeep's only other seat. Its heater functioned more or less, but worked best if you also had the foresight to wear a down-filled jacket, boots, and gloves. She wore only a thin wool overcoat, fashionable but relatively useless, leather gloves, and heels.

"Tell me again why I am freezing to death in this relic."

"The roads are slick. This has four-wheel drive, and Abe hasn't had time to plow his driveway. So, it's more likely to get us there."

"You could have warned me, you know."

"I did. I told you we were going to the country. I figured you'd dress accordingly."

"Going to the country? Do you consider Picketsville the big city? It's all country out here."

They passed the Crossroads Diner and he caught a glimpse of Flora shaking her finger in the face of someone Ike could not recognize—probably one of the people who wanted her establishment relocated.

"Point of reference only, ma'am. You big-city folks reckon all of us out here must is hillbillies but the troof is—"

"Don't start, Schwartz, I'm too cold to play games with you."

"Nevertheless, for the people who grew up here, Picketsville is the city, or as close as they want to get to one. For them, country is out in the valley, on the farms, or up on the mountains. Have you been up there?"

"Skyline Drive count?"

"Just barely."

"I went with you to that restaurant, Le Chateau, once. It's out in the sticks."

"Better."

"How come you never took me there again?"

"It's a restaurant for first meetings, celebrations, great occasions and…"

"And what?"

"You are very hard to pry away from your desk and duties. It takes time to eat a fine meal correctly."

"So, it's my fault?"

"Um…I had dinner at the Crossroads Diner tonight. I may not eat again for a week."

"That bad?"

"You have no idea."

"Good. It serves you right for not taking me to Le Chateau tonight before we decided to mush to Nome."

"You think you're cold now. Try two and a half hours, maybe three, over unplowed mountain roads to that place."

"You have a point. You're forgiven."

◇◇◇

Sam slouched down in her chair until her chin settled on her chest. She eyeballed the phone on the coffee table in front of her. Guilt is not an uplifting emotion. In her case it made her wish she could continue her downward slide and disappear into the floor. She had not told Ike everything. She would eventually, but she needed to talk to Karl first. She'd halfway expected to hear from him by now, but since reading what had popped up on her screen this afternoon, she wasn't sure she wanted to. Her problem, the source of her guilt—her guilts, to be precise—had two parts. The first stemmed from what she had discovered, or thought she had discovered, while looking for traces of Kamarov. She knew for a certainty that Cutthroat was not someone's internet alias. She had seen more. Cutthroat had people assigned to it and those people had names which meant it must be a group, a program, a…a black program? Her second had to do with one of the names she saw, only for a split second, in fact, but long enough to recognize—*Hedrick, K.* The name had jumped out from the screen like a happy puppy. Only it did not make her smile. Hedrick, K. could only be Karl, and that signaled his involvement in the search for Kamarov. That, in turn, meant the program they feared resided deep in the FBI and, again, meant the Bureau could be the enemy. She flinched at the thought. Less than a week before, she'd scolded Whaite for using that term about the FBI and now…If what she assumed to be true could be confirmed, everything Whaite said would be correct, and, worse, she stood to lose the brightest spot in her life.

She picked up her phone and held it against her cheek. What would he say? No, what could he say? If he had been assigned to a black program, he probably would have to lie to her. On the other hand, if she didn't call, she might never know and then they could go on as usual…"Just call me Cleopatra, da queen of de Nile." Hoping it would just go away wouldn't help. She considered blotting out what she knew from her memory—if that were possible. If she called, it all could end. Ike said something about finding out what her instincts were telling her, and she'd said she didn't do instincts. So what now? "Just the facts, ma'am." She dialed his number.

◇◇◇

All the windows on the first floor of the farmhouse were lighted when Ike pulled up at his parents' place. He helped Ruth down and retrieved her overnight bag from the back of the Jeep. Together they climbed the steps to the porch and the front door swung open as they reached it. A gust of warm air enveloped them along with Abe Schwartz's famous baritone.

"Well, now, it looks like you all made it just fine. Come in, come in." He circled Ruth's shoulders with one arm and swept her into the hall. "Ike, you take that case up to the front room." He led Ruth into the front parlor. "It's got its own bath, Ms. Harris. I figured you might want that."

Ruth shed her coat and gloves. A fire danced on the living room grate and she moved to it, holding her hands toward the flames.

"Your son made me sit in that ridiculous truck of his all the way out here. I nearly froze."

"He brought you here in his old Jeep?"

"He did."

"Must've had a reason."

Any thought Ruth had that she might receive a sympathetic ear from Abe Schwartz evaporated. As much as Ike and his father argued about every topic from politics to the funny papers, at their core they were as alike as two peas in a pod. Ike returned and gave his father a brief hug.

"I got no solace from your father about the cruel and unusual punishment you subjected me to on the way out here."

"Call the ACLU." He turned to Abe. "City folk, they just never will learn that Gucci and Dior just aren't fit clothes for country folks."

"Well now, Ike, you know we got some sensible working clothes in the back closet. I reckon we could tog the lady out, if you think. Hate to see her suffer."

"You two stop it right now or so help me, snow or no snow, I will walk back to town."

"Not a good idea," the two men said in unison.

"Why do I have a feeling I just signed on to ride to California in a converted Hudson Super Six with the Joads?"

"I'll fix you a drink and then I want you to meet my mother… before it gets too late."

Too late was to be understood in more than one way.

Chapter Eighteen

Ike's mother held court ensconced in what used to be the back parlor. A hospital bed dominated the center of the room. The rest of the furniture had been removed except for an overstuffed Victorian loveseat and a recliner of uncertain age, each placed in one of the room's two remaining corners. An incongruous combination, but the first served for visitors and the second for Abe, who would sit with his wife for hours and often late into the night. A lamp cast a soft glow from a side table and the bed had been raised so that she could sit up, see, and speak to her visitors.

Abe ushered Ike and Ruth into the makeshift hospital room and closed the door.

"You are Ruth Harris." Ike's mother smiled at Ruth. Her skin looked like old parchment. Ruth smiled back and took her hand. She could smell death. Ike's mother would not see her next Passover.

"You have that look," she said from the depths of her pillows.

"Sorry?"

"You can feel it, can't you—Death. He's here in the room waiting for the old bat to give it up, but I'm not ready to go, so he'll have to wait. Don't worry, Abe and I talk about it all the time. Now, Isaac here gets a little jumpy when I bring it up. It comes from being young and unwilling to face the inevitable."

Ike started to say something, but his mother held up her hand to silence him.

"Ruth is a nice name. I wanted to change mine when Abe and I married. My nose-in-the-air, bigoted family held with Hitler that the Jews were an inferior race and cut me off forever."

"They never accepted you two?"

"No. You have to understand they were from a different era and were very right wing even for that one. They were closet Nazis, if you want to know the truth, and thought the late unlamented Führer was just the victim of a lot of bad press. Hard to believe, isn't it, but there you are."

"There are people like that out there now," Ruth said and recalled one or two prospective faculty interviews.

"Oh yes, always will be. But I wanted to tell you about my name change. When they tossed me out of the family, so to speak, I decided I would change my name. Not just my surname but all of them. Well, I started calling myself Naomi. Isn't that a lovely name?"

"Yes, yes it is. Why Naomi?"

"Well, that's the good part. Do you know your Bible?"

"Um…to tell the truth, no."

"Not to worry, practically no one does anymore. Just enough to misquote it. Well, the story is this—a man from Bethlehem went with his wife and two sons to live in Moab. That's another country across the Jordan from Israel/Judea, a gentile country. The wife's name was Naomi. So anyway, both of their sons marry Moabite women and things were going pretty good but then all the men died. Not important for now to go into the how of it. So broke and widowed, Naomi decides to go home. Her daughters-in-law walk with her but she says they should return to Moab where they have family and so on. One of them—I forget her name—"

"Orpah," Abe said.

"Thank you, honey. Orpah went back to Moab but the other woman, Ruth, said, 'No, I will stay with you and where you go, I will go, and where you lodge I will lodge, and your people will be my people, and your God will be my God.'"

"I told her if she wanted to use that old story, she should be Ruth, not Naomi," Abe said. "See, Naomi was not the one making the big switch. She was just going home. It was—"

"You hush, Abe, this is my story. And I liked the sound of Naomi better. Ruth could be anybody. I had a roommate at Wellesley named Ruth and she was as WASP as the DAR. Naomi is a departure and likely to catch my family's notice. Ruth wouldn't do it."

"But you never did it." Ike winked at Ruth. "Tell her why."

"Never you mind, Isaac. That's all over and done with. It's the principle that I am illustrating here."

"She and Dad were married no more than three months when there was a huge scandal in Richmond concerning a certain lady of the night who was caught *in flagrante delicto* with the governor. Her professional name was Naomi. The press started calling her Naughty Naomi."

"Had to put the kibosh on the name. I'd just won a seat in the House and couldn't take no chances on a misunderstanding and stupid questions from the press boys," Abe added.

"If you two would just excuse me, I'd like to finish my story."

"Yes, ma'am." Together.

Ruth smiled.

"So, it didn't matter in the end. My family lost all their money in get-rich-quick schemes my moronic cousin, Randolph, persuaded them to buy into, and they ended up selling their mansion in the Greenspring Valley to Baltimore's best known and, forgive me, notorious, Jewish family. Isn't that just a wonderful irony?"

"On that happy note, we will let you rest, Momma."

"Now Isaac, I will decide if I need to rest. You two men go on back to the living room and talk politics or maybe something a little less lethal, and leave me to have a little heart-to-heart with Ruth. Go on, scat."

◇◇◇

Sam let the phone ring twenty times. Ten was her usual limit, but for Karl, she'd wait. What had happened to his answering machine? He had an answering machine. Why didn't it pick up? She had the headset poised to disconnect when a voice crackled at her. A woman's voice.

"Yes, hello?" She sounded young. "Who is this?"

"Is Karl there?" Sam's heart sank into her shoes.

"He's not available. Who's calling?"

"Sam."

"Sam? Come on, who is this?"

"He hasn't told you about me, has he?" She would fight back even though she really only wanted to hang up and have a good cry.

"Sorry, no Sam on my list." The line went dead.

So that's that. She thought. New assignment indeed. Tied up for the time being—right. She wanted to be angry, she wanted to drive to Alexandria and scratch the woman's eyes out, and she wanted Karl back. She put the phone down, picked up her box of tissues, and went to the kitchen where she proceeded to down a pint of rocky road.

◇◇◇

Steve Bolt drove to the store at the foot of the mountain. Sonny Parker greeted him when he walked in. "Where you been, Steve. People been asking about you."

"Where's Wick?"

"Goad? Poker night. He's probably fleecing your buddy Oldham out of whatever money he has."

"He ain't my buddy, you hear? Anybody says otherwise and they're in trouble with me."

"Okay by me. So where you been?"

"Had an errand to run, and then I had to lay low for a while."

"None of my business but—"

"You got that right. I need some kerosene and some canned goods."

"Well, now Wick, he said I wasn't to give you no more credit—"

"I have cash money. Look here." Bolt flashed a wad of twenties.

"Okay, you know where everything is. Help yourself. You might have to pump some kero though. Couple of city folk were in here a while ago and drained the barrel. I asked them what they wanted with that much. I mean if they was camping…they weren't from around here so I figured they were campers or rented one of them retreat cabins over on the state road. But even then they didn't need that much. Well, you know them city people. Got no more sense than bunny rabbits."

Steve filled a bag with baked beans, corn, Spam, and peach halves. Sonny had been right, the barrel stood dead empty. He started to work the pump.

"Funny thing about them men. I figured they'd head back down the road to wherever they were staying but they didn't. They took off up the hill toward your place. I reckon they got lost. They'll be helloing back down here in a minute or two."

Steve filled his kerosene can, gathered his bags of canned goods, and took them to the counter. He laid ten twenty-dollar bills on the counter.

"This will catch me up with Goad and then some. You mark it down in the book—two hundred dollars. Then minus out all what I owe."

A dark sedan roared past the store, downhill.

"I told you they'd come by here. Shoot, they must be in a big time hurry."

Steve looked out the window as the car flashed by. In the dark and poor light he could not see much. He did notice that the license plate was not Virginia or North Carolina. If he didn't know better, he'd swear they were DC plates. He froze for an instant, then rushed to the door and looked up the hill. His house would be just around the bend. He couldn't see the house, but he did see the pillar of fire rising above treetops just where his house should be. A sudden flash and a shower of sparks leapt a hundred feet or so straight up, like Fourth of July fireworks. Steve left his groceries and kerosene on the counter and drove away—downhill.

Chapter Nineteen

Early the next morning, Ike found Ruth sitting in a rocking chair in the living room. She had a blanket across her knees and a book in her lap. "Sleep well?"

"No, as a matter of fact, I did not."

"You're worried about the CIA connection, about Charlie. Listen, I was up half the night thinking about that and I—"

"That's not what kept me up. This is." She held a book out to him. "It's a Bible. Your mother gave me a Bible. She said I should read the book that's named after me."

"The Book of Ruth? I rather think it's the other way around."

"You don't think the compilers of the Bible had me in mind?"

"Possible, but not likely. Of course prophecy was a much more powerful gift then than it is now so…who knows?"

"I've been reading it, last night and again this morning. Not just the Ruth bit—but parts of the rest of it—strange book. You know all about the Book of Ruth, I guess?"

He nodded.

"So you know that Ruth married a man named Boaz and one of their descendents was King David, of David and Goliath fame." She frowned and closed the book. "I've never read any of it—the Bible, I mean—never felt the need. I come from a long line of committed secular humanists. Do you think she sensed that? Is that why she gave it to me?" Ruth shook her head—in annoyance or puzzlement, he couldn't be sure. "Or is it because she's dying? That's it, don't you think? You know that would put a special valence on it."

"Put a special what on it?"

"You said prophecy just now. People approaching death see things, know things, allow impulses they would normally suppress to surface, and then they say and do things that sometimes border on the prophetic—you understand?"

Ike nodded again. He wasn't sure he did, but Ruth had the bit between her teeth and he thought it best to let her finish her thought. She sat for a long moment staring at the fireplace.

"Ashes," she murmured. "Heat's gone from them. Cold as death. They serve no useful purpose other than to remind us of yesterday's fire." She studied him for a long moment, as if she were seeing him for the first time. She stood, stepped across the room, bent, and kissed him on the lips, hard. She looked at him fiercely with a pair of no-nonsense eyes.

"Ike, the last thing she said to me was, 'Don't you think David is a nice name?'"

◇◇◇

The sun shone in a cloudless sky. The temperature rose to the mid-forties and winter temporarily deserted the Shenandoah Valley. It would return, certainly, but not with the uncharacteristic vengeance it had displayed during the previous two days. Whaite's car, his beautiful show car, managed to survive ice and snow with no apparent damage. Now, as he drove south to Buffalo Mountain, its paint job received regular and massive applications of muddy, salty water. The road's shoulders still had piles of melting snow left by the plows. They formed weirs that held small ponds of dirty slush. He had to drive through them, sending geysers of water up under the body, across the road, and over the shoulder. Approaching cars showered his when they careened into several inches of similarly trapped road water. His windshield wipers began to streak. Adding washer fluid helped, but only slightly.

He pulled around behind Goad's store and, again, parked out of sight. Inside, Goad stood behind the counter staring at his ledger and punching numbers into a small calculator.

"Wait a minute, 'Whaite a Minute,'" he said without looking up. "I've got to add up an account. Steve, the guy you were asking about, came in here last night and paid his back bill. Then Sonny said he acted like he'd seen a ghost and high-tailed it out the door. Left all his things right there on the counter, too. Turns out his house caught fire. He was standing right where you are when he seen it go up."

"Caught fire? His house?"

"Yep, went up like a wild fire in dry timber. Whoosh! The whole place is nothing but ashes and bits of plumbing sticking up here and there."

"This happened last night?"

"About midnight. Sonny said Steve took one look and took off downhill, like the witches was after him, and he ain't been back. You'd think he'd come back to look, salvage what he could, but he ain't. Well, maybe he'll be in later to pick up his stuff." Goad licked the end of his pencil, made an entry and closed the ledger. "I saw that car you're driving. Is the Sheriff's Department up in Picketsville looking to draw attention to itself?"

"No, it's mine, Wick. Not wise to bring a patrol car out of our jurisdiction and my truck is busted."

"Well, it's something. Don't see many lipstick Chevelles anymore."

Whaite offered his card. "If Bolt does come in, give me a call, will you? I need to talk to him."

Goad pocketed the card. Whaite knew he might call or he might not. Mountain loyalties were stratified and Whaite had been away too long and was law enforcement now. He could only hope. "You weren't here last night when he came in?"

"Me? No sirree, I was out playing poker. I went on my weekly sojourn to lighten the pocketbook of one Donnie Oldham. Now there's a coincidence for you, Mister Deputy. Here old Steve pays me off and last night, so did Donnie—pretty near a thousand dollars—cash money. I proceeded to relieve the boy of another two hundred 'fore he quit. He thinks I cheat."

"Do you?"

"Not with him. He's the worst poker player on the East Coast, reckless. I don't need to."

"What's he like, besides being a bad poker player?"

"He's an idiot. Got this hot temper and always starting in on people. In the good weather he dresses up like some mountain man. He's like one of them whatcha-call-ums, a reenacter, you know? Bib overalls, wide brimmed black hat, bushy beard—the whole bit—and toting a pistol in his pocket. Like I said, he's an idiot."

Whaite thanked him, reminded him about calling, and drove up to Bolt's house, or what was left of it. Where there had been a single line of tire tracks before, there were multiple sets now. The fire engines, which evidently arrived too late to do any good, had nearly blotted out the others. He thought he saw a tire print or two that were neither Bolt's VW nor the fire truck. Someone else had been to the house after Whaite left and before the fire company arrived. That could mean the house was torched. There'd been no smoke from the chimney the day before. That meant the space heater was not operating, so how else could the fire have started?

He needed to find Steve Bolt.

◇◇◇

Ike and Ruth left the farm late. Abe insisted on making a huge country breakfast. She just picked at her food. She could not say goodbye to Ike's mother who, Abe reported, still slept and he didn't want to disturb her. He promised to tell her everything Ruth said. She poked her nose out the door, shivered, and allowed herself to be togged out in a parka, a pair of boots, and wool gloves from the back closet. Her coat now lay in her lap and a plastic bag held the remainder of her things, including the Bible.

"It's late, I'm sorry," Ike said over the noise of the engine, which always sounded like a surplus tank until its motor warmed up.

"It's okay, I called and had Agnes rearrange my schedule."

"How is Agnes these days?"

"Much the same. She is a sterling personal secretary—"

"Administrative assistant."

"Right, administrative assistant. She is efficient, honest, cares about me. You would be wise to mend your fences with her. I know for a fact that if she takes it into her head to make your life miserable, she can and will."

"What I can't understand is what did I do to earn her enmity? I'm polite. I don't take her paper clips without asking and I never, ever, ask her to fetch me coffee. That pretty much defines the sensitive man, I think."

"She's afraid of you, if you must know."

"Afraid? Of me? Why?"

"The same reason I am. You are a dangerous man, Schwartz."

"I missed something here. When did I become a danger to you and Agnes?"

"Agnes sees you as a threat to me because she cares about me, so the danger transfers to her."

"I'm lost. Start again."

"No, you'll have to figure it out on your own."

Ike sighed and shook his head. "Lunch then. I'm meeting Weitz. Join us." He pulled up to the front entrance of Callend College. She turned to him. He did not like the expression on her face and was sure he did not want to hear what would come next.

"No, not today, Ike. And about tonight, your protecting me and all that—look, I appreciate it but I need some alone time. Don't worry, I'll have the college cops camp out on my porch until this thing blows over or the bad guys kill me. But I don't want to see you for a while."

"The first part's okay. I didn't sleep that well last night either. I kept running what happened back then over and over in my mind. I'd pushed it all away but around four in the morning, I remembered. I couldn't have seen what happened from where I was sitting, but I was sure I saw what happened. I am sure Charlie is clean. And if he isn't, well…"

"Well what?"

"There's nothing I can do to stop him, anyway. The best protection in that case is to give the appearance the thought never crossed our minds. But that doesn't mean we can't see—"

"No, no. The two aren't connected." Ruth gazed out the passenger side window. Her brow furrowed, mouth drawn tight. She exhaled—not a sigh—a soft whoosh. "To tell you the truth, your mother spooked me a little. I need to make some decisions and I need to do it alone."

"Decisions?"

"Don't push, Ike."

"We're still fine?"

"We're good. That's not the problem. It's about yesterday's fire, and flannel nightgowns, and if I don't get out of this rattle-trap right this minute, you are going to see me cry and I'll be damned if I'm going to let you do that—not today, anyway."

Chapter Twenty

Essie Falco hung up the phone and wig-wagged at Ike as he came through the door. She leaned across the booking desk, which put a significant strain on the top buttons of her blouse, and handed him a stack of pink message slips and a note stating that Sam had called in sick. She resumed her seat and straightened her uniform. Ike had watched that scenario dozens of times and had finally concluded the blouse must zip up the back and the front was sewn shut. The buttons were just for show. He raised an eyebrow.

"I already called Billy and he's okay about working a double. He said he needed Sam to owe him one."

"Did she say what her problem was?"

"No, sir, she didn't, but if I was to guess…"

"Is this a woman's intuition thing, Essie? Because if it is—"

"Ike, have I ever been wrong on things like this?"

"Probably, but I can't remember. So your guess is…?"

"It's man trouble. I bet you a jelly-filled doughnut that FBI guy who, as you know, I never did trust in the first place, has dumped her."

"Why would he do that?"

"Ike, he's a FBI. They can't get all tied down with no country police. It had to happen sooner or later. Give her a day or two and she'll see it's for the best."

"You think?"

"Bet on it."

"A jelly-filled, you said."

"One jelly-filled against whatever doughnut you prefer."

"You're on." They shook hands and tapped knuckles to seal the deal.

"You call her and see if I'm not right."

Ike did not call. Whether Essie had it right or not, he didn't want Sam disturbed just yet. Ruth would have castigated him for not caring, but he figured if Sam was really sick, she'd want to be left alone. He would, and if it was man trouble, as Essie supposed, he would be the last person in the world she needed to talk to.

He proceeded to work his way through the stack of call slips. Half he dealt with by dropping them in the trash. The remainder he sorted by urgency—his, not the caller's—and began returning the calls. He saved the mayor for last. A robbery at the college that summer, and the attendant publicity with its television and news media, had briefly catapulted Picketsville into national prominence. Before that, it had languished as a small town bypassed by Interstate 81 and remarkable only for its rustic charm, a few local characters, and Callend College. The latter had entered the twenty-first century as possibly the only, or certainly, one of the very few, all women's colleges still extant. How much longer that status would endure comprised the bulk of the conversations engaged in by the locals at the Crossroads Diner and the faculty in their musty halls of academe up on the hill. In the meantime, the town had attracted all sorts of land speculators, deal makers, and some shady types Ike hoped would soon slither out the way they came in.

The mayor had issues. He had them with the members of the Town Council, he had them with the county, the Commonwealth, and most particularly, he had them with Ike.

"Ike, doggone it, you know how this town works. You can't go ally—alnate—"

"Alienating?"

"Making enemies of council members. Brent Wilcox said he visited your shop last week and you weren't...um...receptive to his—"

"Meddling in the affairs of the Sheriff's Office. You're absolutely right, Tom, and if you had the gumption eating grits every morning since you were weaned from your mother's tit is supposed to give you, you'd tell that twerp to take a hike."

"Now, Ike, don't you start in on me. I been your biggest supporter and fan—yes sir, fan—but I have a town to run here and whether you've noticed it or not, things are changing. We have to go with the times. Wilcox has big ideas and sees the future, like."

"He's an over-educated stuffed shirt, Tom. His ideas are as modern as hula hoops—you remember them, don't you? And if you let him and his sycophant buddies up on the hill have their way, Picketsville is going to turn into a phony tourist town whose chief attraction will be an outlet mall done up to look like Tara."

"Look like who? Look here, Ike—"

"The plantation in *Gone with the Wind*. No, I won't look. Tom, this town has to grow and change but it needs its own vision and a plan, not some cookie cutter idea imported from a New York land speculator."

"New York? What's that about New York?"

"It's where he came from, and what he did, among other things, before he decided to move south and civilize us."

"How'd you know that?"

"I run your police department, remember? It's my job to check out suspicious characters."

"Well now, I don't think suspicious—"

"Some advice from someone who knew you when…don't get into this guy's pocket and, more importantly, don't let him get into yours. He's bad news, and it's only a matter of time until he will crash and burn, and when he does, he'll take all sorts of folk down with him."

"Ike, you're over the line on this."

"Tom, remember you heard it here first." Ike hung up before the mayor said something they'd both regret later.

He told Essie to tell the mayor, if he called back, to say that he, Ike, would be out of the office. He looked at his watch.

He had fifteen minutes to meet Weitz for lunch. He heaved himself up from his desk chair, which squealed in protest. He reminded himself for the one hundredth time to fix it, signed out, and left.

Frank Chitwood owned Chez François, Picketsville's other restaurant. It attempted French cuisine which the locals referred to as Frank's Southern Fried Frog's Legs. Weitz met him in the foyer and they took a table in the rear.

"I would stick to the roast beef, if I were you," Ike said and pulled his red checked napkin into his lap. "I read the book you sent over, thanks. Buffalo Mountain must have been an interesting place before the war."

"No snails?"

"If you feel brave, go for it."

"I'll stay with the beef. Or is it *boeuf?* The mountain? Yes, it was. What I discovered, Sheriff, and should have known from my other studies, but somehow missed, is that stereotypes derive from reality. The idea of feuding hillbillies with their jugs of moonshine, shotgun justice, and the whole costumery come from a people who were at one time, more or less, exactly as they are depicted in the cartoons."

Their waitress arrived dressed in what Ike assumed Frank Chitwood thought must look like a Parisian maid. She looked more like an Apache dancer. She took their orders and retreated.

"If you look at old films from that era," Weitz continued, "black and white, maybe even a silent one, the people depicted as living in the mountains back east, the hillbillies, if you will, really dressed and acted and looked very much like the ones in the films, only they were real, not acting in some buffoonery. At the remove of more than three quarters of a century and the two generations who've never read the late Al Capp's *Lil' Abner,* we think the image must have been overdone and our natural predilection to slip into politically correct thinking means we reject the whole as something bordering on a kind of racism. I am not, by the way, suggesting that what Hollywood and television have done to the accents and humor of the era is representative—shows like *Hee Haw* and so on. They do, in fact, overplay the people—out of a sense of cultural superiority, I suppose. At any rate, the truth is, allowing for all that, mountain folk did look and live pretty much that way at one time."

"Except for the notion that political correctness is 'natural,' I agree. Is there anything you can tell me about the descendents of those folks still in the hills that will help me find a murderer?"

"Well, they are still pretty close-mouthed. Outsiders will not find it easy to get information, and they still distrust the police. They'd rather see to things themselves."

"I'd need an insider to crack that?"

"And not a policeman, yes."

"Then I have a problem."

Their lunch arrived. Weitz seemed to want to ask Ike something and twice started to speak, then shook his head and resumed dipping into his soup.

"Ask it," Ike said, amused at the academic's indecision.

"It's none of my business, Sheriff—"

"Ike. Everyone calls me Ike."

"Thank you. Leon, then. Ike, you and Dr. Harris, ah…How do I ask this…?"

"Let me guess. Are we what the rumors suppose? That help?"

"Yes. I'm sorry. There're faculty members who have this inane notion that the intelligentsia should not be seen fraternizing with the *hoi polloi,* mere mortals, you might say."

"Except when they seduce their students, but of course, that doesn't count any more than an eighteenth-century squire impregnating a milkmaid."

"Yes, there's that, too, I suppose."

"You can report the following: the sheriff, tugging respectfully at a forelock and shuffling his feet, eyes downcast, begs their lordship's collective pardon, and suggests, respectfully, that they get a life."

Weitz grinned. "I'll do that. Sorry, but I promised I'd ask.'"

"Since we've opened up the area of reporting back to our side the activities of the other side, there is something you can do for me. What can you tell me about Brent Wilcox's relations with the faculty?"

"Ah, that's something I am happy to talk about. He has a following in the group that, by the way, is most concerned about your *bona fides*, they are...Let me start again. Except for the men and women in the business school, faculty members are incredibly naïve when it comes to business and money. We deny it, of course, because we think we are smarter than people. Wilcox has caught the fancy of some of them because of his presumptive knowledge of real estate and land brokerage. They are looking for some windfall income by investing in something called the New Options Investments."

"He is recruiting investors?"

"Yes, no...I think so. I would assume they will surface soon enough."

"Leon, I will happily keep your nosey friends posted on my relationship with their president, within the bounds of decency and discretion, of course, if you will keep me posted on Wilcox. Oh, and don't buy in yourself. He's a scam artist."

"Hadn't planned to. I am smart enough to know when I'm not smart enough to know, if you follow me. I will keep you posted. There's no need to reciprocate at your end. Their fertile imaginations will serve them better than the truth."

Ike said goodbye and left wondering what new can of worms he'd just opened, and if he might end up having to arrest the mayor.

Chapter Twenty-one

Sam expected a call from Ike. None came. That left her both disappointed and relieved. On the one hand she thought no call meant she might not rank high enough in his mind to warrant a "how're you doing?" On the other hand, if he had called, she would be duty bound to tell him about Cutthroat and Karl. The thought of Karl sent her back to her tissues. She blew her nose and called the office. Billy Sutherlin answered. "Hey Ryder, what's up with you? You got the 'blue-flu'?"

"Is Ike there?"

"Nah, he's off to a meeting with one of them faculty dudes, probably trying to get the low-down on Ms. Harris."

"Billy, forget that. President Harris is a really nice lady and Ike—well, he's lucky she sees something in him."

"He's lucky? You women always stick together. So, when are you coming back?"

Good question. She knew she needed to get back to work, to put Karl out of her mind. "I'll be in tomorrow."

"Okay, that's good. Say, now that you owe me, I want to get down to Talladega for the NASCAR meet. I need you to cover one day for me."

"No problem."

"It's a weekend, Ryder. It might interfere with your love life."

"And I said no problem. You just plan on having a big time inhaling exhaust fumes."

"You're sure?"

"You heard me. Put Essie on, will you?" Sam needed to talk to a woman. Essie was the closest one available. Essie listened for a minute and whooped something about a jelly-filled.

◇ ◇ ◇

Before he left Picketsville for Harvard and a different life, Ike had his hair cut at Melvin Cushwa's barbershop on Main Street. Everybody did. It was the only barbershop in town. There were five chairs—the old-fashioned kind that had the big adjustable bolster on the back where you could rest your head while the effects of a hot towel worked their magic on your face and soul. Mel and four other men honed their straight edge razors on leather strops, applied hot lather with badger hair brushes, and gave everybody the identical haircut. When he returned to Picketsville, Ike discovered Melvin had retired to Florida, the other men had drifted away, and a Pakistani who talked too much and giggled had assumed ownership of the shop. One haircut by Pradesh convinced Ike he needed an alternative.

He'd discovered Lee Henry quite by accident. She was in the Shop n' Save when he stopped in for some ground beef and hamburger rolls. He'd just had his hair cut and she happened to look up from a conversation she was having with several of her cronies. She frowned and shook her head. "Mmm, mmm, mmmmmm! That there is the worst mess I ever saw on the top of a man's head in a long time. You need help, honey."

He ran his fingers through his hair. "I do. Question is, short of driving to Roanoke, where will I find it?"

"You come see me. I'll see if I can fix that disaster." She dug a crumpled business card from her purse and handed it to him. "Don't wait too long, sugar." She turned to her companions and Ike heard her murmur, "He's been done by that Indin."

A week later, he pulled into her driveway. Her house had started out as a split-level but the area usually assigned as a utility room had been expanded to the rear and was fitted out like a salon. Not a barber shop. There were no chairs raised by pedaling hydraulics, no men's magazines lying about. Just shelves loaded with shampoos and conditioners, brushes with wide-spaced, knobby teeth and the perpetual odor of wet hair. If he had any second thoughts about using Lee, however, they were immediately dismissed by her raucous personality and endless optimism. She cut hair for men and women. "I'm unisex," she'd said. "That means I only do it with one guy at a time." And she'd bubbled over with the kind of laughter that would do more good in a hospital than an entire pharmaceutical company. She told stories, the latest gossip, and jokes. She and Ike struck up a friendship that became an important part of his life. When she finally kicked her alcoholic and abusive husband out, Ike was there to console. He sometimes would drop in "for a trim" simply to get away from the dark side of his life.

Today, he needed a haircut.

"Well, look at what come in with the north wind. Say, Ike, you must be feeling right at home with all this snow since you lived up north all them years."

"This isn't a snow, Lee. This is a dusting. A real snow is when it piles up to your hips."

"Well, I don't ever want to see no real snow then. Sit down, put your feet on the foot rest thingy, and let me get to work." She tucked a vinyl sheet around his neck and spritzed his hair.

"Okay," she said, and Ike knew he was in for *the story*. "Did you hear about the Tices' daughter and her car?"

"No, what about her?"

"This is a true story, Ike. Swear to God. Georgie Tice gave little Tiffani—that's with an 'I' instead of a 'Y' and a little heart instead of a dot over the 'I'. He gave her a Ford Mustang when she turned eighteen. Not a new one but nice, you know. Lordy me, the times I had in a Mustang…my, my…Well, anyway, she'd been away to college over in Charlottesville and came home for the weekend. Drove home, mind you, in the 'Stang. She pulls up and old Georgie hears the worst noise you can imagine. Bangity, bang, bang. He runs out and that old Mustang is jumping and rocking. It sounds like the rods and lifters are about ready to fly out the top of the engine. She pops out all gushy and such and George just stands there. Then he goes to check the car to see what's wrong. She comes back for her bags and the car's about to shake apart. He says, 'Tiffani, you see this oil pressure gauge? It's dead on zero.' And she says, 'Oh that. Don't you pay no attention to that old thing, Daddy. It ain't worked for weeks.'" Lee burst into her patented laugh. "Cost him twenty-five hundred dollars for a new engine and he made her go to the Vo-Tech at night and take an auto mechanics course before he'd let her drive again. Ain't that a scream?" She put the electric trimmers to work on the back of his neck. "So what's new in the policing business? You got any juicy stuff for me?"

"You know more about what's going on in the Sheriff's Office than I do. You tell me."

"Well, there's the body you took out of the woods a while back. Anything new there?"

"How'd you hear about it?"

"I got other customers 'sides you, Handsome. Picketsville is a small town. We don't have much in the way of secrets here."

"Nobody's supposed to know about that."

"No? Too late on that one."

"What else?"

"Mavis Bowers told me she was out that way the night before. I don't know what that woman was doing out there in the middle of the night. Getting out of the house, I expect. Her husband is a hard shell Baptist and she's an E-whiskey-palian and needs a pick-me-up every now and then. I expect she slipped out for a nip, bless her heart."

"What did she tell you?"

"Oh yeah, she said she saw a truck parked on the side of the road. Not likely it was kids slipping into the woods to get it on—too cold—so it must have been someone else."

"Did she say what kind of truck?"

"No. Mavis doesn't know about vehicles."

"But you do."

"Twelve years living with an alcoholic over-the-road trucker—I do." She combed his hair and trimmed his eyebrows. "Got a jungle started there, Ike. Means you're getting old."

"Tell me something I don't know. What do you hear about Brent Wilcox?"

"Oh, now you got a good one. What do you want to know?"

"Anything I can't pull off the internet."

"Let's see. Where to start? He's been out to the old Craddock place a time or two. It don't seem likely he's interested in any of them girls, so it must be something else has caught his eye. And then he's been moving all around town asking questions about folks—you especially. Why is that, do you suppose?"

"Probably because I'm the guy who's most likely to bust him. He would not like that to happen."

"He's been squiring Agnes Ewalt around."

That was news and definitely not good news. Agnes was too close to Ruth. Ike pushed away the images that struggled to form in his mind.

Agnes and Wilcox!

Chapter Twenty-two

Andover Crisp had a problem. In fact he had a whole laundry list of problems. It had not been his idea to extract Kamarov from Novosibirsk in the first place. That had come down from the director's office. One of his know-it-all recruits sold him on the idea and he ordered the black ops division to go in and bring the Russian spook out. Only then had Crisp received orders to make the damn-fool operation work. Nobody had the sense to find out what the man did or did not know. He'd promised something on 9-11 but hadn't as yet produced anything that couldn't have been gleaned from the internet, if you knew where to look. He did have some interesting things to say about a deep sleeper in the CIA a while back. The sleeper had been on station for a dozen years and moved into a very sensitive area and done considerable damage to the Agency's missions. A number of field operatives had their cover blown. It was useful information, but…putting together Cutthroat, including the extraction, had cost the Bureau a cool ten million, none of it logged on the budget, which meant a whole lot of departments were going to buy a whole lot of non-existent paperclips. And the end wasn't in sight. Now the Russian had flown the coop. No one knew where or why he went. Crisp's only hope of recovering the asset was to follow the money and hope Kamarov wasn't as clever as he'd come to believe.

The director had started calling him at home and in the middle of the night. That's how it began. When the director decides to dump someone—he starts calling in the middle of the night. Then memos appear in your email. Memos you never saw or wrote. Of course, the idiot who thought up this Looney Tunes operation would be insulated from any responsibility. The only bright spot Crisp could see was that the idiot would be promoted and then the next moronic operation to emanate from on top would land in his lap.

The phone rang. The director?

"Crisp here."

"He's on the move again."

"Where?"

"He seems to be headed south on I-77 toward Charlotte. He's using one of his credit cards to take cash advances from ATMs."

"Why the credit card? Why not the bank card? All the big money is in the bank. He'll need the credit card later."

"Can't say, sir. Here's something else. He used a different card to book into a motel near I-81 last night."

"Motel? What the devil is going on here? Shut down the credit cards. Make him use the bank card. I don't want those bills coming in—not at the rate he's running them up."

"Yes, sir. Anything else?"

"That's all for now, Kevin, thank you."

Crisp pushed his chair back and steepled his fingers under his chin. Something did not fit. What had he missed? He closed his eyes. He needed to think. He lit a cigar—a definite no-no in the new director's tenure, but Crisp and his unit were out in the country and there would be no nicotine police to tattle on him. He breathed in contraband Cuban smoke and closed his eyes. Something…what? He ran through the few facts he had. He wondered if there might be another interpretation to them that he might have overlooked. He sat, eyes closed and fingertips together, for a long time. His secretary came into the office, recognized the posture, and left. Finally, he emerged from his reverie and picked up the phone.

"Kevin, I have another assignment for you. I want you to search again for John Does. You're to stay cloaked, you understand? I don't want anybody to know we're looking. Hack into police department computers if you have to, for unidentified men, bodies, whatever, and call me back if you find something. Oh, and concentrate on the greater Richmond area particularly."

Was it possible Kamarov was already dead and consigned on some departmental blotter as just another derelict? Did he traipse off to Richmond to get laid again and end up mugged in an alley instead? Did some bimbo strip him of his cards and leave him in the gutter—another homeless man with no ID—now just a body cooling in the morgue? That scenario would solve at least half of Crisp's problems. He rubbed his hands together, whether in anticipation or hope, he wasn't sure.

◇◇◇

Whaite stopped at the volunteer fire station and greeted the men on duty. He recognized some of their names but none well. Returning to the mountain had not been a trip down memory lane. His childhood had been hard. Not that his parents were abusive—on the contrary—but they worked a hardscrabble farm that barely put food on the table. As soon as he was able, Whaite started working at the Exxon station. There, he learned the basics of auto mechanics. The meager wages he earned, he handed over to his mother, who would peel off a dollar or two for him to keep. The farm finally failed and his folks moved on to Baltimore to work construction. Whaite stayed on the mountain looking after the house and working at the gas station until he heard about the police academy and a chance to step up in the world. Picketsville needed a deputy and would sponsor him. He snapped at it. He'd served under Sheriff Loyal Parker for a few years. Parker was a bully and knew less about police work than anyone in the office. Ike's election came at just the right time. Whaite had already started a job search when Ike took over.

There wasn't much to be learned from the crew on duty. They told him that by the time they got a call and made it to Bolt's house, the roof had already collapsed. They shut down and sat out the fire. The only job left for them to do was keep it from jumping to the trees and starting something in the forest.

"Too bad," one of them said. Whaite thought he looked like one of the Childress boys but couldn't be sure. "Steve had that place about all fixed up. He had his permit to hook up to propane and everything. He did a nice job, too. Them space heaters need watching twenty-four seven. If they don't set the house on fire, they'll get you with the carbon monoxide. He shoulda known better."

"And if it wasn't an accident?"

"What? Who's saying so?" The other men looked up at Whaite.

"I was out there yesterday. His space heater was off."

"You went to his house?"

"No, I checked out the chimney. No hot air, none of the swirls it makes when it rises that you see, especially on a cold, sunny day."

"Anyway, not seeing smoke or exhaust from the chimney don't prove anything. It coulda been on pilot, or a thermostat, and kicked in after you left."

"Could. You been in his house, do you remember a thermostat? I mean, if he was going to hook up a propane tank, why would he go to the expense of buying a space heater with a thermostat?"

"You got a point. And Steve, he didn't earn too much. Better lately, when he got that part-time handyman job with the guy up in Floyd."

"When I was up there, there were tire tracks leading out, but not back. This morning I saw your truck's tracks and traces of at least one other set. That car went in after I was there and before you arrived, and it wasn't Bolt."

"I remember them tracks. Didn't mean anything to me at the time."

"Wick Goad says Sonny Parker sold kerosene to some strangers just before that and he saw them head up the mountain."

"Who'd want to burn Steve out?"

"I don't know. I thought maybe you guys could help."

"How?"

"What can you tell me about the man he works for?"

"Nothing. Steve, he's pretty tight about him. Just said he paid pretty good and he didn't have to do too much."

"Did any of you ever see him?"

The men looked at one another, lips pursed. Finally one cleared his throat. "I did. Just one time and not too good. Here's the thing. I don't want to get in the middle of some old mountain thing so you didn't hear it from me."

"Some old mountain thing?"

"You know how it was—well, it sometimes pops up again— old feud or something. So, like I said, I didn't get a clear view of him but he looked like a Harris."

Chapter Twenty-three

Saturday mornings marked the end of the week. That was the good news. The bad news, another week would start in twenty-four hours. Ike took a deep breath and pushed through the glass door of the Crossroads Diner. He was immediately assaulted by the mixed aromas of coffee, bacon, and frying onions—and loud voices. Not the usual chatter about local gossip, politics, and Hokie football, but voices raised in anger. Flora Blevins held her finger a quarter of an inch from Brent Wilcox's nose.

"Let me tell you something, you carpetbagger, this diner ain't going nowhere."

"You might be persuaded to the contrary when I bring in paper defining the town's right of eminent domain."

"Maybe. And you might be persuaded to the contrary by a right-up-your-caboose-with-a-pump-action twelve-gauge."

"Are you threatening me? Ms. Blevins, I can swear out a warrant and have you arrested. A felony conviction would make your case for holding out extremely difficult. There are all these witnesses." Wilcox turned to the assembled breakfast clientele. "You heard what she said." He caught sight of Ike and turned to him. "Sheriff, I insist you arrest this woman for assault. She threatened me. These people are my witnesses."

"Anybody hear Flora threaten Mr. Wilcox?" No one replied. "Looks like you must have been mistaken, Wilcox. None of these good people heard a thing. You were probably speaking too softly."

"You heard her. I know you did."

"Sorry, I found myself so enthralled by the scent of fresh brewed coffee I lost track of everything else."

"She threatened me and I plan to swear out a warrant."

"Be my guest. Miss Falco over at the station will help you with that, but I think you're wasting time. It'll be a 'he says, she says' thing in the end."

For what seemed a full minute but couldn't have been more than a few seconds, Wilcox glared at Ike. "I'll have your badge, Sheriff."

"If you think you're up to the job, go for it. In the meantime, I'll be watching you."

Wilcox stumped out, cursing.

"Who is that creep, Ike? Where's he get off coming into my diner that I have been running since my old daddy died and left it to me, and tell me to move it or he'll tear it down?"

"He's what they used to call a shill, Flora. He makes things happen by bluff and bluster. The law of eminent domain is nowhere as simple as he wants you to believe. He can't do anything without the Town Council approval. They can't invoke it without a master plan. They can't implement a master plan without hearings and on and on. As much as Wilcox and his speculator friends want to grab up real estate, there are more who will put the pressure on the Council to keep the Crossroads in place." The patrons nodded and a few applauded. "There, you see? And I loved the bit about the twelve-gauge up the caboose. Nice touch."

"You didn't do so badly there yourself, Ike. Breakfast is on the house."

A free breakfast called for a celebration of sorts, so Ike sat in a booth instead of his usual place at the counter. He wouldn't have to order. Flora always brought him the same thing every morning. Once he tried to shift to the Valley Triple Stack—three humongous pancakes awash in butter and syrup, but Flora brought him two eggs over easy, bacon, grits, and whole wheat toast—buttered. He gave up. Flora held as her dietetic credo—eggs, bacon, grits, and toast were the only sensible way to begin a person's day. She did not want to see Ike slip into bad dietary habits, so whatever he ordered, she overruled and served him his usual.

Ike had not called Ruth the night before. She wanted to be alone and he'd decided to respect that. He'd meant to call Sam but forgot. He considered calling Charlie and decided to wait until later in the morning. He did connect with Whaite, who told him he thought Steve Bolt worked for Kamarov. That was news, assuming someone saying the man he worked for "looked like a Harris" qualified as a lead. Bolt's house torched probably had more immediate significance. Why would anyone want to do something like that? Unless the man *was* Kamarov. Then… then what? So far, only Sam, Whaite and he…no, that wasn't right…Sam, Whaite, Ruth, Charlie, and he knew Kamarov was dead. Unless Bolt killed him and dumped the body in Picketsville figuring nobody that far away would make the connection. But then, who set fire to his house?

He mopped up some egg yolk with a toast crust and paused, hand in midair. He lowered it and pulled a clean napkin from the dispenser on the table. He retrieved his pen and wrote down the four possibilities he'd identified as likely sponsors of the black program.

1. *Central Intelligence Agency*
2. *Federal Bureau of Investigation*
3. *Defense Intelligence Agency*
4. *National Security Agency*
5. *Other?*

He put a plus after the CIA, a double plus after the FBI, a minus after the DIA, and a double minus after NSA, rating each as likely candidates. The *Other* category he added in case their search drifted into the area of those unnamed and unaccounted for programs he knew existed in the darker recesses of the government but rarely identified.

Where did Bolt fit? He finished his breakfast, endured a dirty look from Flora for not finishing his grits, and asked for a second cup of coffee and a piece of paper. When the coffee arrived, he transferred his list to the paper and studied it. He pulled Charlie's secure cell phone out and turned it on. He fumbled in his pockets and found the number he'd been given to call and punched it in. There followed an empty space and then Charlie answered.

"It's about time I heard from you. What have you been doing?"

"Long story, Charlie, and I'm not in a place where I can tell it, but here's what we have so far." He filled him in on Sam's tracking and what seemed three other entities stalking Kamarov's money transactions. That meant at least two of them believed he was alive. He assumed one belonged to Charlie's people. He told him about the arson at Bolt's house. Could Charlie think of any reason why someone who might have been working for Kamarov would have his house burned to the ground? Charlie said he was stumped.

"Suppose they were looking for something, couldn't find it, but believed it was hidden in the house? To make sure it never surfaced, they burned it to the ground. If I'm right, they'll be after Bolt next."

"Where is he?"

"Bolted—no pun intended. He's gone to ground. But my deputy said he drove an old VW beetle. Shouldn't be too hard to find. Any news on your APB?"

"Nothing yet. You realize it will be easy for whoever is after him, too. If they can tap into our computer as easily as your gal tapped into theirs, an APB might have already led them straight to him."

"You have a point. I'll think about it."

"Who's your candidate for the second group? I assume you think you know who the first is."

"Actually, I don't. Here's my list." He read the five names and his ratings.

"You can pull the plus off of CIA. I checked."

"You'd say that even if it weren't true. The plus stays, but my guess is FBI. They have the most to gain by discrediting the CIA and that's what I think this is all about. You guys are jockeying for position and prestige in the big restructuring of the intelligence community game and would be only too happy to leak some dirt about the other."

"Okay. Maybe you're right. But—"

"But that does not explain Bolt and arson. I know, so, I'm adding another name to the list." Ike retrieved the list and his pen and wrote.

"Who?"

"Who indeed? Who has the most to gain by killing Kamarov? Not you. You would turn him or trade him for someone they have that you want. Not the FBI. If they bought him, they'd want to keep him for now and then put him in the witness protection program. So who gains from a dead Kamarov?"

"Are you going to tell me, or must I beg?"

"Begging would help. His former bosses, Charlie. They are the losers. They had Kamarov bottled up, but perestroika and the fall of Communism made them forgetful, or careless."

"I vote for careless."

"Okay, so instead of liquidating him as they would have in the old days, they send him off to an uncomfortable retirement. Then he turns up here. If you were Kamarov, what would induce you to come to the States?"

"Money, a new life, it couldn't have been very upbeat for him in…what was that place?"

"Novosibirsk."

"Right. You talked to Alexei in the old days. What would be your guess?"

"I think he might have been approached by whoever did this. I think he might even have set up the meet himself. He persuaded the people—we'll assume the FBI for the moment—that he had information that would embarrass the Agency. He wouldn't have much of anything that could be used against them, so FBI seems the likely choice, not you. They snap him up and whisk him to wherever. Then things get screwy."

"Thanks for letting us off the hook. How screwy?"

"He moves to Floyd. Apparently, they did not keep him on a close leash or they would have noticed our asking about Randall Harris. That means...what? I don't know. Could he have had a second ID they didn't know about? That seems unlikely. Anyway, they haven't."

"Haven't what?"

"Picked up on the fact that local police are pursuing Randall Harris and his friends."

"Oh."

"Anyway, he's shipped off to Floyd. Do you think the Bureau doesn't know who makes up an important portion of the population down there? It had to be at his insistence."

"I still don't follow...wait...you think he used them to get to us?"

"Who's he angry at, Charlie? Not the Agency, I don't think."

"He finagled his way over here to blow the whistle on his former bosses?"

"Somehow they found him and killed him. They dumped him in a place as far away as they dared to go from Floyd—small town with limited police. They couldn't possibly know they picked the one town on the East Coast where there was someone who knew him by sight."

"Wow. Okay, but that ends your search, you know. Even if you could get witnesses and evidence enough to arrest, the minute you get close, they'll invoke diplomatic immunity and ship their muscle home."

"But at least they'd know we know."

"Why bother, Ike?"

"Charlie, in the insane world you inhabit, and I used to, you get to know people. When you are an operative, you don't make friends, but to the extent two men on the opposite side of the fence could be, Alexei and I were friends. He tried to help me and paid the price. I owe him. If it's at all possible, I'm going to get them."

"Your call."

"One more thing."

"What's that?"

"What if Alexei had documents."

"If he thought he was in trouble or if he was killed, he might want to share them with the press! Blow the lid off everybody."

"And?"

"He'd keep a copy hidden somewhere."

"And someone torched Bolt's house."

"To get rid of the copies?"

"Works for me."

Ike hung up and stared at the list. As neatly as he'd spun it out to Charlie, he knew it didn't add up. They may have wanted to, but the Russians did not kill Kamarov. And where was Steve Bolt? The television blared out an infomercial from the local tourism bureau. He caught sight of a long shot down the Blue Ridge Parkway and a few seconds of a humpbacked Buffalo Mountain looming in the distance. At that moment it seemed menacing.

Chapter Twenty-four

Whaite felt his frustration rising. Every time he thought he had a lead, someone stalled him or disappeared. He needed to talk to Bolt but nobody knew, or would admit to knowing, where he could be found. The volunteer fire company up on the mountain didn't think Whaite had done them any favors by suggesting arson. Now they would have to call in the County to investigate. He tried to reach Ike at the office. Essie said Ike was out and she didn't know where. She put Sam on, who sounded like a bad soap opera.

"I don't know anything," she mumbled.

"What's up with you, Sam? You sound like you missed winning the lottery by one digit."

"Karl," she said. Whaite thought she might be crying. "He's what you said and worse." She hung up.

Karl? He didn't remember saying anything about Karl. Whaite redialed and tried Essie again.

"What in the billy blue blazes is going on up there?"

"She's got man trouble with that smart-alecky FBI guy, and Ike owes me a jelly-filled."

"I don't think I want you to translate that. I ain't had my second cup yet. Look, I need some help down here. Get Ike to call when he gets in or Sam when she's normal."

He drove on to Willis. If he couldn't find Bolt, he'd do the next best thing and find Oldham. He pulled in at the first establishment that had salt- and mud-encrusted trucks and older model cars parked in front. He wanted to talk to the locals, the ones who drove pickups and beat-up Malibus. He pushed in through the door, which scraped on the linoleum. Code violation, he mused. Men sat around drinking an early lunch. All eyes focused on him. Conversations stopped, started up again, but the eyes never left him. He nodded to several, pulled up to the bar, and ordered a coffee.

"You'll have to wait," the proprietor said. "I just this minute started a fresh pot." Whaite smiled and nodded again.

"No hurry."

Whatever the laws were regarding smoking in public facilities, they clearly did not apply there. A haze of acrid blue smoke hung from the ceiling. He could only escape it by slouching down. Three men sat at a table next to him. He smiled, stuck out his hand.

"How do, Whaite Billingsly. You from around here?"

The men inspected him. "You wouldn't be Howard Billingsly's boy, now, would you?" one asked. Howard, in this part of the world, was pronounced Haired.

"Howard from up near Slate Mountain?"

"That's the one."

"No, I'm his nephew a couple of times over. My daddy was Dink Billingsly from over to Buffalo Mountain."

"Well, I thought you looked familiar. You ain't from around here no more, though, are you?"

"Nope. Moved up to Picketsville."

"Now I got you. You're a deputy up there."

"That's me."

"That your car—the fancy one?"

"It is."

"Don't look much like a police car to me."

"It's my own. Long story on why I'm messing up the paint job with salt and cinders."

"Chevelle—what year?"

"Sixty-seven. Got the big 396 engine."

"She's a goer, I'll bet. So, what're you doing down here, if I ain't being too personal."

"Looking for a guy we think might know something about a corpse we got on ice up at Picketsville."

"Dead man? Who? Again, if I ain't being too—"

"Not sure. Rumor has it might be a Randall Harris. Ring a bell?"

Conversation in the immediate area stopped. The men stared at Whaite and then quickly averted their eyes.

"There was a Randall Harris up near Floyd, but he weren't no real Harris. He come from somewhere else and talked funny, like he come from some other country, or maybe Boston—one of them foreign places, you know?"

"You see him around here much?"

The man studied Whaite for a full mountain minute, evidently weighing which way he would answer.

"He's dead, you say?"

"As a door nail. Somebody shot him more'n once."

"Can't help you, son."

"Figured as much. Just thought I'd ask. You wouldn't happen to know someone named Oldham, Donald Oldham, now would you?" Whaite felt sure he was on the cusp. The answer might or might not come. It depended on how this man or any of the others, who were pretending not to eavesdrop, felt about him, or about Oldham. The first man shrugged and sipped his beer. A younger man with sawdust in the cuffs of his trousers looked up.

"I know him," he said. "He's that new boy who works up at the mill some days."

"And?"

"Well, he's lived here for a spell. His old man ran a gas station down on the corner. When it burned down folks figured Donnie put the torch to it. He lives up past The Pub, about a quarter of a mile further on and down that side road where you see the rusty Purina feed sign."

"Thanks. Why 'new boy'?"

"He's, like, a new boy on account of his family come from outside, you know, Ohio, I heard. But he took to calling himself a mountain man. Claims to be descended from one of the old families—Moles, I think. He swaggers around with that old five-shooter in his pocket he must've picked up in a pawn shop somewhere and talks about setting the record straight."

"What record would that be?"

"Who knows? He's loony."

The first man broke in. "Oldham is all talk. He ain't close to being no mountain man. He might wave that popgun of his around and bully somebody smaller than him, but he ain't got the courage of a whorehouse cat. He'd steal your wallet if you ain't looking, and maybe cheat you out of a few beers, but that's it for Donnie O, I'll tell you."

Whaite's cell phone played two bars of "You Ain't Nothing but a Hound Dog." He thanked the men and took his call outside. It had warmed up and water dripped off the roof and down his collar before he could clear the building.

◇◇◇

Ike had finished his call to Charlie Garland. He asked for, but did not finish, a third cup of coffee. Back at the office he took Whaite's message. Before he could call, Sam burst into his office.

"I was afraid to say anything before, Ike. I thought, well, it's his job and he should do it, but then if he had anything to do with—"

"Whoa. Slow down. Whose job?" Sam filled him in about Karl and her discovery he was connected to Cutthroat.

"You're sure it's Karl. The FBI is a big operation and—"

"It's him. He told me he'd been reassigned. His name was on the roster."

Ike spent an uncomfortable fifteen minutes trying to console her. He wished Ruth were there. She would know what to say. All Essie had to offer was an "I told you so" and when could she collect.

"Collect? What?"

"My jelly-filled."

"Go away, Essie. Answer the phone. Do something out there."

Sam settled down and filled him in on what she knew and what she suspected. The programs were still tracking the money transactions. She hadn't found anything new, but she had an idea she wanted to try. Finally, Ike called Whaite.

"No news on Bolt?"

"No. I am going to find the other guy, Oldham. Maybe he can lead us to Bolt."

"What do you have on him?"

"Mixed bag. He's either a bad dude or a phony. The going sense around here is mostly the last."

"Well, in case they're wrong, be careful."

Ike put the phone down and tried to unscramble the pieces. Somehow he knew that before he'd put this one to bed, he'd have to connect Bolt, Kamarov, and Cutthroat. The secure phone buzzed.

"Ike," Charlie said. "Don't mean to butt in so soon, but I started thinking about the Russians—"

"I know. It won't work."

"Not the way you put it, but maybe another."

"How?"

"Do you have access to Washington papers?"

"We permit them in town on occasion."

"Late edition Thursday or Friday morning. There's a short report about a suicide in Rock Creek Park. Then, later that morning, some goons broke into the dead guy's apartment, grabbed the girlfriend, tossed the apartment, and left her trussed up with a two-inch-wide strip of duct tape across her mouth, naked as a jaybird."

"So, the District police aren't buying a suicide."

"Nope."

"Charlie, tell me the significance of this. If I want to read the story, I have to go up to the college and make nice to the librarian, who doesn't like me."

"Why doesn't she like you?"

"Enough already. She's a he, by the way. What are you getting at?"

"The dead guy was a reporter, freelance columnist. He wrote in his date book he was to pick up something in the park. I'm guessing it arrived and he took a bullet afterwards. The apartment would be a 'just in case.'"

"And Bolt's house up in flames another 'just in case'?"

"It's a thought."

A bad one. A dangerous one. If someone was after Bolt, Whaite could be in danger. He called Whaite, but he'd shut down his cell phone—new town ordinance—radio not responding, apparently out of range. For the first time since they'd found Kamarov's body in the forest, Ike thought he might be in over his head.

Chapter Twenty-five

Hollis had finally figured out how to navigate with crutches on ice. He'd removed the rubber ends and driven a sixpenny nail in their place. He cut off the head of each and sharpened it to a point. The arrangement worked like two ice picks. But once the ice melted, the sharp points were useless. They skidded laterally on concrete and forced him to hop on one foot until he regained his balance. On turf they were worse. They punched a starter hole which then allowed the crutch ends to sink an inch or so into the ground, pitching him forward. He found a pair of pliers and tried to remove the nails but discovered that they were set in too firmly. When Donnie Oldham walked into his garage, he was attempting to refit the rubber end pieces by pushing the nails through their centers.

"What're you doing?"

"I'm trying to fix these crutches back." He slipped off his shoe and used the heel as a hammer to force the rubber tip back on the crutch. It slid into place but now the shoe was nailed to its end. He twisted it back and forth cursing the shoe, the crutch, and Donnie, who'd made him break his leg in the first place.

"They're after you, you know," he said as the shoe finally jerked free and hit him in the face. "Ow!"

"Who's after me?"

"Some guy was in Jake's this morning asking about you and Steve Bolt."

"So what?"

"He was a police."

"How'd you know that?"

"Ralph, he did the talking, Ralph and Bart from the mill, him too. Ralph said he was a cop."

Donnie scratched his head and, to the extent it was possible for him to do so, looked thoughtful. "Why would a cop want to find me?"

"Don't know. But Harris' name came up, too. So maybe they want to know about them credit cards."

"What did this guy, the cop, look like?"

"Sort of ordinary, tallish, pretty lean, and he wasn't wearing no uniform. He said he was from Picketsville."

"Who said?"

"Ralph."

"Is that the best you can do, Hollis? I swear you are the ignorantest person I ever met."

"Well, that's for you to say. He was driving a big red car. That help?"

"You dope. Police don't drive red cars. Even Picketsville police don't and that's a pretty backward place. Firemen drive red cars. He must have been a fireman."

"Well now, that makes some sort of sense. Steve Bolt's house was set on fire the other night. Maybe he's a fire police. He's probably checking out arson and, naturally, your name must've come up."

"They're not called fire police, you idiot, and why *naturally*?"

"I reckon everybody knows you set your old man's gas station on fire, so—"

"Nobody knows that. It were never proved."

"Okay fine. Still, this fire police is looking for you, so watch out."

"Big deal. The day comes when I can't take care of some jerk in a red car, I hang it up. I come for the card, by the way."

Hollis replaced his shoe, rummaged around in his pocket, and tossed the card to Donnie. "Here, take it. It don't work no more."

"Why didn't you just saw that nail off, dummy? What do you mean, it don't work?"

"Well, I reckon we might get us some more snow and I want to be ready."

"Right. What about the card not working?"

"I tried it this morning and the machine said 'account closed' and I should return it to the issuing bank. So here you are, Mr. Issuing Bank."

Donnie frowned. How many of the other cards were canceled, he wondered. He'd have to try them. Tomorrow was Sunday. Did the ATMs work on Sunday? If the door was closing, he'd need to pull out as much as he possibly could before it slammed shut. Then he'd see about that fireman.

◇◇◇

Sam shook her head. What a mess. She sighed and retrieved *Cat's Eye* from the floor where it had landed previously. A bad read was better than no read, she reasoned.

> *Sledge felt, more than knew, that someone had slipped into his room. The scent—the scent of a woman—he'd know it anywhere, jasmine. He'd caught a hint of it this morning in the souk—penetrating the rich smell of garlic, roasting goat, and Near Eastern body odor. That was just before the sniper had cut down Rodriguez and all hell broke loose. And now—here it was again.*
>
> *Adrenaline began to pump through his veins. The animal urge to strike lay, like a feral cat, just beneath the surface of his brain, making his heart race, and pricking up the hairs on the nape of his deeply tanned neck. Only a small candle flickered fitfully on the dresser. Too dark to see anything but he realized that, for the moment, his life depended on the woman—probably a woman—or it could be Dickie Farquar-Smythe. He was known to splash on a little jasmine from time to time, the little poof, but he was supposed to be studying Maori stone carvings in New Zealand. Whoever*

it was believed Sledge asleep. He kept his breathing steady, regular, his muscles tense.

Then he heard the rustle of nylon against nylon. Female legs crossing and re-crossing. Definitely a dame. He lay perfectly still, waiting—waiting for her to make the next move. His fingers gently stroked the one-of-a kind rosewood crosshatched grips of the Kimber under his pillow. He flicked the safety off—the click muffled by six inches of expensive Norwegian eiderdown. Next, another series of rustles—clothes probably—and two thumps—shoes being kicked off. The sheet and blanket on the other side of the bed raised and lowered and the mattress took the woman's weight. Not too much weight. One ten, one fifteen at the most, five feet four inches tall, and buff.

Cat-like, he spun and had the woman's throat between his thumb and forefinger in a classic Chi-Cha move. Her body went rigid. He suddenly realized she was naked and beautiful—the way only Eurasian women were beautiful. Hybrid vigor. He recalled learning that in his advanced agronomy course at Yale.

"You have thirty seconds to tell me who you are or I close my fingers and send you into Miss Chinatown heaven," he rasped menacingly.

"Oh, don't hurt me," she whimpered and closed her almond eyes. Her full round breasts pressed urgently against his chest.

"Don't pull that fainting Chinese virgin crap on me, Babe," he hissed.

"How you know…?" Her body went limp.

"I can read a yin and yang as good as the next guy," he smirked, and tapped the tattoo on her thigh.

She gasped at his touch. "You have me in you power, Scot."

"You know me?"

"Everybody know Scot Sredge."

"Yeah? So what do they call you, Sweetheart?"

She stretched her gracefully long arms and slipped her palms behind her head. One hand stroked her earlobe caressingly.

"Kin Tok ee." She whispered.

There was something wrong with the accent. Not Mandarin or Cantonese but something...Her pelvis began the quintessential primal circuits, age-old and unmistakable in their meaning, forcing any thoughts of accents and origins from his brain. She took his hand in hers and slid it slowly across her belly.

"Be gentle," she moaned and fell back on the silk sheets.

Sam snapped the book shut, heaved herself out of her chair, walked to the kitchen, stepped on the treadle of her garbage bin, and dropped the book in to join the eggshells, coffee grounds, and trash accumulated over the previous two days.

"Why won't I ever learn?" The lid clanked shut. She polished off the last pint of Ben and Jerry's and went to bed.

Chapter Twenty-six

Dawn. Steve Bolt, fully dressed, huddled on the bed, his knees drawn up to his chin. He stared out the window at an unfamiliar landscape. He had not slept the night before. He'd picked this particular motel strictly on impulse, reasoning that if he didn't know where he would be next, anyone tracking him wouldn't either. He shifted his gaze and stared at the phone. He didn't know who to call. His house had gone up like tinder. Those men must have poured on kerosene by the gallon before they set it off. He rocked back and forth. Now someone was after him and he didn't know who—or why.

Everything had been working just fine until that idiot Donnie Oldham screwed it up. It wasn't a complicated deal. Harris had hired Bolt to run errands, do chores, and keep an eye on his place when he went out of town. He seemed to have plenty of money and Bolt could always use more of that. After a few beers at The Pub, he'd hatched what he believed would be a sure-fire plan. Harris was leaving on one of his once-a-month trips to Richmond. He set Donnie up to snatch some credit cards when Harris was gone. Even though Bolt had a key, he had to make it look like a break-in, so he smashed a window, went to town to establish an alibi, and waited while Donnie slipped into the apartment to lift the cards. But instead of delivering the goods, he'd come scurrying into the Burger King all flustered and red in the face.

"There weren't no cards in that desk where you said they was, Steve. The place done been tossed and I couldn't find nothing worth nothing."

Bolt couldn't understand it. Harris had left town the day before. Twenty minutes previously he'd set up the broken window, and now the place had been turned upside down?

He got up as calmly as he could and led Donnie outside.

"What do you mean there's nothing there? I was over to that apartment an hour ago and it was just fine."

"You must not have looked in because it ain't now. Go see for yourself."

Never should have told that moron Donnie Oldham about Harris, he thought. Not that he had the brains or the guts to do anything. But still, ever since he told him and the easy job he had, and the cards that he'd sometimes be sent to get money from the bank machines with, things had gone really bad. Donnie Oldham was ten miles of bad luck.

Bolt straightened his legs and stretched full length. He really needed to sleep. The bed springs squeaked. He tried counting the water stains on the ceiling but to get them all he'd have to sit up again and he didn't want to. He tried to remember.

Harris always feared something or somebody. He'd given Bolt instructions—what he should do if anything happened to him. He'd put them in a bulky envelope with some papers. Bolt kept it in the glove box of his VW. When he reckoned Harris would not be coming back, Bolt retrieved the package. It contained a credit card, two thousand dollars in cash, and a second envelope with instructions he should follow: Hand off the inside envelope to some guy in Washington.

His instincts told him to take the money, pull out as much cash as an ATM would advance him, and stash the rest. Then he thought what if…? There could be all kinds of people involved in this. If he didn't follow the instructions, they might come after him, so he did as he was told. He'd driven to Washington in a snowstorm and finished the job—simple. And now they were after him.

He wondered if he'd made a mistake using the credit card to check into the motel. He'd heard they could be traced. They did that on TV shows all the time. A knock on the door so startled him, he nearly fell off the bed.

"Housekeeping." A woman's voice.

He peered through the viewer in the door. What kind of housekeeping knocked on your door at six a.m.? A young woman stood in front of the door, her head turned as if she were looking down the walkway.

"Come back later," he said, still watching her. She paused, nodded, and turned back to face the door.

"I am sorry, but I must clean now. The manager needs this room."

"No way. I booked for three nights and I ain't checking out. You have the manager call me."

A second later the door flew open so violently it seemed to explode. The knob hit him in the solar plexus and he went down gasping for breath. Before he could recover, hands gripped both arms and dragged him out the door, across the parking lot, and tossed him like a sack of potatoes into the trunk of a car. In seconds his wrists and ankles were bound with zip ties. Before the lid slammed shut he recognized the make and model. He was being kidnapped in a Lincoln Town Car. The good news: all newer cars come equipped with a release mechanism that would allow him to escape. The bad news: unless he could reach the knife in his boot, whoever shoved him in had made it impossible for him to use it.

◇◇◇

The early morning took some of the edge off the cold as Blake unlocked the front doors of the church. Whereas his ten o'clock service generally did not have parishioners arriving more than five minutes before its start, eight o'clock attendees could arrive anywhere from fifteen to thirty minutes early. This morning was no exception. Darla Throck puffed up the ramp at half past seven.

"Sorry to be late," she gasped and pushed into the church.

"We won't start for another half hour," Blake said. Whether she heard or not, he could not tell. She bustled down the aisle, made an awkward genuflection, and collapsed into a pew. It happened to be the one normally occupied by Mildred Tompkins, and Blake imagined there would be some looks and words exchanged when Mildred arrived. She was a matriarch and held a proprietary claim on that particular pew and place. By quarter to eight, Darla began to fidget.

"Service is at eight," Blake said. Darla sat up and looked confused.

"You might be more comfortable over here," he added and pointed to a neutral pew on the other side of the church.

"Oh, I thought it was at seven-thirty. Over there?"

"Yes."

"Thank you. Why did I think the service was at seven-thirty?"

Blake shrugged and resisted the temptation to say something unkind. Darla settled safely in her new location just as Mildred arrived. Blake thanked the Lord for small favors and retreated to his office.

At five minutes to eight, Blake watched as Colonel Bob's car wheeled around the corner and pulled smartly into a parking place. It did not even come close to hitting anything and drove at a normal, even a little above normal, speed. He wondered if Colonel Bob had new glasses or had just been lucky. When he saw the object of his speculation exit from the passenger side, he frowned. When T.J. Harkins emerged from the driver's side and the two of them walked up the steps to the church together, he understood.

"You puzzled, Padre?" Colonel Bob said, face innocent. "No surprises, I can't see so good anymore—no news there—and T.J. here—"

"Sergeant," T.J. corrected.

"Quite right there, Sergeant. Sergeant T.J. here has been assigned as my driver."

"Rose and Minnie know about this?"

"Oh, well, certainly. We have that all worked out. T.J. brings me to church at eight and then drops me at the Crossroads Diner after. I always go there on Sunday morning. Eat one of those heart attack breakfasts they're so good at, drink coffee, and chat up Flora. Tell me something, Padre, it's been a while since I could really see her. Is she still, ah…handsome?"

Blake could not say. He knew Ms. Blevins by reputation only and couldn't remember if he'd ever seen her or, if he had, knew what she looked like. He did know that except for the one time when he took Mary Miller there for coffee, the diner stayed pretty devoid of good-looking women, much less handsome ones. The Crossroads was a guy thing.

"I don't know, Colonel—sorry."

"Well, no matter. If I can't see her, it doesn't make much difference, does it? Ben Franklin said all cats are gray in the dark. I say, all women are beautiful if you're blind."

"How bad is—"

"You mean, am I blind as a bat? Not yet, Padre. Macular degeneration in both eyes. On a good day I can see mostly shapes and could drive if I had to. Doc's given me pills that are supposed to slow it down, but putting on the brakes isn't the same as throwing her into reverse."

"I'm sorry."

"Yes, well, where was I? Oh, so, after he drops me, T.J. will fetch the ladies to church and then circle back to take me home. We have a schedule all worked out, see?"

He unfolded a piece of paper and handed it to Blake. Days, times, and events, in large print, filled the page. Blake felt an enormous sense of relief. T.J. provided a solution to a problem—no, an answer to prayer. Colonel Bob's increasing disability worried him. T.J. had removed one more problem from his plate, at least for a while.

T.J. peered into the church and scanned the parking lot. "Mr. Blake," he said, "is Miss Deputy Ryder here today?"

"Not yet. She comes at ten if she comes at all." He thought a moment. "That's usually every other Sunday, so I don't expect to see her today. Is there something you wanted?"

"Yes, sir. If you see her, would you ask her about the ride in the police car she said she would give me?"

"Well, what I will do is have her call you. Shall she call you at your home, at your aunt's, or at Colonel Bob's?"

T.J. frowned. Multiple choices created a problem for him. He could sort them out most times, but he needed a minute or two.

"You have her call me on my cell phone," Colonel Bob said. "I'll see she gets hooked up with my sergeant here. Okay, T.J., now my pew is over on the gospel side near the back...you don't know which side that is? Well, I can see we have some educating to do here. See, all churches are..."

◇◇◇

Ike slipped into Callend College's library as unobtrusively as possible. He hoped Sunday morning would mean fewer students and the absence of the librarian. He was right on both counts. He found the back issues of the *Washington Post* and read the stories Charlie had mentioned. Neither was particularly helpful. A writer was found dead—apparent suicide. The man had shot himself in the head and the woman, naked and mad as a wet cat, was found as Charlie had described her. Her apartment had been methodically trashed. She couldn't describe her attackers except to say they wore ski masks and were not gentlemen—an understatement of monumental proportions. She later reported the event in greater detail on the five, six, and eleven o'clock news appearing, he read, smart, attractive, and very professional. Ike guessed her boyfriend's murder had been a good career move for her.

He returned the papers to their hanging rods and chanced a trip to Ruth's office. He did not think she'd be working on a Sunday, but you never knew. He walked the length of the long corridor toward the administrative wing. His shoe soles squeaked on the newly waxed floor. "Cop shoes," Ruth would call them. On either side, classrooms, their doors closed, measured his progress. He peeked through the glass when he reached Ruth's outer office. No Agnes Ewalt in sight. That did not mean Ruth wasn't in, but it did increase the probability. He tried the knob. It turned and he walked in. Ruth's door was ajar. He softfooted to the sill and tapped on the door.

"Who?" Ruth clearly did not expect anyone.

"*C'est moi.*"

"Come in here. I have a bone to pick with you, Schwartz, and what's with the phony French?"

"I just want to be sure that you, unlike your faculty friends, do not mistake me for an uncultured rube. A little French, perhaps a quote from Elizabeth Barrett Browning—*How do I love thee? Let me count the ways—*"

"Can it. What are you doing here?"

"As I said, brushing up on my couth. I was using your library."

"Bully for you. Do I want to know the real reason?"

Ike lowered himself into one of the two matched crewel upholstered chairs and stretched out his legs. Afternoon sun filtered through partially closed blinds. Very peaceful. A large room with oriental rugs, rosewood paneling, and a carefully contrived Georgian ambiance. Its only discordant note was a modern clock on the mantle. He wondered if the town would spring for an office this nice for him. He knew they wouldn't.

"The reason? No, and the bone you have to pick?"

"My building…it's being…altered, no, transformed, hell… it's not the same."

"How about transmogrified? It's being transmogrified. You didn't expect that?"

"Trans…is that what you were doing in the library—humping up arcane vocabulary?"

"Humping up arcane…you're not doing too badly there yourself. No, I was reading your Washington papers, if you must know. What's different about your building?"

"The back wall…you remember how that used to be? There were restrooms at either end, a utility closet, a stairwell, and an elevator shaft to the floors below in the center."

"I remember."

"They're gone."

"What's gone?"

"The elevators, the stairwell, they've disappeared. Everything else is exactly the same. I thought they'd built a new wall in front of the old one but if they had, the restrooms would be bigger or something. They're just gone."

"Maybe they moved the three floors under the building to a new site. Jacked up the top floor and skidded the—"

"Stop. Are they really that good? I mean to make that wall look exactly like—"

"They are that good."

"So down in the bowels of the earth under my new—my new what?"

"Art museum."

"Ah. Down in the depths, under my new art museum, spooks in trench coats and fedoras are going about their business. What are they doing down there, anyway?"

"I have no idea and before you ask, I can't find out for you."

She stretched arms over her head, swiveled once around, and fixed him with her *this is important* look.

"I've been thinking about your mother."

"New insights into the mystery of the Book of Ruth?"

"She loves you very much, Ike."

"I don't see the connection. Holy Writ is not my long suit, but even I know it's a reach from the Book to that statement."

"Men are so dense. You really don't get it?"

"Clueless."

"Understatement. Take me to lunch and I'll find out why it took you so long to get in touch with me since that night."

"So long? You said you wanted to be alone for a while and—"

"You really are clueless."

Chapter Twenty-seven

Steve Bolt tried to be as quiet as possible as he shifted around in the car's trunk. He managed to extract his Buck knife from his boot and cut the zip ties around his ankles. Reversing the blade and severing the wrist bindings had been a challenge that finally succeeded, but only at the cost of a mean gash near his right thumb. The last thing he wanted was for his kidnappers to hear him thumping about. If they thought he could move, they would probably stop, rebind him, and then he'd never get free. And freedom was what he had in mind. As nearly as he could tell, they'd been driving south. He couldn't be sure, but he knew they'd turned right out of the motel's parking lot and had stayed on a more or less straight course ever since. Once his hands were free, he managed to twist around so that he could reach the trunk release lanyard. The car accelerated. He'd have to wait until it slowed or stopped. The car swerved left and seemed to be climbing. They must be going east now. East meant the Blue Ridge Mountains. He grabbed the trunk deck from the inside to keep it from flying open, and pulled the lanyard. The latch thunked and the deck lid tugged at his fingertips. The car did not slow—a good sign. He gripped the lid and waited.

Five minutes later the left turn signal started blinking and the car slowed. Bolt prayed for oncoming traffic to force it to stop. His prayers were answered. The car paused momentarily. Then, as it accelerated into another left turn, he rolled out of the trunk and onto the road. He'd been cramped in the confined space so long, his legs refused to respond and he barely regained his footing. He spun around and stared at the car. Without conscious effort, his mind registered both the license plate and the men's voices.

The car completed its turn and pulled off the road. The doors flew open and two men pushed their way out. In the split second it took for them to focus in on him, his adrenaline kicked in, conquered his stiffness, and he lurched into the woods.

He knew the intersection the instant he tumbled onto the road and thanked a god he rarely acknowledged otherwise for deliverance. He'd just cleared the Rocky Knob entrance onto the Blue Ridge Parkway and landed in the mountains. He was home. Once in the woods, there was no way those men would ever find him. He slipped behind an oak and risked a glance back to the road. Two men stood next to the Lincoln. One had a cell phone to his ear, his arms gesturing wildly. The second jerked out a pistol and snapped off six shots in Bolt's general direction.

Bolt checked his pockets. He still had most of the two thousand left. He pulled out the credit card and tossed it away. Buffalo Mountain lay just to the south and that meant safety. Over the years it may have been tamed and even civilized, but there were still places in the hollows and coves where a man could hide and where there were people who would help him. With nearly two thousand in cash, he could disappear for months. He grinned and began working his way into the trees. Those men would never track him. Never.

◇◇◇

No one ever accused Donnie Oldham of being a genius. Next to Hollis, he might appear bright, but compared to, say, a tree stump, he came up short, which would explain why he took off early Sunday morning to use Harris' credit and bank cards. He figured if he put some distance between Floyd and the cards, he would have a better chance of cashing out. Close to the issuing bank—he'd finally figured out what that meant—the other ATMs would know about the accounts being closed. But further away, they might not have got the word. So he decided to drive to Charlotte.

He arrived downtown at noon. He hoped no one would notice him or his out-of-state tags. The first ATM he saw was one owned by the issuing bank for a VISA card. He knew Hollis said the card should be returned there, but he thought the account had only been shut down for non-bank ATMs and it would work in the ATMs it belonged to. This one ate the card. He stared in disbelief as the message appeared on the little screen informing him to see the bank manager at his earliest convenience. He drove his fist into the screen. It did not break, but something in his hand did. He cursed and shook it and kicked the wall.

He drove around trying to decide what to do next. He continued cursing and pounded on the steering wheel with his good hand. He wished he'd pulled out more money the first time he'd used the cards. At the next ATM he tried a MasterCard. The machine was not one belonging to the issuing bank. It returned the card with the same message Hollis received. He had the same response with the American Express and a second VISA. Finally, he tried the bank card and held his breath. He asked for and received three hundred dollars. He tried again and was rewarded again. When he'd withdrawn twelve hundred dollars the machine asked him to wait. He didn't. He snatched the card and strode across to his truck. No sense pushing his luck. Tomorrow—no, he'd wait until Wednesday and then he'd try again. In his delight at again having money and prospects, he forgot the pain in his hand. The security camera built into the ATM, however, recorded all four of his withdrawals. He failed to see the black Suburban that drifted up to the ATM just as he turned the corner. Luckily, the occupants of that vehicle did not see him either and would have to wait until the following day when the bank opened to discover that Donald Oldham, not Alexei Kamarov, had withdrawn the funds.

◇◇◇

Whaite Billingsly was not a man to use the Lord's name in vain. He attended the Baptist church out on the highway every

Sunday and, when he could, on Wednesday night as well. He didn't drink, smoke, or chew. In his youth, before he left the mountain, before he'd met Darcie, married, and had children, things were different. On the mountain, drinking came as natural as breathing. A boy became a man when he'd had his first full blown drunk, shot his first buck, and visited one of the Grainger girls. But that was all behind him now. He worked hard, took care of his family, and had a good future.

Head down under the hood of his pickup, he stared in frustration at the engine. Somehow the head bolt had been torqued too tight and he'd sheared it off. Until he could pull the head off the engine, the new gasket would lie useless on the front seat. The moment the socket suddenly gave way with the bolt head in it, he seriously considered leaving the Baptist church for a few minutes and addressing the Almighty in the old mountain way. Instead, he closed his eyes and counted to ten—three times. He'd have to drill out the old bolt, no easy job, and rethread. Then he'd need to visit the parts department at the Ford dealership or hit the junkyard again and pick up a new one. None of that could be done on a Sunday afternoon. He wondered, just for a second, if the Lord would really mind if he were to drink a nice cold beer. He reckoned he wouldn't, but Pastor Jim would. He used to keep a small stash of bottles, for just such occasions, in a little refrigerator he had in the garage. Now all it held were sodas and the kids' juice boxes.

His wife called him in for early supper. He'd promised to go with her to the evening service as well. Why not? The truck wasn't going anywhere tonight anyway.

"There's a man says he's with Floyd County on the phone for you. Don't be long. I have to be early to church."

Whaite filled a water glass, plopped in ice cubes, and went into the front room to take the call.

"I got it," he yelled, and waited until he heard the click signaling the phone had been hung up in the kitchen. "Hello."

"Deputy Billingsly, the word on the street is, you've been trying to locate Steve Bolt."

"Yeah, that's right. Do you know where he is?"

"We located him but we were too late. Somebody found him first and took him."

"Kidnapped or killed?"

"Kidnapped at least. Can't say about the other. Judging by the way they went into his hotel room, he could be a dead man by now. If he ain't, he will be soon."

"He was my lead in a shooting. Now what do I do?"

"Can't help you there, partner. You have any other leads?"

"Donnie Oldham, maybe."

"Well, I can help you with that twerp. I'd like to talk to him myself."

"Can we meet sometime tomorrow?"

"Sure enough. There's a beer joint on the main road called The Pub. Donnie drops by there pretty near every day. You meet me there at three. I go on shift then. Somebody there will know where he's at."

"Can you give me directions?"

The county man described the location. Whaite retrieved a pencil stub and fumbled for a piece of paper to write on. He pulled a scrap from his pocket, frowned at the numbers on one side—license plate maybe—and wrote the directions on the reverse.

"Three tomorrow—The Pub. Got it. Thanks." He hung up and headed toward the dining room.

Chapter Twenty-eight

Monday morning and another week gone. Ike sighed and pushed open the door to the Sheriff's office. A gust of warm air and Anne Murray's rendition of "White Christmas" assaulted him. Essie had her CD player going full blast and stood on the booking counter stringing plastic holly and pine fronds over the assignment board. When she bent over to extricate another strand, Ike thought it a good thing she'd decided to wear slacks today instead of her usual miniskirt.

"Morning Ike, Merry Christmas and Happy Cha-nooka."

"It's pronounced 'Hgan-a-kah,' with a guttural H at the front, but thank you, anyway."

"Whatever. Sam wants to see you. By the way, where's my—" Ike put a fresh Krispy Kreme jelly-filled on her desk. "Oh, good, there you go, thank you, too."

"What's up with Sam?"

"She's coping, I reckon. She said she has an idea about the stiff in the morgue. Who is that guy, anyway, and why haven't we put out the usual—?"

"Keep it under your hat, Essie. It's very important. You hear me?"

"Yes, sir, boss. Lips sealed and all that, but I still don't see why—"

"Let it go, Essie."

"Oh, right. Where you want the mistletoe at?"

"The question is where do *you* want the mistletoe at? I'm not expecting a lot of action, but you surely might."

Essie did not blush. She nodded, raised one eyebrow, and pursed her lips. "Well, the party'll be mostly here behind the counter and the punch bowl will be over there, so I reckon it ought to go about here." She reached up and marked the spot on the ceiling with a pencil she pulled out from behind her ear.

Ike headed for Sam's work area, her cell that housed the array of electronic equipment that both fascinated and frightened him. He stepped through the door. On an ordinary day, she would be hunched forward, eyes glued to one of the screens. Today, she sat sideways in her chair staring at, but apparently not seeing, the stack of files and CDs on her desk.

"Are you okay, Sam?"

"I'm good."

One look at her red-rimmed eyes and the pile of tissues on the floor next to her made it very clear she wasn't.

"Essie said you wanted to see me."

"Um…let me think. Oh yeah, Whaite called in. He has some information on Bolt that didn't sound good and he's off."

"Off? Where and what about Bolt?"

"Whaite switched shifts with Charlie Picket. He said he had a call from a county policeman down in Floyd about Bolt. Appears someone snatched him from a motel. Nobody knows who or why, but they're betting he's dead or soon will be."

"This is getting crazier and crazier. Why would anyone want to torch Bolt's house, snatch him, and then kill him—if, in fact, that's what happened. What does he know that is so important?"

"I don't know. Anyway, speaking of bolts, Whaite's out looking for a head bolt for his truck. He said he sheared one off yesterday trying to get the head off the V-8. After that, he said he was meeting up with the cop in Willis to track down one of Bolt's friends. He hopes the guy will start sorting this mess out. So, he won't be in today at all and he's driving his Chevelle. He said he'd check in with you if he came up with anything, but otherwise, he'd see you tomorrow."

"Good. You said you had an idea. You want to share that?"

"Oh, yeah." Sam blew her nose. "Look, I've been tracking what we assumed were cash transactions on Harris', that is, Kamarov's, various bank and credit cards. Then on Friday or Saturday all but one of them closed out, but before that, they were pumping out money and credit like crazy."

"And?"

"Two things. Why did they shut him down? Did they finally figure he was not among the living? Except the fact they're after Bolt suggests they don't know. Second, some ATMs have security cameras, miniature TVs, built into them. They record every person making a transaction and put a time stamp on it. I thought we might see if we can get a bank or two to let us have a peek at the tape and maybe pull a picture of whoever is doing it and, well, at least have a lead."

"Cameras. Of course. Good job. Call Whaite and tell him to check that out…" Ike saw the expression on Sam's face change. "Problem?"

"I thought I might do that."

Ike studied his resident computer geek and realized he'd grown so used to her working her electronic magic, he'd forgotten he'd first hired her as a working deputy. The computer stuff was supposed to be extra and nowhere near as elaborate as it had become.

"Good idea. I should have thought of it. Thanks. Where did all these transactions take place?"

"They are all over this end of the state, some close by—that is, in the area south of Roanoke—some as far away as Charlotte, North Carolina."

"You don't need to go that far. Hit the nearest ones. I think it's safe to assume that whoever made the withdrawals is the same guy at all of them."

Sam perked up. He supposed just getting away from the quiet hum of her machinery and a chance to move outdoors would be a welcome change—would help her put Karl out of her mind. She tucked in her uniform blouse, buckled her duty belt, holstered her Glock, and waved good-bye.

"You be sure to tell Essie where you are going and check in." He felt like a father seeing his daughter off on her first date. "I'm getting old," he muttered.

◇◇◇

Andover Crisp added a terrible weekend to a miserable week. His in-laws descended on him unannounced. That included his chronically unemployed brother-in-law, who declared that work, unless it had something to do with the arts, was beneath him. The fact he possessed an extraordinarily limited knowledge about anything artistic accounted for his seeking but never finding gainful employment. Only a modest trust fund and a foolish, indulgent mother kept him from joining the ranks of the homeless—a class of people, he made clear to anyone who would listen, that he despised.

By Sunday night Crisp felt the need to hit the brandy bottle pretty hard. This morning his head felt like a troupe of Kumi-Daiko drummers were rehearsing in it. If that weren't bad enough, his people in Charlotte had missed Kamarov the day before. He knew he must still be in the area but not moving south as they'd supposed. So what was he up to? Kevin knocked and entered.

"Mr. Crisp, you want the bad news or the really bad news?"

"What's that supposed to mean?"

"The men in Charlotte, the ones who missed Kamarov yesterday, went to the bank, the one he withdrew the money from, and they looked at the surveillance tapes from the ATM. They just sent some stills taken from the tape. Here." He pushed three grainy photographs across the desk.

"Who? Who is this guy?" Crisp exploded.

"Nobody seems to know."

He studied the pictures. A man-boy, he would have said, short, small ears, with wispy hair in a forelock, and a blank look on his moon face. He forced himself not to make an odious comparison with the banjo-playing character in *Deliverance*.

"God love us, this has to be the guy he hired to watch his stuff."

"Could be. I hope so."

He studied the pictures again. "The guy is wearing bib overalls, for crying out loud. Do you believe it? I didn't know they still made them." He pushed the photos away. "Kamarov is no dope. He wouldn't be out in the open if he's trying to jump ship, and he certainly wouldn't hit the machines by himself. He'd get someone to do it for him. He sent his factotum, what's his name?"

"Steve Bolt."

"Right. This has to be him. Tell them to start an all-out search for a Steve Bolt, ASAP. If we get him, we'll have Kamarov. You can take that to the bank."

"Yes, sir, but—"

"What? But…"

"If it isn't Bolt, we'd have to consider another, very different, scenario, I'm afraid."

Crisp scooted his chair back until it slammed into the credenza behind. He tilted back and closed his eyes and clenched his jaws. He nodded twice, sat back up, and shot forward to the desk.

"You're right. If this isn't Bolt, then we have to assume the worst and cut our losses. Tell Ops I want a paper on my desk in an hour." He sighed and tapped his fist on the smooth mahogany desktop. "Kamarov was our only real asset. If he's dead, Cutthroat is, too."

◇◇◇

Essie Falco was aware of Sam at the counter and looking over her shoulder. Essie was caught up in her copy of *Cat's Eye*.

Sledge looked at the body in the snow. She was as beautiful in death as in life. He hated destroying beautiful things, but she'd earned her bullet. It reminded him of the time he'd knocked his grandfather's prized Ming Dynasty vase on the floor. The old man had been furious. If he'd known the vase disaster was due to Scot's attempt to grab Margie the maid, he'd have killed Scot. Granddad kept the pulchritudinous Margie for himself.

But Kin Tok ee had lured him out to this lonely ski slope so her accomplices could take him down. Well, she learned the hard way that Scot Sledge didn't go down that easy. The three snowmobiles had caught up with them after they cleared the big mogul run. Scot saw them out of the corner of his eye and had laid down a rooster tail of powder as he cut across in front of the lead machine. Moonlight etched the black tree trunks against a gray starless sky. The gunners in the second unit traced his path with bullets, fresh powder spitting up in little geysers inches from his feet, until, too late, the gun's trajectory arc caught the men on the snowmobile in front and splattered their custom Columbia white survival jackets with black-red splotches. It was a simple matter, then, to slalom through the dark Austrian pines until the second crashed head-on into the bole of one of the larger ones. Shattered bark and the scent of pine resin filled the air. It reminded Scot of the rosin bag he used when he pitched his no-hitter in the minor leagues. Those were the good days, he recalled nostalgically.

The last pair of Albanians he'd taken out with two quick, and decidedly deadly, over the shoulder shots from the Beretta he kept in his ski boot. How could they know he'd skied the pentathlon in the last winter Olympics on this very course?

But she knew.

Yes, and she knew her buddies didn't have a chance against him. Yet she'd brought it on anyway. So, why had she gone ahead with this crazy plan? Following orders? Okay, he could see that. It's what they did in this insane game of dead man's chess they played. One moment you're lovers, the next fierce adversaries fighting like bull rhinos to keep the world in balance!

But then she'd pulled the gun!

He reached into the snowbank where her last spasm had caused it to fall and turned it over in his hand. The clip was

missing. *He ratcheted the receiver back—empty. She'd deliberately goaded him into killing her. Why? He looked at the
gun again. A piece of rice paper fell out of the clip channel.
The words were Chinese but he could make out the childish
scrawl,* Because I love you.

*"Why do they all end up like this?" He studied the pool of
blood spreading through the virginally white snow. Her eyes
fluttered and she reached for her ear lobe. She said something.
Sledge knelt beside her.*

"What?"

"Kin Tok ee," she whispered.

*"Yes, yes, I know who you are, Sweetheart. What do you
want to tell me?"*

*"Kin Tok ee." Her fingers seemed to flicker at her ear and
then she was gone.*

*No more moonlight ski trips for you, kid, he thought bru-
tally. But what was she trying to tell him? Something…but
what? And then there was that accent. That was it! She'd been
trying to tell him all along but he hadn't quite figured it out.
Tug at the ear lobe—sounds like…Kin Tok ee—sounds like
Kentucky, of course. She was trying to tell him that his search
would end in Cat's Eye, Kentucky, the town the Chinese mafia
made its own when the tough Mainland Chinese police forced
them out of Hong Kong. He pointed his skis downhill. He
had a plane to catch.*

"Wow," Essie gushed. "Don't you just love Scot Sledge? I
think this one is the best ever.

Sam smiled. "Best ever."

Chapter Twenty-nine

Best ever. Sam grinned at this minuscule ray of sunshine in an otherwise dreary week—Scot Sledge—best ever! She pulled out of the parking lot and headed to the intersection of Main Street and the Covington Road and turned east toward the interstate. It felt good to be out in the fresh air with something different, something important, to do. With any luck, by the time she finished they'd have a real lead. Traffic was light and she rolled down her window and let in some air. She noticed the decorations on the street and realized she had not even started thinking about Christmas. The thought plunged her back into gloom. She and Karl had had plans for Christmas, but now…She stepped on the gas, to hell with Karl. She'd find plenty to do. She'd fly home and see her parents. No, they'd want to know about her boyfriends, and the last time she'd visited, they wanted to know when she planned to return to her old job at the college. Police work was no occupation for a lady, they said. She'd replied that being a lady wasn't her ambition.

As she turned over holiday possibilities, realizing that in her circumstances, she had few, if any, choices, she passed a gray Crown Vic going the other way. No doubt about it, government issue. She glanced sideways as it swished by and for a moment she could have sworn she saw Karl, not driving, but in the passenger seat away from her. At the relative speed the two cars created, her view into the other car lasted less than a tenth of a second. She shook her head and focused on the road.

"No way."

For the next hour she drove south. The first three ATMs she checked out did not have surveillance equipment. She figured out that unless they were attached to a building with access from the rear, ATMs would not be so equipped. At least that was her surmise after the fourth unsuccessful stop. She drove to the first bank on her list and pulled in. The ATM faced the street under a shallow awning. She watched as three people transacted their business. When she looked back at the bank's front door she saw a man watching her and writing something on a pad. He ducked back into the relative shadows when he realized she'd spotted him. She slid out of the car, tucked in her blouse, and went into the bank.

Once inside, she walked to the desks at the rear. She noticed the man with the pad now had his cell phone out and poised, ready to make a call. She turned and faced him.

"Police," she said and pointed to her badge.

"I saw you watching the ATM and I thought you might be a mugger."

"The uniform didn't tell you anything?"

"Well, it could be a fake or…" He put his phone away and took a place in one of the teller lines.

"Can I help you?" Sam turned but didn't see anyone. A young man about her age stood in front of her staring at her chest. It wasn't his fault, he must have been at least a foot and a half shorter than she, and that was the only view available to him. She slouched down a little to reduce the distance and the view.

"I'm hoping you can help me. You have a surveillance camera mounted on your ATM. How long do you save the tapes?"

"That would be a question for Mr. Harmon."

The young man retreated into the maze of desks to a small office and spoke to someone inside. Sam squinted but could not read the nameplate on the door. She'd need to get her prescription checked. A bulky man in a rumpled checked suit and a bad comb-over emerged from the office. When he caught sight of Sam he whistled.

"Well now, if you aren't a tall drink of water. Franklin, here, says you want some information about our security tapes. Can I ask why?"

"Yes, sir. We are tracking a set of stolen credit cards and a bank card. One of them was used here last Wednesday or Thursday. We'd like to see who that was."

"Last week? You're in luck. We have those tapes in the back room. Sorry I can't help you look, but we do have a tape deck and a monitor if you'd like to have a go."

"Would it be possible to print out a still from them?"

"Off the TV? Gee, I don't know how you'd do that."

"I have a laptop, cables, and a program that will let me do that. I'd need to borrow a printer."

"No fooling? Well, help yourself, Missy. There's an empty desk next to the tape deal."

Sam let the *Missy* remark go where she deposited the *tall drink of water*, but she wished, for a split second, she were not a police officer so she could lay this jerk out. She spent the next hour scanning the tape and downloading images onto her hard drive. She passed on the printer when she saw its condition. She could print out any of the pictures she had when she returned to the office. When she finished she thanked Harmon and drove to the next location and repeated the process. By three in the afternoon, she'd seen enough. She had pictures, but Ike wasn't going to be happy. There were two people using the cards.

◇◇◇

Ike sat on the floor of his office, oil can in hand. He swiveled his chair, heard the squeal, and applied more oil on what he believed to be its source. He managed to reduce the volume but not eliminate it.

"Ike, where you at?" He saw what he assumed to be Essie's feet at his door.

"On the floor behind the desk."

"You okay?"

"Fine, fine. I'm just trying to quiet this chair down."

"Ike, I do believe that chair was left here by General Jubal Early when he rode through town with his cavalry. Why don't you spring for a new one?"

"I like this chair. I just don't like the squeaks and squawks."

"Ms. Harris is on the phone for you."

Ike heard the mild disdain in Essie's voice. He wondered how long it would be before his staff and friends got over their town-gown problems and accepted Ruth. He stood up, spun his chair around, flinched at the squeal it produced, and sat. He pulled out the middle desk drawer, rested his feet on its edge, and picked up.

"Ike, have you been setting Agnes up?"

"Come again? I assume we are speaking of the Agnes who sits outside your office."

"Who else?"

"I could make you a list, but go on. Why do you think I've set her up? And for what?"

"She spent an hour and a half in an interview with some federal types who wanted to know about her relationship with Brent Wilcox. I didn't even know she had a relationship with him—or anyone else, for that matter."

"Word around town is the smooth Mr. Wilcox has been squiring her about. I meant to call you about that."

"Why would you call me about Agnes' love life—if that's what it is, although I can't see—?"

"He's a bad apple, Ruth. I wanted you to steer her away or at least warn her before he got into her purse."

"You mean pants, don't you?"

"I said purse. I meant purse. The rest is none of my business. Wilcox is a phony and is looking for suckers to invest in real estate schemes."

"Why don't you tell her yourself?"

"You figure that one out. Agnes…me?"

"I see. You need to brush up on your social graces, Schwartz. Agnes is a very nice lady and—"

"Dislikes me the way dogs dislike cats. It's in her genes."

"Which brings us back to her pants."

"What?"

"Sorry, bad pun—genes, jeans. When are you taking me out to dinner? We have things to talk about."

"We do? Tonight, then. Bring an agenda so I won't disappoint you by being unremittingly dense."

"What are we doing for Christmas?"

"Ah, put that on the agenda. I have some thoughts about that."

"Really? You'd do Christmas for me?"

"For you, anything, but, sorry, I was thinking about my mother, not you."

"How is she?"

"Hanging on. It's like she's waiting for something."

"She is."

"She is? For what?"

"Later, Sheriff, duty calls. And lay off Agnes."

Chapter Thirty

Whaite found the bar and pulled in beside a county cruiser. His caller leaned against the hood and did a double-take when he slid out of his bright red Chevelle.

"Picketsville going for showy muscle cars for their officers?" the county guy asked.

Whaite had grown weary of explaining. "Hey, it could be worse. I hear there's a police department in Wisconsin that put their guys in Volkswagen beetles. Oldham inside?"

"Don't know. I've been waiting for you. Say, if that buggy is standard issue, I'm ready to transfer."

"Don't hold your breath."

The two men stepped in out of the cold, damp afternoon. The Pub looked like every other blue-collar bar in the country. Pinball machines dinged in one corner. A bar ran from the front to the back. A mustached fat guy with a damp towel over his arm stood behind it. The air reeked of cigarette smoke, beer, and wet wool. Men in work boots and flannel shirts, denim, and overalls hunkered over their drafts and looked at the two policemen with thinly disguised malice.

"Feeling at home?" the county officer said.

"Once, not anymore. I guess we better just jump in. There's no way we'll ever win this bunch over."

"Gentlemen," the fat bartender said, sounding like a butler at a posh party, "your pleasure."

"Information," Whaite said. He turned toward the dozen or so pairs of eyes. "We are looking for a man named Oldham. He's not wanted for anything and we are not here to hassle him. We're hoping he can help us find someone who, we are afraid, may be in trouble."

"Got the first part wrong, copper," a man with a five-day beard and red-rimmed eyes muttered.

"What part would that be?"

"You said you were looking for a *man*. Donnie ain't no man." Four of the other drinkers sniggered in agreement. "And, in the second place, that little creep is no more likely to help you than flap his arms and fly."

"Okay, I hear you. But can anyone give us a hand here?"

The bartender cleared his throat. "I do believe that I might be of assistance. Most of my customers, however, find they can speak more freely with a drink in their hand—if you follow my meaning."

Whaite ordered two beers. "One for me and one for him," he said pointing to the county officer. "Give mine to the guy over there." The first speaker nodded his head in appreciation. The county cop drank his.

"Well, now, this is the way of things," the bartender said. He fixed his gaze on a fly-specked calendar on the opposite wall. An off-print of the famous Marilyn Monroe nude pose appeared just below the year—a classic—like his car. Before he'd married Darcy, Whaite had that same calendar in his workshop. He gave it to his brother-in-law at his stag party.

"The young man you seek was in here last night. He had a considerable sum of money in his possession and spent it freely and, I should add, foolishly. Fortunately, he became enormously intoxicated before he spent it all and we sent him home. He lives just a few hundred yards down the road from here."

"That'd be past the old Purina feed sign?"

"Correct. I also took the precaution of removing his truck keys. It is parked outside, the dark green one with the obscene graphic on the window."

"May I ask you a personal question?" the county man said. "Where'd you learn to talk like that?" The remark produced a round of guffaws from the men in the bar.

"I, sir, am an actor by trade. This employment is but a passing phase. Do you know Shakespeare's works?"

"You got me there, partner. So how long has the phase been going on?"

That evoked another round of laughter. "He's been waiting ten years for Broadway to call, ain't that right, Eddie? He thinks he's Richard Burton or somebody."

"He could play Falstaff," a young bespectacled man holding a set of crutches said, and looked embarrassed.

"Old Hollis here reads books. Ain't that right, bookworm?" The object of the remark made no reply.

"Thank you," Whaite said. He turned back to the bartender and in a lowered voice asked, "Who's the kid in the corner?"

"That is Hollis," the fat guy murmured. "He is a bit of an *idiot savant.*"

"A what?" the county guy asked.

"He is brilliant at some things—books, for instance, but doesn't have the common sense of a turkey. Did you know that domesticated turkeys have been known to drown in a rain storm? They look up, open their beaks, and next thing you know, they're on the ground, dead as doorknobs. Pitiful. His father, however, is a genius. He manages several bank websites as a private contractor, I think. But poor Hollis…knows so much and understands so little."

Whaite realized he would get no more information from this crowd. The two police officers left.

Clouds piled up in the south—a bad sign. Storms that came from the south were always messy. Whaite buttoned his parka and pulled on his gloves. "You want to go to his house?" he said.

"You know, I don't like the look of that sky. If the snow comes, I'll need to be out on the roads. I'll leave the interviewing to you."

Whaite watched as the county car drove away. He looked at the truck at the end of the lot and walked to and then around it. Whatever faults Oldham might have, misuse of his truck wasn't one of them. Only a small dent in one fender marred its body work, and except for some sandbags, the bed was clear of trash; no coffee cups or fast food bags in the cab either. Oldham had installed a tool box that rested on the side rails and spanned the width of the truck behind the cab. It did not quite reach the floor of the bed. Whaite leaned over the side and peered in. There was something. He could barely make it out, but it did trigger something in his subconscious. He tried to remember.

He drove to Oldham's house. The street was lined with tired one- and two-story clapboard houses. Most showed signs of their occupants' attempts at maintenance—paint mostly, a few flower boxes filled with winter-killed stalks. Oldham's house sagged in front. When it had received its last coat of paint was anybody's guess, but certainly not in this decade or the one before.

Whaite mounted the steps and pounded on the door. He waited, tried again, still no response. He walked around back and knocked on the back door. While he waited, he inspected Oldham's backyard. He thought he caught sight of a face in an upstairs window in the house behind. He lowered his gaze and inspected the grounds. He could see where Oldham parked his truck. The ground was clear of snow. A blue tarp lay folded nearby, and empty motor oil cans and beer bottles were scattered about. He turned back to the door and knocked again. He saw movement in the shadows on the other side.

"Oldham," he called. "No sense hiding, I saw you."

The movement materialized into a shape and the shape into a person, and a disgruntled Donnie Oldham unlatched the door and opened it a crack.

"What do you want?"

"Just a little talk. I need to know about Steve Bolt and Randall Harris."

"I don't know nothing. Go away." He started to push the door closed.

"How about I come in and we talk," Whaite said, and put his shoulder to the door. It opened and Oldham, shoulder to the door but in stocking feet, slid backward.

"Hey, you can't do that. Police can't do that and you ain't even a police."

"Sorry, but you're wrong on both counts. If I have probable cause, I can come in."

"Well, that's as may be, but I told you I don't know nothing."

"Randall Harris is dead. Shot five times with what appears to be a .38 caliber pistol."

"So? I never met the man."

"He's been dead over a week, but somebody's been using his credit cards. You have any ideas about that?"

"I think I'm calling my lawyer. This is harassment or something. I don't know anything about any Harris and I ain't seen Bolt since Saturday a week ago. Now you'd better leave."

"Somebody took Bolt out of a motel Sunday morning—a couple of big bad somebodys. Do you reckon they'll be looking for you next?"

"Bolt's dead?"

"Probably. Are you refusing to cooperate with a police investigation? You want that in the file?"

"You'd better leave. I didn't do nothing and you can't prove I did. Like you said, Bolt's dead so that's that. You better get out of here."

Whaite dropped his gaze to the floor for a moment and contemplated Oldham's shoeless feet. Then he remembered. If he was right, he'd need a search warrant. He let himself out the door.

"You'd better watch your back, cop."

Whaite walked back to his car and drove into town. He needed to think. He parked and turned on his cell phone. It chirped—missed call—Ike.

"Whaite, what's up?"

"I think I'm on to something here, but I need to check one or two things out first."

"Come on in. Sam has pictures of the people using the cards. Maybe they are people you met or know."

"I'll check them first thing tomorrow. Look, my shift doesn't end until eleven. I want to check one more thing and then I'll be in."

"Okay, but be careful. It'll be late and they're predicting more snow. I'd hate to see you wreck that pretty car of yours."

"Not a problem, I'll drive real careful. See you in the morning."

Whaite clicked off and drove back toward The Pub. He parked around the corner where he could watch the front door. Sure enough, within five minutes Donnie Oldham scurried up the street, retrieved his keys, and drove away. Whaite saw him turn the corner. Oldham was headed home. He checked his watch. He'd have time for a bite to eat and then…he'd see what that truck could tell him.

A roadhouse that looked like it might serve decent food stood a mile and a half up the road. By eight o'clock Whaite returned to the corner to watch The Pub's front door. At nine-thirty Donnie Oldham strolled up the street and entered. *Wait a minute, Whaite.* He would hold for ten minutes to be certain Oldham had settled in, and then he'd move.

It started to snow.

Chapter Thirty-one

Donnie Oldham stomped into The Pub and brushed a few flakes of snow from his jacket. He worked his way to a back booth and flopped down. Big Dolores slipped into the bench opposite and gave him a crooked-toothed smile.

"I'll have a drink," she said.

"Don't let me stop you."

"You still buying, big spender?"

"What makes you think I'd buy?"

"Well, last night you were the life of the party. You musta dropped a couple hundred in here."

"You think I'm stupid, Dolores? I couldn't have spent more than fifty or so. Someone took my money when I wasn't looking. I aim to find out. Let's see what's in your purse." He snatched her Brighton knock-off and dumped the contents on the table. Except for a lipstick, four dollars in crumpled ones, three tens, and a six-pack of condoms, Dolores had nothing much to share.

"You probably left it home and figured you'd get the rest tonight, didn't you?"

"What are you talking about?"

"Listen, you all think I was drunk and all, but I remember everything. Mountain men can hold their liquor. I remember you was all over me last night, you coulda took my money easy."

"The only thing all over you last night was throw-up after you had your fifth sidecar. Mountain man, my sweet patoot…here," she said, and threw the ten-dollar bills at him. "These are the ones you stuffed down my bra last night. You didn't have no problems about me and money then, did you? You wanted to cop a feel and thought that'd be the way, like I'm dumb or something."

Donnie felt the anger rising. He couldn't prove anything, but he knew. He scanned the crowd. The door opened with a bang and Hollis thumped in on his crutches.

"Hey, boy," the barkeep barked, "what's amiss with your crutches? You're punctuating the floor with little holes."

"They're…um, defective," he said, and swung them forward, planted them in front, and began his forward motion.

"Unless you want to pay for sanding and refinishing the floor, you will cease and desist."

Hollis jerked the nail-studded crutches from the floor and hopped over to Donnie's booth.

"Donnie, you should have been here this afternoon. That fire police was in here with the county cop asking about you."

"So what. I talked to that guy. He don't know nothing. Stupid is what he is."

"Yeah, but it's him that's asking about Steve Bolt and then about Harris…I don't know. Maybe you should get rid of those cards, you know?"

"No way. Steve told me about a guy in Roanoke who buys old credit cards. He has a program like your dad's that puts new information on them or something. He'll give me fifty bucks for the dead ones. I'm keeping the one that still works until it don't."

"I don't know, he's a police, you know, and—"

"Forget that guy. Like I said, he don't know nothing, can't prove nothing. Hollis, I need your help on something important. Someone stole my money last night. I think it must have been Dolores but she probably had help. See if you can find out who."

"Donnie, I don't think anybody did that. You were pretty lit up last night. You bought drinks for the house at least three times and you and Dolores had a lot yourselves. You put money down her dress. How'd that feel, anyway?"

"Never mind that. You know Dolores." Actually, Hollis did not. He may have been the only man in the room who didn't.

"See, I figure that fat slob behind the bar must have padded the bill. No way could I have dropped six hundred in here in one night."

Donnie fumed. The bartender and Dolores were in it together. He saw that now. How many others were, too? He drained his shot and a beer and stared at the room. He hated them all.

"What are you looking at, creep?" a big guy in a camouflage jacket asked.

"What's it to you, cupcake?"

The man unfolded from his chair. He was big, bigger than anyone Donnie had ever seen. He reminded him of Jaws from the old James Bond movies.

"Gentlemen," the bartender said, "there'll be none of that in here." The big guy sat down. Now Donnie was angry.

"What I want to know," he shouted, "is who took my money last night."

Amid laughter from nearly all the tables, men raised their hands, ten or more.

"Don't forget Hank," one said. "He got him some, too."

"You took it?"

"No, you moron, you spent it like it wasn't even yours, which, I reckon, it weren't, and we would thank you for a nice evening except you acted like a sick puppy and we had to send you home."

Donnie stood next to his table ignoring Hollis' attempts to get him to sit back down. "You can get you some more tomorrow," he whispered.

"I'll show you bozos you can't fool me. I'm a mountain man and when I open a can of whup-ass—"

The room exploded in laughter. Donnie's face turned a bright crimson. He stormed out the door. "I'll be back and you'd better be ready for trouble."

"Ooooo," they said in unison. "Don't let the door hit you in the butt on your way out, mountain man," the camo-clad giant hooted.

In fact the door did just that, which made the men inside laugh even harder, and Donnie angrier. Worse, he'd left in such a hurry, he'd left his jacket in the booth. He couldn't face going back in to get it. Not now, not until after he went home and retrieved his gun. Then he'd see who was laughing last. The icy air and snow had a salutary effect on him. The chill slowed the absorption of alcohol and he sobered up some. He hurried down the street toward his home.

◇◇◇

Whaite had stayed the ten minutes he'd promised himself and then put the car in gear. He let it drift past The Pub, headlights out. When he'd covered fifty yards or so, he turned them on and headed to Oldham's house. He turned into the road and drove past the house. He made a U-turn twenty yards further on and parked the Chevelle in the deepest shadows he could find. The snow had picked up in intensity and soon the car would be covered and unrecognizable. He grabbed a flashlight and checked the clip in his Glock. He stepped out into the storm and made his way to the house.

New snow already dusted the pathway to the backyard where Oldham parked the truck. The blue tarp had been thrown over it and half-gallon milk jugs filled with water were attached with short lengths of cord at each corner and at several points along the side to hold it in place. Whaite checked the street and began working the tarp up and over the truck bed toward the cab. It took a little doing. It would have been easier if he had simply pulled the whole thing off, but he wanted his visit to leave as little evidence as possible. If he'd guessed correctly, he'd be back the next day with a search warrant, and he didn't want any slick city attorney blocking what he expected to find with the assertion it had been obtained illegally.

He pushed the stiff plastic up. He turned on the flashlight and aimed it under the tool box. The shadows were too deep for him to see anything. He'd have to climb into the bed. The sides were slippery from melting snow and forming ice. He needed to get in and get out before too much snow piled up in the bed—a dead tipoff to Oldham and his lawyer, if he had one, that someone had been in the truck. Whaite heaved himself over the tailgate and he lay on his stomach and shone the light up under the tool box. It was there. He switched off the light and clambered out of the truck. Putting the tarp back in place went more swiftly than removing it had.

Satisfied he'd done everything necessary, Whaite shuffled back out onto the street and back to his car. Whatever footprints he may have made would be covered by morning. Donnie Oldham would never know he'd been there. He started the car and headed north.

Chapter Thirty-two

Donnie slipped twice on his way home. His blood alcohol level kept him from feeling the cold as he lurched along the pavement cursing the men back at The Pub. He pictured what they would do when he came back and showed them his pistol. They wouldn't be laughing then, especially that big guy. He'd shoot him first. As he slogged along, doubts crept into his mind. There were a lot of men in that bar and he was sure some of them also had guns. He stopped in mid-stride and tried to figure out how he could show them up but not get hurt himself. If they only knew what he could do…no, what he'd done in his time. He picked up his pace.

He reached his house and turned into the alleyway that led to his backyard. Snow muffled his footsteps. When he reached the rear, he stopped. He saw the light first. It came from the pickup's bed. Then he realized the tarp had been rolled up. Someone was in his truck. He wished he had his gun already. It would be a justified shooting—trespassing—might have to drag the stiff indoors, though. He started forward. A figure loomed up from the bed. The fire police—no, that wasn't right, the guy was a regular cop and he had climbed up into the bed of his truck. Donnie racked his brains for any idea why a policeman would climb around in his truck.

He stepped back into the shadows and watched as the cop replaced the tarp and pocketed his flashlight. At that moment all the anger he felt for the men in the bar shifted from them to this man. He'd take care of him and then…it was perfect. All of those dopes in the bar knew the cop had asked about him that afternoon. If something happened to him…then they'd know what Donnie Oldham could do. He flattened himself against the sagging clapboards next to his garbage cans. The cop hurried away and down the street. Donnie made sure the cop got into his car and then ran to his truck and jerked off the tarp. He pulled out onto the street. He saw the red car's taillights turn the corner. He cranked up the truck's heater and fell in behind, keeping a hundred yards or so between the two vehicles. Out on the main road, he'd drop back and, in a turn, switch off his head lights, then speed up again. He followed that way for a while, and then repeated the ploy only with the lights on. He'd read about that technique in one of Hollis' books about surveillance. He figured to take care of him out in the country somewhere. When the word got back to The Pub, there'd be no laughing at him anymore.

◇◇◇

"It's started snowing again, Ike. We should be thinking about leaving before the roads close."

Ruth wanted dinner, he'd provided it. No gourmet cook, he'd bought Chinese carryout.

"No interest in spending the night here?" They were sitting on either side of a round wooden table in Ike's A-frame. He'd built the house years before as a retreat from the grittier aspects of his life. He kept an apartment in town to be close to his work but slipped away to this spot whenever he could.

"I agreed to come to your hideaway for dinner. I've never seen it in the winter. It's almost as beautiful with the snow in the trees as it is in the spring. But, no, I have things I need to do first thing tomorrow."

"You said we needed to talk. You had items on your agenda or something."

"The agenda was your idea. You're right, but I'm worried about that snow. Take me home."

"Okay. Five minutes. I have something I need to say and then we can go."

"You can tell me in the car."

"You know, for a New Englander, you sure are spooky about snow."

"It isn't about me, Schwartz. I've seen how your people handle it and if I don't get home before an inch hits the macadam, I'm screwed."

"Five minutes. I promise I'll get you back to dear old Callend and beddy-byes."

"Shoot, but I'm warning you—"

"The doctor called Pop this morning."

"Your mother?"

"He's not sure she's going to make the New Year." Ruth started to say something but he held up his hand. "Hear me out. Just in case, we're moving Christmas/Chanukah up. We don't think she'll notice. Pop wanted to know if you'd be there, be a part of it. I said I'd ask. So, I'm asking. Will you?"

"Of course, I will. Give me the days or nights—whatever—and I'll be there. It's a little short notice, so if I have to duck out and come back, will that be all right?"

"That will be fine. Thank you."

"Hey, you're my sweetie pie," she said and kissed him. "The rest of the dessert will have to wait. Now take me home."

"I'm your what?"

"You heard me. Now move."

◇◇◇

Karl Hedrick seethed. His partner sat turnip-like on the motel bed watching re-runs of *Survivor*. He'd thought to go for a walk but the snow forced him back into the motel room.

"This whole operation is so bogus," he said. He didn't expect to get a sympathetic hearing but he needed to vent to somebody.

"It's what the boss wants. It's what he gets," his partner said and switched to a re-run of *CSI*. "I love this show."

"There is no reason for us to be here."

"Talk to the boss."

"I did. He wouldn't listen."

In fact, Karl had more than talked to the division chief. He'd argued, cajoled, and finally lost his temper. In the first place, the great disappearance turned out to be a miscue on the part of a group in the department acting as a bunko squad. The man had, in fact, slipped their surveillance net, but he wasn't that hard to find. Instead of transferring them back on him, the chief decided he would empanel a "task force" and close the guy down. Karl came to the conclusion his boss needed a big operation, a breakthrough, something positive in his jacket. His last two operations had sputtered out like candles in a hurricane.

"I picked you," his chief had said, "because you know the territory. Good thing you put that dame in your book."

"I didn't put her in my book. I don't even know what that means. You're right, I know the area better than anyone and I'm telling you, we don't need to waste time and resources in an operation down there. The sheriff down there is perfectly capable of handling the situation."

"Oh sure. Cripes, Hedrick, he isn't state or even county. He's sheriff of a two-bit town. He couldn't handle dog doo-doo with a scooper."

"You're wrong. He's dealt with some pretty big stuff down there."

"Yeah, and we were there to pick up the pieces."

"Pick up the pieces? You're kidding, right? We stood around with our thumbs in our mouths while he tidied up our mess the last time. I know. I was there."

"That's not the way it appears in the report."

"Then the report lies."

"Careful, son, if you have any notion of staying in the Bureau, you better learn quick—we back each other. The report says the sheriff is a bumbler, that's what he is. Now you pack your stuff, say goodbye to the woman, and go to work."

"But—"

"No buts, here's what you need to know—Rule one, nobody knows where you are. Rule two, you shut down your answering machine and forward all your calls to this number. We'll take care of your messages. Rule three, under no circumstances do you contact anyone in the sheriff's office. Do you get my drift or do I have to spell out the rest as well?"

"I got it."

Karl had done as he had been ordered. He discovered when his answering machine had been unplugged. Calls to him had to go through some idiotic answering service. He couldn't call Sam and she hadn't tried to call him. He paced up and down in the cramped room.

"Sit down, cowboy, you're driving me nuts," his roommate said. "And you are in my line of sight. Look, they're showing a close-up of a bullet track through the dead guy's body. Whoa, that must have been his liver. I love this show."

"So you said."

"Tomorrow, we drop in on the rest of the eggheads at the college. They ought to be able to give us what we need. Word is he's hooked about a dozen of them. Why is it that the higher the IQ, the dumber a person becomes for scams like the one he's working?"

"No idea. My question is, why is it that the longer you work inside the Washington beltway, the less you trust the wisdom and judgment of those who live outside it?"

"You keep talking like that and you will never make a career in the Bureau, Karl. You know that? Ever since you went down there to find that guy, you have been preaching this goody two shoes notion of interagency cooperation. It will never happen. So, the only question left is which of the agencies will get the biggest piece of pie. As far as your sheriff is concerned, if he's so hot, what's he doing being a sheriff in a jerkwater town like this in the first place? You know what? You need to rethink your career options."

Karl thought he might be right. He picked up his cell phone, pulled on his jacket, and moved to the door.

"Where're you going?"

"Out. I need fresh air."

"It's snowing outside."

"Snow job out there—snow job in here. What's the difference?" Karl stepped out into the cold night. He was about to break rules one and three.

Chapter Thirty-three

Sam's phone battery failed. She'd had it on the charger for over an hour. The face plate kept spelling C-H-A-R-G-I-N-G but when she unplugged the charger to make a call, the face plate read LOW BATTERY. She didn't have a landline. She, like thousands of her generation, abandoned hardwired phones and relied exclusively on cell phones. Her phone was a Sheriff's Department issue. Essie had spare batteries in one of her cabinets. She could run down to the office and pick up a new one. She peered out the window and saw that the snow was coming down harder. She decided to wait until the next day to rejoin the rest of the world. She wasn't expecting any calls anyway.

She booted up her laptop and opened the file where she'd stored the pictures of the credit card users. She wasn't interested in the faces anymore. She wanted to see if there might be something else in the pictures, something in the background that might help. The problem with surveillance cameras, especially the small "lipstick" variety used in ATMs, is definition. No matter what crime shows on TV seemed to be able to do with their technology, in reality, a small fuzzy image could only become a large fuzzy image when blown up unless you had some pretty exotic, intuitive software. You couldn't make new pixels, but you could make more and, using the laws of probability, recreate what was lost. The clarity of the primary image—the face in this case—was poor and the background almost unrecognizable. She let her program run, and after a half dozen passes she could make out a truck. If there were other pictures like it in the file, she might be able to pull a license plate. She checked her watch. Whaite should be in the office or out on the road. She picked up her phone to call him and looked at LOW BATTERY. It would have to wait until morning.

◇ ◇ ◇

Except on holidays like Christmas and Thanksgiving, or when someone dropped by, Connie Platt sat by her window every night, her TV on, volume up full. She spent the time watching cars whiz by and old movies. When she was younger, she'd had a life—children, a husband, and friends. But they'd all died or drifted away, and now, in her seventy-fifth year with nagging arthritis, hearing problems, and failing eyesight, she faced life alone. Watching the road and its comings and goings gave her a sense of belonging.

Her road served as a shortcut to I-81 out of Willis. It started with four lanes close to town but by the time it passed her house, it had narrowed to two. Beyond her house were a few clusters of cottages, a small development of what the city folk called townhouses, and a pocket park.

Dusk comes early in December, so this evening she mostly watched headlights and listened as automobiles swished by. Her cat, Precious, attempted a jump up onto her lap. Given its size, which was obscene, and age, which in cat years approached hers, he missed, tumbled sideways, and upset her teacup and saucer. Her attention momentarily distracted, Connie did not notice the pickup, headlights off, passing a bright red car, but she heard a crash. She jerked her head up at the sound of a second one. She peered out the window but the snow blocked her view. She could barely see the road. She thought she saw lights over by the big oak tree across the road, but when she looked closer they winked out. She rubbed her eyes and looked again—nothing. She glanced over at her old black and white TV blaring away in the corner. Steve McQueen had just turned over a race car. Well, she thought it was McQueen. Or was it James Garner or Paul

Newman? She couldn't remember. The TV had a snowstorm, too, but then that had nothing to do with the weather. Her granddaughter, Dolores, promised she'd buy her a new TV last year, but she never did. Never would, silly tramp. A car's horn sounded for a moment and then it went silent just as she shut the television off. She mopped up the mess the cat had made and tottered off to bed.

◇◇◇

Darcie Billingsly sat straight up in bed, eyes wide and staring, heart pounding. Something bad was going to happen. She often had her "mountain moments," when she saw things, felt things, when she just knew that she knew. It was a gift. Like her husband, she'd grown up on Buffalo Mountain and she knew better than to ignore the signs. When she'd given her life to Jesus at an altar call in her eighteenth year, she'd become a strong believing Christian. She thought she'd put away the superstitions and practices she'd learned as a child back in the hollow. Immersion in an ice cold creek should have washed that away. But neither it, nor daily Bible reading, nor her single-minded devotion to her church and faith had affected the gift in any way.

She thought when she left the mountain and moved north, it might leave her. But it didn't. She never told her new friends in Picketsville. They were not mountain folk and they would not understand. She never told Pastor Jim either. She feared his take on the gift would be either painful or humiliating, so she kept those moments to herself. But Whaite understood and would listen. Sometimes he'd tell her about a police problem and she could help him. Tonight, it would be the other way around, if she wasn't too late. She pulled the phone off the hook and dialed his cell phone, then stopped. He couldn't be reached that way anymore unless he was off duty or parked somewhere. A call to his office revealed he was out of radio range as well. She began to cry. If only they didn't have that stupid rule about cell phones. If only Whaite had decided to ignore it.

If only…

Chapter Thirty-four

Ike believed there were two kinds of people in the world, morning people and night people. He knew some folks demurred, claiming the divisions were to be found in other more compelling, or socially significant, personality traits, but reduced to the lowest common denominator, he contended it came down to morning versus night. Ike had a roommate in college who would rise fully awake at first light. He would move about with the energy that he'd sustain all day. Then at nine or nine-thirty that night, he would crash. Ike, on the other hand, rarely went to sleep before two a.m. Left to his own devices, he would sleep until nine or ten o'clock in the morning. It wasn't that he couldn't function any earlier. His mind worked just fine. It was just that the rest of his body wouldn't pay attention for at least another hour.

He'd made a promise to himself, however, that he'd be in the office for the seven o'clock shift change at least three days a week, and Tuesday was one of those days. But this morning his phone woke him, not his alarm clock. A full minute passed before he sorted that out and stopped slapping the clock.

"Hello," he gargled.

"Ike? Are you awake?"

"I am now, Ruth."

"I just had the weirdest dream—no, nightmare is what it was—and I had to call you."

"Do you have any idea what time it is?" Ruth, he knew, occupied the alternative half of the universe, but still…five-thirty in the morning?

"I thought you'd be up by now. You should be. Listen, I had this peculiar dream last night. I need to tell you before I forget."

Why, Ike wondered, do people insist on telling you their dreams? Almost without exception, they hold no interest to the hearer and, more often than not, do not even make sense. The importance the teller puts on them is rarely, if ever, shared.

"Shoot," he said and flopped back on his pillow.

"Are you listening? This is strange. I dreamed you and I were at this function at the governor's mansion, or maybe it was the White House. That's probably not it, is it? Anyway, we were at this big party and they were celebrating your election to the United States Senate—"

"Whoa. I was elected to the Senate? That sounds more like *my* nightmare."

"Don't interrupt. We were there at this place and your father was there, all smiling and greeting all his old political pals. There was a lot of back slapping and you and I…this is scary…"

Ike's phone beeped, informing him he had an incoming call waiting.

"Hang on a second, Ruth, someone's trying to reach me.'

"They can wait, this is important."

"I'll be right back." He hit the flash button.

"Ike, this is Darcie, Whaite's wife. Where is he?"

"I'm not sure. Did you call Rita at the office?"

"I did. Nobody can reach him, Ike, and I know something awful has happened."

"Darcie, hang on. I have someone on the other line, I'll be right back." He flashed back to Ruth.

"I have an emergency on the other line. Can we talk about this later?"

"One minute, Schwartz, or you know what you will *not* find under your Christmas tree."

"Okay, but make it quick. So this scary thing was?"

"We were married, Ike."

"I'm okay with that, at least, dream wise. Is that the nightmare part because—?"

"Shut up and listen. The celebration is going on all around and then it changed, like instead of being there, I'm watching a television show and the voice-over announces us—no, you. He goes on about your dad—the political legend, and then about you—Senator Schwartz—lots of applause—your wife—they didn't even call me by name. Do you believe that? There's some more applause and, then, are you ready for this? Our son—thunderous applause."

"We had a son?"

"We did."

"I gotta go, but you're right. Mixing our gene pools is indeed scary. But hey, if you want to try, I know how babies are made. We could—"

"In your dreams, Schwartz."

"Actually, it was in yours. Is that it?" Ruth had already hung up. "Darcie, are you still there?"

"I'm here, Ike, and I'm scared."

"Stay calm, Darcie. You know he's not in a police car. His cell phone is probably off—"

"No, that's the other thing. I've been dialing it for hours and all I get is his voice mail."

"Well, there you go. It's off."

"No, if it were off, it would go to voice mail, like, right away. But it rings and rings and…" Ike heard the sob in her voice. "See, I have these premonitions and last night I woke up and I just knew he'd been hurt. Now, this morning, I think it's worse. He's—"

"I'll get right on it. It'll be just fine. I'll call you back in an hour when we know something. Now you just get those kids ready for school. In an hour." He hung up and called Essie at home.

"Ike, Essie, are you up?"

"Been up for a while." Essie also occupied the other half of the human race.

"I want you to call Rita and ask her to stick around for a while past the shift change. Then I want you to go out to Whaite's house and look in on his family."

"What's going on?"

"I'm not sure but Whaite hasn't been heard from since late last night and Darcie—"

"She has second sight, I know. She thinks something is wrong?"

"Yes."

"Then she's right. I'm on it." Essie's line went dead.

Ike showered and dressed. He reached for the doorknob when his phone rang again. The caller ID read SHRFF OFF-PKTVLL.

"Ike, this is Rita. We just got a call from the Floyd County Police Department. There's been an accident and—"

"It's Whaite. How bad?"

"Ike, he was dead when they found him. His car must have skidded and he lost control. He hit an oak tree head on."

Ike hung his head. Whaite—gone. "Rita, can you give me a few more hours this morning, I—"

"Whatever you need. I already called everybody in. I figured you'd want to talk to them."

"Thanks. I'll be right there."

◇◇◇

Deputies crowded the office area. They almost never saw each other at the same time. More men entered and stamped the snow from their boots. The room hummed with subdued greetings. Ike stood in their midst and asked for their attention. He filled them in on what he knew, which wasn't much. Rita said there'd been a second call from Floyd County asking for someone to come down to identify the body and inspect Whaite's car. Ike asked his deputies for their cooperation in rescheduling shifts. He said he'd be in touch regarding any services and went on through the dismal litany of things to do, bases to touch with an officer down.

"Sam?" he said, looking around. He realized he hadn't seen her at the briefing.

"She didn't answer her phone, Ike. She may not know."

For an instant, Ike had a moment of panic. Another deputy out of touch—phone not responding.

"Anybody heard from Sam?"

As if on cue, she walked in the door and was greeted by a dozen pairs of eyes.

"What?" she said.

"Okay, everybody, that's it," Ike announced. "Sam, I'll catch you up on the way to Floyd."

"We're going to Floyd?"

"It's Whaite. He was killed in a car accident. You and I are going to ID the body and…other things."

"Not his wife?"

"Not if I can help it. She has kids to look to and…Not now."

Sam's eyes started to tear up. She blew her nose. "I don't guess he'll be needing these things." She dropped the pictures taken from the ATMs on Whaite's desk.

Ike waved her into his office and pointed to his only other chair. He shuffled through the paperwork on his desk—forms to fill out, reports to be filed. He sat and sighed. Charlie Garland's superphone bleeped. Ike closed his eyes. He did not want to talk to Charlie right at that moment. The phone went into urgent mode.

Chapter Thirty-five

Sam rose to leave but Ike signaled for her to stay seated. The phone continued its insistent beeping. He drummed his fingers and after a moment punched the receive button.

"Charlie, this is a bad time. Can I call you back?"

"This will only take a minute." That's what they all say, Ike thought, and watched as Sam fitted a new battery into her phone.

"Okay, but please make it quick."

"Last night two rather hefty men left the Russian embassy in a hurry. They were whisked off to Dulles, where an official Russian jet sat on the taxiway, motors spinning, and waiting for them. They are gone. Our intel people are convinced they are the probables of your homicide. We are closing up shop."

"That's it?"

"You said be brief."

"Not enough. What about the black program? Aren't you interested in tracking that down?"

"Not my department, Ike. We'll stay tuned in, but we think Kamarov was their only real asset. With him gone, the program will disintegrate. If he told them anything, they know it already. If he didn't, they never will. End of story."

"It won't work, Charlie. Too many loose ends, and besides, I want a crack at the person who did it."

"The goons on the plane will be met by our people at the other end, maybe not right away, but some day."

"What about Bolt? What about the credit cards?"

"I expect we'll find out what that's all about eventually."

Ike shook his head. "We are in a mess down here right now and I haven't the time or the inclination to debate this with you. I just lost my best deputy in an automobile accident. Coincidently, he was the lead tracking Kamarov. That worries me. Now, we will have to start all over again. I'm telling you this so you will know that if you don't see any progress at this end, it's because we have paused, not stopped."

"I'll be pulling for you."

"That's all you have to say?"

"Um…no, I need the phone back."

Ike shoved the phone into a desk drawer. "We're on our own now, Sam. I don't believe for a minute that Kamarov was a simple takeout by his own people. It's possible, even logical, but—"

"I heard. There's the cards and Bolt. The FBI ran the black program, we're pretty sure of that. The last time I looked, they were still trying to find our corpse. Lately, there's been an unusual amount of traffic looking in the John Doe reports of area police departments. Eventually they are going to tumble to us. They're not convinced his people did him, and since they have the same capacity to ferret out the Russians as the CIA, why don't they go away, too?"

"Point taken. You are absolutely right. We are not done with Kamarov."

◇◇◇

Ike let Sam drive and they covered the roads to Floyd in relative silence. Ike found himself fighting conflicting emotions. He was alternately angry, guilty, and saddened by Waite's death. It seemed so unfair, so unlikely that a routine, no, make that marginal, investigation should end in death. Whaite had been following a lead three degrees removed from the real interest. Ike had sent him on the job, and now he wondered if he'd been wrong to do so. And he thought of Darcie Billingsly and two children under eight. What a waste.

"Boss?" Sam broke into his thoughts.

"Yeah?"

"I heard your half of the conversation with your friend at the CIA. They think that Harris' or Kamarov's killing had nothing to do with the people running the black program?"

"Pretty much, yes."

"I guess I'm happy about that."

"Because of Karl?"

Sam sighed and slouched a little in her seat. "Yes. He's a no good double dirt bag, but I'm glad he's not a murderer, too."

"Well, yes. You know, Sam, it's just possible you have him pegged wrong."

"I saw the name, Ike—Hedrick, K."

"Well, you know, he has a job to do. He can't pick and choose. If he's ordered to join a special operation, he doesn't get a choice."

"Yeah, I know, but what about the woman on the phone?"

"There is probably some perfectly reasonable explanation for that."

"Like what?"

"I don't know, Sam, I'm just trying to be neutral here. I had hopes for you and Karl and I'm not willing to let them go just yet."

"Can't see it. Sorry."

Ike decided he'd never make a living as Dear Abby. Luckily they arrived at the county police barracks and had other things to occupy them.

The sergeant at the desk referred them to Officer Martz, who happened to be in. Sam and Ike found him two-finger typing at his desk. Ike introduced himself and Sam. Martz stopped his pecking and led them to the morgue. Ike made the official ID and set up the transfer of the body to Unger's Funeral Home in Picketsville. Siegfried Unger had taken over the business from the Quade family, who'd run it for three generations. Since the fourth didn't want anything to do with it, they'd sold to Unger, who renamed it. Folks thought the name change somehow violated a tradition and got to calling Siegfried Unger, Six Feet Under.

Ike and Sam spent a few minutes staring at Whaite's waxen face. He realized how helpless people were in death. If he could, he would have reversed every decision he'd made about the investigation, and Whaite would still be alive.

"It's part of the job, Ike," Sam said, reading his mind. "Whaite knew that, we all do. It's what we do." Ike nodded, but he didn't feel any better.

Martz took them back to the main building and ushered them into a small conference room.

"Here's what we have. It isn't much, but before we write accident on anything we check—you know—just in case. Well, we canvassed the houses in the neighborhood. Nobody saw or heard anything. I guess the snow muffled the sound. One lady lives almost directly opposite the scene, so we spent some time with her. Now I have to tell you, she's old, hard of hearing, and maybe has a little trouble seeing as well."

"My favorite kind of witness," Ike said.

"Right, I know what you mean. Anyway, this woman said she must have witnessed the crash. I asked her what she meant saying, 'she must have witnessed the crash.' She didn't report it so what happened? Well, she thought she heard something but when she looked out the window, except for the lights going out, she couldn't see anything. 'What lights?' I asked. Now I have to tell you it was confusing. She did not see the skid, she says, only heard it. She said her cat distracted her and she took her eyes off the road for a second. She said…" Martz pulled a notebook from his pocket and consulted it.

"She said, 'There was the little bang and then, another, bigger, bang.' She couldn't figure out what the first one was all about. I asked her to describe the first one and she said, 'like a crash when cars hit each other.' That isn't much in itself except a minute later she said something like, 'it's funny, because before I turned off the TV, a pickup truck drove by going the other way and its side was all banged up and it looked like it had hit something.' Any of this work for you?"

"You left out the part about the lights."

"Oh that. Yeah, she said she thought she saw lights, but when she looked closer, they were gone. By the next morning she figured she'd seen a soul passing. Mountain people—superstitious lot."

Ike felt the butterflies begin to swarm in his stomach. "It might not have been an accident."

"I told you, the lady is a quarter deaf and half blind. She had her TV up full blast and apparently had been watching an old auto racing movie. She lives alone. I don't know how much is memory and how much is imagination. She kept referring to the driver as Steve McQueen. You follow?"

Ike still felt the butterflies. He turned to Sam. "Deputy? Any thoughts?"

"I think we need to look at Whaite's car."

Chapter Thirty-six

The rest of the week slid by, gray and cold. Slush and dirty snow lined Picketsville's streets. Even the multicolored lights and decorations looked old and tired. Things seemed to move in slow motion. Essie stepped up and took over the day to day. She made the arrangements for the memorial service. She talked to, soothed, and supported Darcie. Pastor Jim from the Baptist church arrived and consulted. By Thursday all the important details had been taken care of. Ike felt relieved. That afternoon a woman in a black leather slacks suit sailed into the office. Essie directed her to Ike. She flashed her ID and asked for Charlie's secure phone.

Ike handed it over. The day before, Sam had taken its back off and studied its circuitry. Ike had an uneasy feeling she'd also found a jack of some sort in there somewhere and had hooked it up to her computer. Whether she'd downloaded its encryption program or not, he didn't know and he didn't want to know. The last thing he wanted was the feds in his shop arresting his deputy.

Essie watched the woman's every move, in and out.

"Miss Agency-Ain't-I-Something didn't get that hottie outfit at the Dollar Store, did she?" she said. "I bet you can't even get one like that in Roanoke."

"That's 'inside the beltway chic,' no doubt about it."

"Inside whose belt? Are you talking dirty, Ike, or am I missing something?"

"Inside the Washington Beltway—the navel of the universe, font of all true wisdom."

"Okay, I got you, I think."

Ike and Sam had inspected what was left of Whaite's vehicle. Muscle cars from that era had two things working against anyone hoping to survive a crash in them. They were heavy, with too much of the weight in the front end. In a head-on, a 396 V-8 engine could easily blow through the fire wall and wind up in the driver's lap. Worse, the Chevelle was pre-air bag. It barely made it into the seat belt era. Whaite never had a chance. They saw where the Jaws of Life had been used to get him out—too late to save his life. There was a very suspicious scrape along the driver's side front quarter panel. They decided to keep that bit of information to themselves until they had time to assess it and make a plan. Right now, they did not want all the other deputies angry and out for blood. The chances of finding a hit-and-run driver were not good. They needed another angle and they hadn't found one. Ike clenched his jaw. He'd find whoever did it. Nobody was going to take down one of his people.

◇◇◇

T.J. stared out the second storey window down into the backyard of the house behind his. He had no idea how long he'd been standing there. The passage of time did settle easily in his mind. He owned a watch. He could tell time. But that was a discipline he had learned over a dozen years to please others. Time ticking away meant nothing to him. Memory difficulties, however, were not among the many deficits visited on him in his young life. On the contrary, his memory functioned perfectly. So, if he knew he was to be at a certain place at a certain time, he would not forget. He would look at his watch with almost compulsive regularity and when the large and small hands were in the alignment he needed, he would respond. He, like the inexpensive timepiece on his wrist, was amazingly punctual.

He stood close to the window, only vaguely aware of the cold sheet of air that coursed across its face and chilled the room.

Like time, heat and cold were not prominent features in his awareness. Not that he didn't know the difference; it just didn't seem to register. He shivered briefly and shifted his weight from one foot to the other. The wind rattled the window frame and swirled around the narrow confines of the small backyard below. The blue tarp on Donald's truck lifted and flapped angrily in an icy gust, fell, and covered the truck once more.

Donald parked the truck right where T.J. remembered. Donald's mother used to sit and drink there.

Hey there, T.J., how you doing?

I'm doing just fine there, Mrs. Donald's Mother.

Well that's good to hear, boy.

What's that you have in that bottle? Is it water?

Oh yeah, it is. It's special water, T.J. It's fire water. Hee, hee.

T.J. never did see the fire come out of the water and he wondered about that sometimes. Mrs. Donald's Mother didn't act like other mothers, not like his. She laughed and sometimes fell asleep in the backyard with her fire water and Donald would come home and yell at her and T.J. would go to the front of his house because he didn't like the words they said when they yelled. But she wasn't there anymore. "Gone to the Loony Bin," Donald had said. T.J. asked his mother what the Loony Bin was, and she said it was not a nice word and why did he want to know, and he said it was just something Donald said about where his mother went.   An institution, she said. Later, his father said he, T.J., belonged in the Loony Bin, too, and his mother had cried.

T.J. missed the Christmas lights. Donald's father always put up lights on the house. They would run all the way around the porch and up on the pointy part of the roof and out front. He had a Santa that laughed and had a light inside him, too. In town, in front of the post office, they used to have a manger and all those people, wise men and shepherds and, of course, the baby Jesus and his mom and dad. They didn't put that up anymore, either. He never understood why, though his mother told him a hundred times.

"T.J., I've told you a hundred times. It's against the law now."
Why would statues of all those nice God people be against the
law? He put it down in that part of his brain with all the other
things that he could not understand, like the moon changing
shape. Cause and effect worked at a simple level. Brakes on—car
stops, no brakes, car hits something. He could grasp an immediate outcome. Long term was another matter.

The wind tore at the covering on the truck again. T.J. watched
as it lifted and fluttered like an uncleated sail. Donald's special
truck—the one the girls at The Pub liked so much. T.J. wondered, if he saved enough money working for Colonel Bob, if
his mother would let him buy a truck like Donald's.

When Mrs. Donald's Mother lived next door, before she went
to the Loony Bin, there were flowers in the yard. Now the thin
dusting of snow only covered Donald's bottles—the brown ones
he drank from and then threw aside.

The canvas covering snapped in the wind and nearly tore
away from the few milk bottle anchors that still held it. Donald
stepped out on the small gray painted porch and down the stairs
into the yard. He did not look happy. He looked like he might
be ready for the Loony Bin. T.J. moved back from the window.
He did not want Donald to see him. He did not know why, but
some primal instinct, some response in the deeper recesses of his
brain, the part not involved with cognitive processes, sounded
an alarm and he yielded to it instinctively. For the first time in
his life, he understood that Donald was not his friend.

He watched as Donald lifted the tarp from one side of his
truck and inspected the passenger side door. T.J. stared at the
truck, too, taking it in. He felt a little sorry for Donald. Too
bad, it was his special truck.

T.J. had perfect vision. The eye doctor told him, "T.J., you
have perfect 20/20 vision." The woman who checked his eyes
when he got his driver's license said the same thing.

And his memory functioned just fine.

Chapter Thirty-seven

It had been a particularly bad week for Sam. Her phone died. Her car developed a funny noise she couldn't identify, and the closest Subaru dealer was in Roanoke. Sam stared at her phone. She'd tried to sort out the voice messages. They were all garbled. She deleted the lot. The new battery went dead in less than five minutes when she installed it, faster after that. So her problem lay somewhere within the phone itself. She wished she had a phone like the secure one Ike had been using. She had managed to unscrew the back cover plate, half expecting it to explode or release a deadly gas when she did. Nothing happened, which was her first clue there wouldn't be anything useful for her to remove. She did find a computer receptacle built in it and had managed to fit a cable from her desktop to the phone. It required the same hookup as her Palm Pilot. She'd been able to explore the contents of its microchip, but every attempt she made to download or copy the program was blocked. She did pick up one or two ideas, however.

She checked in with Ike, who told her to draw another phone and turn in the old one. She should also post the new number and… She said she got it. Essie gave her a new phone—actually an old phone, but in better shape than the one she'd turned in. Her eye caught sight of Essie's dog-eared copy of *Cat's Eye* propped up on a shelf over her desk. Sam picked it up and flipped through the pages, noting the turned page corners where Essie had marked particularly salacious passages.

"You know, Essie, this is crap, unreal. This guy, Sledge, gets himself shot, stabbed, and God only knows what else and…nothing. Nothing happens. No six weeks in rehab so his gunshot wounds can heal. No remorse, no chance for failure, not a qualm, doubt, or hesitation. He just keeps pegging along, seducing air-headed women and filling page after page with one idiotic bulletproof moment after another."

Essie took the book from her, a frown on her face. "But—"

"But you and I know that in the real world, our world, people get hurt. They bleed and die and suffer and usually because some moron or some greedy, angry, or evil bastard decides to do something irrational and stupid. And then, people get hurt—maybe die. But we're real…the things we do every day…what Whaite did every day…"

At the mention of Whaite's name Essie's customary one-hundred-watt smile faded.

"It cost him his life and there was nothing romantic or heroic about it." Sam felt tears in her eyes as she finished.

Essie stared at the book, leaned forward, took it between thumb and forefinger, and without a word dropped it in the wastebasket.

Sam nodded and pushed through the door. Outside, she wiped her eyes, took a deep breath, and called her parents. They would need her new number. There wasn't anyone else to call. She thought about Karl and managed to pump up her anger sufficiently to keep from crying again.

◇◇◇

Karl Hedrick snapped his phone shut and yelled at no one in particular. He'd been calling Sam for days, leaving voice messages. Sometimes the phone would ring and then drop the call. Sometimes it would switch him directly to voice messaging. His partner got wind of what he was trying to do and reported him. Karl found himself driving back to Washington, where, he was sure, a thorough reaming awaited. He made up his mind he'd give as good as he got. He called Sam one more time and discovered her phone had been removed from service and would he like to try a different number? What had happened, he wondered. One day everything is fine, the next, it's all gone.

He called his own number. Maybe today there'd be a message, an explanation.

"Yes, hello?" A woman's voice, she sounded young. "Who is this?"

"Karl."

"He's not available. Who's calling?"

"No, I'm Karl. Karl Hedrick, I'm calling for messages."

"Come on, who is this?"

"You are the answering service, right? You are answering my phone. Is that how you always answer it?"

"You're sure you're Mr. Hedrick?"

"Positive. I just checked my driver's license and that's the name on it. Now, are you the answering service or not?"

"Well, yeah."

"Aren't you supposed to announce that? Not just say hello?"

"Some of the girls do, but I think it's so, you know, like formal, so I just say hello."

"You realize that anyone calling me would have no idea that you were a service and might reasonably assume you were in my apartment when you picked up."

"But I'm not in your apartment, am I?"

"How would I know that?"

"What difference does it make? I mean who wants to hear 'Answering service, may I take a message?'"

"I would, because then I'd know who I was talking to and not make the mistake that I think others may have. Who told you to answer like that?"

"Nobody. I just thought, you know, it sounded more casual like."

"Do you have a protocol you are supposed to follow?"

"A what?"

"Skip it." He disconnected.

Karl had started his trip back to DC by taking Route 460 through Lynchburg. As he approached Appomattox it hit him. He pulled into a turnoff and sat staring through the window. If Sam had called him at his apartment and that airhead had picked up the call, she might reasonably think…He let his head fall against the steering wheel. He could not reach Sam. He had to be in DC for his meeting with his chief on Monday first thing, and he had been barred from connecting with her in the meantime. Somehow, the gods of love had abandoned him. He checked his watch. At the rate he was going, and with a stop for food, he'd make Washington by seven or seven-thirty. He'd take the weekend to think about the mess his well-meaning but tunnel-vision boss had created for him. But one way or the other, he planned to be back on this road, headed in the other direction, by Tuesday at the latest. He put the car in gear and continued north.

◇◇◇

Ruth called Ike after dinner. Her usual in-your-face tone, while not totally missing, seemed significantly subdued. She had called, she said, to find out how he was holding up. Ike, in turn, banked down his *I gotcha* and they talked quietly for fifteen minutes. He did not bring up her nightmare, although the thought crossed his mind. She refrained from suggesting her faculty might have an issue with any of a number of police procedures. Overall, it was a remarkable quarter of an hour for them.

"What's new in the search for the Russian guy's killer?"

He filled her in and shared his doubts about Charlie Garland's take on the homicide. "It's really complex. Charlie is making it way too simple."

"Perhaps you're making it way too complicated?"

"Me? No. What makes you say that?"

"Suppose, just for the sake of argument, you are all wrong about your black programs and sub-rosa plots and schemes. What are you left with then?"

"Not much. What I can't figure is why anyone would want kill Whaite."

"Maybe they didn't want to kill him, just hurt him and his fancy car, or he met up with a drunk driver, or it really was an accident."

"Anything's possible. The person he was tracking was a lead, not a primary, you see?"

"Yes, but I say again—suppose you have it backwards and this second or third degree lead is more than that?"

"Where is all this analysis coming from?"

"I'm an historian, Ike. I know that most great events arise from relatively trivial causes. An anarchist with a political agenda having nothing to do with the balance of power in the Balkans assassinates Archduke Ferdinand and all hell breaks out in Europe. The end result is a communist Russia, a world war, and a society that would never be the same. So don't assume that a person removed from the center of things can't be a significant player."

Ike thought she might be on to something, but like many ideas people not familiar with his line of work offered, he needed to think it through.

"We have the service for Whaite tomorrow. Pop suggested sometime early next week for the holiday do. You okay with that?"

"Sure. What…is there anything special I should wear?"

"Wear?"

"Well hell, Ike, I don't know how those things go. I know my Santa suit won't work, but a scarf over my head? You all will wear a yarmulke, I guess."

"Actually, it's called a kippot, and no, we won't. Just dress the way you would for a party. I've invited Leon Weitz, by the way. He wants to meet Abe. Thinks he's local history."

"You know he is. Are you okay, Ike?"

"Sure, fine."

"You say so. Why don't I believe you?"

"You are a suspicious woman who has a secret thing for policemen."

"Not much of a secret anymore, sad to say. I liked sneaking around with my fascist cop. Does a nightcap by the fire sound good?"

"It does. Your fire or mine?"

"You don't have a fireplace, do you?"

"I could make one. There's a skylight in my second bedroom that would work as a chimney and I have the barbeque grill…"

"My study, fifteen minutes—no, make that a half hour. I need to get ready."

"On my way. And if you want to wear your Santa suit—"

"What Santa—?"

"You said you could wear one to the—"

"I was speaking metaphorically."

"Wear your metaphorical Santa suit, then."

"Half an hour, smartass."

He hung up. He could use a break. He shrugged on his parka. The phone rang again.

"Sheriff Schwartz?"

"That's me."

"You don't know me but I need to talk."

"And you are?"

"This is Steve Bolt. I heard about your deputy and I think I'm in trouble."

Chapter Thirty-eight

Ike let the words sink in. Bolt had somehow managed to survive. What did that do to Charlie's theory about Russian assassins?

"What kind of trouble are we talking about?"

"I know something about Harris, and your guy was asking about him and me."

"What can you tell me about Harris?"

"I figure it's worth something, don't you think?"

"It's worth a great deal to us. So talk to me."

"No. I meant it ought to be worth some money. I can tell you things that can maybe solve who killed him."

"You know he's dead? How do you know that?"

"I hear things."

"But you know he's dead for certain?"

"Okay, I give you this one for free and then you can decide if a thousand dollars is a fair price for the rest. See, I did odd jobs for him, you know. Like, if he didn't want anybody to see him but he needed money, he'd give me his bank card and the pin number and I'd go withdraw what he wanted."

"You didn't skim a little on the side?"

"I thought about it, but he always paid me good, so no, I didn't."

"That's it? That's the free information that's going to convince me to hand over a thousand dollars?"

"No, no, let me finish. He gave me this package to deliver if anything ever happened to him, see. He set up this, like, code deal where if he didn't do something two days in a row, I was to deliver it. Well, two days went by and so I figured he must be dead."

"Did you deliver the package?"

"I might have. How about my money?"

Ike sat down and scratched his head. He was getting hot. He unzipped his parka. He looked at his watch and realized he was five minutes away from being late at Ruth's. He needed time to mull through what Bolt said. He remembered the *Washington Post* articles he'd read. Could there be a connection? He made up his mind to bluff.

"So you drove to Washington and dropped the package off to someone in Rock Creek Park. Have I got it right?"

Ike waited. Silence at the other end. Ike knew he'd guessed correctly.

"That guy's dead now, did you know that, Bolt? He's dead and his apartment was trashed. Are you listening?"

"Hey, I don't know about that. I just —"

"Listen to me. You can forget about money. You need to think about your future and if you have one. Right now, with the evidence we have, you are looking good for a murder." He heard Bolt try to interrupt. "I said, listen to me. That's worse case, I can probably hang this one on you—if not directly, at least as an accessory after the fact. Now, there's a rumor you're dead. If I let it out that you're not, do you suppose some folks just might come gunning for you?"

"I didn't do nothing wrong. I took the package like I was told and delivered it. That's it."

"And your house got torched and two beefy guys dragged you out of a fleabag motel. Doesn't that suggest something to you?"

More silence. Ike wondered if he'd hung up. "Bolt, you still there? I have one more thing to say to you. The deputy who was killed came from your part of the world. If someone killed him, what do you suppose will happen next? He was a Buffalo Mountain man."

"Oh, sweet Jesus. Somebody else will be killed."

"What happened?"

"I told you, I took the package to—"

"No. Before that."

The line remained quiet. Ike could almost hear the gears grinding as Bolt thought through his options.

"Okay. See, Harris, like once a month, he would go to Richmond to, you know, get it on."

"Get it on?"

"With women."

"He visited prostitutes?"

"Yeah, I guess. Port of Richmond—bars, stuff like that. Anyway, before he left, he'd use his cards, the bank card especially, to get cash. Then he'd leave them behind in a desk drawer. I guess he thought they could be stolen in one of them places. He was probably right. I had a friend who went to this massage place in Roanoke and they pretty near cleaned him out."

"Identification?"

"No, he didn't even take a driver's license."

"He did this often?"

"Yeah. Like I said, once a month or so."

"So Harris is supposed to leave for Richmond, and then what?"

"Well, now I think he did leave but he never came back. That's my take on things. Anyway, I knew where he was going so I says to that nut case Donnie—"

"That's Oldham?"

"Yeah. I says, 'We'll wait 'til he leaves then fake a burglary,' only we were too late."

"How, 'too late'?"

"When we got there, the whole place was, like, turned upside down and the cards were gone."

"Oldham didn't take them?"

"No. I made him turn out his pockets. He didn't have nothing except a cigarette lighter and silver penknife he copped."

"He didn't double cross you and get to Harris early?"

"I don't see how he could. I mean he ain't too bright. How'd he know who he was—he never met your guy before that."

"You're sure?"

"Um…I guess so."

"You're not sure?"

"I don't know. What do you want me to do?"

"You have a good hiding place now, I expect. Get back in that hole for the weekend. Monday, you call me again and we'll arrange to meet—someplace safe."

Ike hung up before he could answer. Ruth was going to give him a hard time. There would be no point in calling. He'd just have to go, take his medicine, and then, after a drink, and a little schmooze, who knew?

◇◇◇

Saturday morning arrived cold and clear. People began to assemble along the street for Whaite's funeral. They exhaled in steamy columns as they mingled back and forth. Essie Falco asked Ike if she could rent a horse from the riding stable. She said she wanted to saddle it and put boots in the stirrups backwards like she'd seen in funerals on television. Ike turned her down.

"Essie, we all loved Whaite and want to honor him but it's eight miles from Six Feet Under's to the Baptist church and another eight to the graveyard. In this weather and moving at the rate of a walking horse, we won't get the service over until tomorrow. Besides, that's really for military funerals. Sorry."

She looked crestfallen and started to say something when Billy Sutherlin put his arm around her.

"Come with me, sweetcakes. I got a better idea."

Ike watched the two leave. God only knew what Billy's idea might be. Ike supposed he'd probably want to veto it, too. At the same time, he realized the two were close to Whaite and whatever it turned out to be, he should probably keep quiet.

Police vehicles from surrounding jurisdictions began arriving an hour before the start of the procession. Their occupants filed into Unger's to greet Darcie and view Whaite. At ten o'clock, they would form a motorcade and follow the hearse and limousine to the Baptist church for the service and then to the cemetery. A bus carrying four men in kilts and seven men in full dress uniform arrived—the pipers who would play "Amazing Grace" and the men who would provide a twenty-one gun salute at the graveside. Ike was impressed.

He thought about his years in the CIA—about the men and a few women he'd known who had been killed in the pursuance of their job. He thought about Eloise, his wife of a hundred days. Not one of them was celebrated by an assemblage of agents in uniform. No string of cars from other agencies, other jurisdictions, escorted them to their grave. No bugler played taps. No kilted pipers piped them on their way. Just a few friends, a few words, and a brief letter of thanks in the mail a week later.

But the law enforcement community…that was a different story entirely. It knew how to take care of its own.

Before he left the office, he straightened his tie. He was in full regalia, uniform, duty belt, and cap. He made a point of never wearing his "Smokey the Bear" hat; it embarrassed him just to think about it. He was very lax about uniforms in the department as well—his and others. Billy, for instance, wore cowboy boots and a Stetson. Other deputies varied their uniforms to suit their taste. Only Sam Ryder consistently showed up for duty correctly dressed, although her shirttail usually flopped out over her belt. He put on the embarrassing hat, straightened it, and stepped outside. That's when he saw his deputies waiting. Every one of them in uniform, correct head wear, shoes polished, and standing at attention. He couldn't help himself. A lump formed in his throat and he realized how proud he was of them all. He snapped them an awkward salute. They returned it. For him and for them, it was a first.

At that moment, Billy's "idea" turned the corner and fell into line with the growing number of police cars filling the funeral home's parking lot and lining the street. At least a dozen late nineteen-sixties Chevrolet Chevelles appeared, their motors throbbing. Most were red, but a few black and blue ones punctuated the line here and there. Billy had contacted Whaite's car club and they were there to pay their respects—not to the police officer—but to the car owner whose vehicle routinely bested them in showoffs. Whaite's wrecked but still brilliant red car, loaded on the bed of a Rollback, brought up the rear. Someone had strung a black garland across its shattered windscreen.

He gave Billy a thumbs-up. Essie, her arm around Billy's waist and tears in her eyes, beamed.

At a signal from Siegfried Unger, an auxiliary policeman stopped the traffic on Main Street and the procession began. The hearse and limo pulled out and, one by one, police cars and motorcycles, lights flashing, and finally the Chevelles. The whole formed a line a half mile long and headed to the highway. It was a sad but noble day for Picketsville.

Chapter Thirty-nine

Everitt Barstow scurried up to Brent Wilcox outside the Dollar Store. Wilcox plastered on his best smile and waited for the ponytailed academic to tell him what had upset him.

"Brent," Barstow said, and looked nervously over his shoulder, "what's going on?"

"Sorry? Nothing is going on."

"Listen, for the last two days, two ham-fisted G-men have been up at the campus interviewing all of us. They are asking about the investment package you've put together—how much we've invested—things like that."

"What did you tell them? You know, Everitt, the only way this deal can go down and generate the returns I mention in the prospectus is if we keep it absolutely under the radar. If anyone gets wind of the details, other investors will—"

"I know, I know, I remember the pitch. But these guys were from the FBI. You know how I feel about them. I didn't give them anything. Obviously, Big Brother has gotten wind of your idea to access the federal parks and wants to stop you. But still, I'm not sure the others are as sharp about this as I am."

"What are you saying, Everitt?" Wilcox's smile stayed frozen in place even though his face muscles had started to cramp.

"I think I need to pull out—just temporarily, of course. It's the name thing, not the money."

"The name thing? What do you mean?"

"If there is a leak to the press, for example...like, say the sheriff gets hold of this and talks or something...The word around town is, he's got it in for you...How would it look if a tenured professor were to appear in the story? I have a small reputation in the ecology community. Removing natural resources from federal lands, no matter how carefully managed, is not going to read well. I don't want my name to appear. So if you would just refund my investment—"

Wilcox let his smile slide off his face. "It's Saturday, Barstow. I can't transfer a sum that large until Monday. And, anyway, I think you are making too much of this and should reconsider."

"Not until Monday?"

"Close of the business day on Monday, yes. It's the best I can do. Don't worry, your money is perfectly safe. Look, the feds have a responsibility to assure that any program that involves government property is fiscally sound and, I should emphasize, solidly funded. If too many people like you panic...see...I think you should take the weekend to think it over."

"Not until Monday, you said."

"Monday, right."

Barstow did not look happy as he turned and scuttled away. Wilcox waited until he drove off in his Saab. He checked his watch and headed for the bank. The cavalcade of police vehicles pulling out of Unger's Funeral Home, their light bars flashing red, white, and blue, rolled toward him. That many policemen in one area and, worse, heading toward him, made him very nervous. It felt like an omen. He took it seriously. He hurried into the bank's relative warmth.

◇◇◇

Sam had started attending church because Karl wished it. He was the one with religion. She'd drifted away from the church and its trappings after a comparative religion course in college. She said she objected to the formalities. Later, the formalities purged from her life, she found it easy to drop the substance as well. Karl was a believer in his own way. In Picketsville the two went to the Stonewall Jackson Memorial Episcopal church. When she joined him in DC, they would drive to Fairfax. Now, with him out of her life, there was no reason for her to attend at all. But Whaite's funeral had stirred an old need and so, on Sunday morning, she found herself parking beside the handsome limestone church. She climbed the few steps to the red-painted doors and was nearly knocked backwards when they flew open. T.J. Harkins stepped out. He saw her distress and must have realized he'd opened a door too hard—again. Apparently, he did that frequently.

"Oh, I am sorry," he said, and then, seeing who he'd nearly knocked over, added, "Miss Sam, I am sorry. Are you okay?"

"Yes, thank you, T.J., I'm fine. How are you?"

"I am here to deliver Aunt Rose and Aunt Minnie to church and now I have to pick up Colonel Bob at the diner."

"Well, I won't keep you, then." Sam reached for the door's handle.

"Miss Sam?"

"Yes?"

"When are you going to take me for a ride in the police car like you said?"

"I did promise you that. We've been very busy and it's been a sad time for me, and I forgot."

"Are you still sad?"

"A little, yes."

"When you're finished being sad, can we go for a ride in the police car?"

"This is a special sadness, T.J. It won't go away for a long time. But I'll tell you what I can do...tomorrow at three o'clock...you have a way to know when it's three?"

"Yes, I do. I have this watch." He rolled up the sleeve of his coat and showed her his watch. "I can tell the time. I know three."

"Fine, then, tomorrow at three. Can you come to the police station? We'll take the ride then."

T.J.'s face beamed. "I will be there at three o'clock tomorrow which is a Monday, Miss Sam."

◇◇◇

Ike needed time to think. He felt trapped in his tiny apartment and didn't want to risk the roads to his A-frame in the mountains. The call from Bolt confirmed his doubts about the Russians. He believed they may have had something to do with Kamarov's death, but Ike felt sure someone else did the actual shooting. He needed some fresh air. The morning's cold had moderated to a bearable crispness. He pulled on his parka and decided to drive back to the cemetery. In the confusion of playing host to more than fifty police officers from more than a dozen jurisdictions the previous day, he never had a chance to say goodbye to Whaite. Then the mayor wanted to talk about the government's harassment of Wilcox and did he know anything about it? He didn't, but was glad. The mayor did not like that answer and reminded him there was an election coming up and Ike would be wise to choose his friends carefully. Ike reminded the mayor, in turn, where he was and what such an occasion required of him as the town's top executive. Both had parted in a state of high annoyance.

He parked on the access road. The tire tracks from all the previous day's vehicles had widened it to include a yard or two of the grassy verge. Muddy footprints marked the path to the site where Whaite had been laid to rest. Odd expression, he thought, *laid to rest*. Is that what death is, rest? That would make it something to look forward to. He stood staring at the freshly turned earth, head bowed. He'd need to replace Whaite. Not now, though. Let him rest. He would miss him and his country, no, mountain wisdom and patience. He'd lost a good man, maybe his best. The sun dipped behind a cloud.

He turned to go to his car and then abruptly turned back and walked to the corner of the graveyard where Eloise was buried. His wife, dead now nearly five years…had it been that long? He wanted to sit on the stone bench he'd placed there as a memorial, but it had an inch of melting snow on it. Instead, he stood. It had been a while since he'd visited the grave, and there were things he still needed to do. He took a deep breath and finally asked for her forgiveness. If he'd been smarter, if he'd been quicker, or if they'd never met, she'd still be alive and well, and probably enormously happy somewhere raising a passel of Irish-American kids. But he had not been the things he needed to be for her, and now she lay beneath six feet of ice-cold earth. He shivered at the thought. So beautiful, so young. *Laid to rest.*

"Do you like Ruth?" he asked. The wind picked up and howled through the pines in the state park to the west. "I want you to like her. She's not anything like you. She's smart and bitchy...she's like an old-fashioned whetstone. She grinds at me. I'm a dull axe, I think. She keeps me sharp. And I think she is what I need right now. Do you understand?" The cloud passed and the sun shone again.

"Thanks."

He walked back to the car. As he did so, it hit him. He hadn't been thinking about Kamarov at all, but he knew at that moment why Charlie's theory didn't work.

Chapter Forty

Sam lingered at church. The wind had picked up and, in spite of its central heating, the church had been chilly. She had the time, goodness knows, and a cup of coffee would warm her up, she thought. Whether she would admit to it or not, she needed people. Blake Fisher, apparently sensing her discomfort, wandered over.

"How are you, Sam?"

"Fine, Father Blake." The *Father* part she'd acquired from Karl, and it sounded oddly discordant to her lapsed Lutheran ears. "I'm fine, thank you," she added. It was not true but the best she could do.

"You must try Tina's oatmeal-raisin cookies. They are famous in the church, maybe in the county—I'm not sure about that—but they should be. I have my private stash Tina makes for me up in the office, but I plan to scarf off as many of these as possible now, save the others for later." Sam saw the smile and felt grateful for the attention. She did not need a cookie, but then…They moved to the table with its tray of cookies and coffee urn. He filled a cup for each of them and offered her a cookie.

Rose Garroway, overcoated, hatted, and gloved, slipped up beside Blake.

"Harry Potter," she said. "A word to the wise. Joe Bartlett is on his way over here and he's got the little English wizard on the brain."

"What?" Blake said.

"Joe. He heard the school library has shelved the Harry Potter books and he wants you to sign a petition to have them removed." She glanced over at an impatient T.J. and Minnie standing by the door. "He asked me and I said I liked the Potter stories, and he said they glorified satanic practices and the occult. Oops, here he comes now. And here's T.J. He'll want me to leave. Bye."

Joe Bartlett moved toward Blake like a heavy cruiser doing twenty knots on a calm sea. Members of the congregation were washed aside in his bow wake and all but tumbled into each other as he passed. The look on his face made Blake cringe. He glanced around for an escape but could find none. In his greed to garner more than his fair share of cookies, he had pinned himself and Sam behind the refreshment table, an easy target for Joe's big guns.

"I guess you've heard, Vicar, about what's going on in the library at the school?" Joe said, breathless and red-faced.

"No, Joe. Is there trouble?"

"Harry Potter," he said, fixing Blake with a righteous stare. "They are letting our kids read books inspired by the devil."

"What's the problem with the books, Joe? I've read them and seen the movies. They are not great literature, but I can't see…"

"Vicar, I am amazed. You've read them?"

"Yes, have you?"

"Certainly not. I won't have sorcery and magic in my house."

"You haven't read them but you are prepared to have them banned? Why?"

"Come on, Vicar, surely you know. They are about wizards and witches—all the denizens of the Devil's army—children at risk, and all that. I have a petition here I want you to sign."

"No, I don't think so, Joe. I won't sign."

"You won't? I'm disappointed, Vicar. And I'm sure the Mission Board will have something to say about that."

"They may, Joe, and you are certainly free to bring it up, but I will not sign. Would you like to know why?"

"Um. Sure, I guess, but I can't see how you can stand there and let something like this happen. Don't you care what happens to our children?"

Joe poured himself a cup of coffee and grabbed a handful of cookies, half of which he stuffed into his mouth, the other half into his pocket.

"We are in the Advent season now. You know what that's about, of course?"

"One of those historical things, I guess. For me, we are getting ready to celebrate the birth of Jesus, so I don't understand all this stuff about repenting."

"Well, stay with the birth of Jesus, then. Who came to worship him in the manger?"

"Shepherds, angels…"

"Anyone else?"

"Three kings came with gold and frankincense and myrrh."

"Not kings, Joe. Kings is not how the Greek reads. They were magi."

"Well, okay, wise men, then."

"Not quite. *Magi* shares the root from which we get the word magic. They were magicians, stargazers, astrologers—wizards are what we would call them today. And they brought gifts. What do you suppose those gifts were meant to symbolize?"

"Gold is for the riches of the world, frankincense is for worship, and myrrh is to remind us that we all will die but we will die in the Lord. It's in that hymn."

"That is the traditional Christian view, but I don't believe that's what the magi had in mind. The ancients believed gold had magical properties. For example, they believed gold could remove poison from beverages, so kings drank from gold chalices, not to show their wealth, but to benefit from its magic. Alchemists tried for centuries to turn base metal into gold. They believed they could do so because there was some sort of residual magic in the metal and the right incantation and procedure would make the conversion possible.

"Frankincense was burned in the Temple in Jerusalem and pagan temples all over the known world and especially at oracles.

At Delphi, for example, a priestess would sit in a smoke-filled room, with candles or lamps set in front of large, split geodes, the origin of crystal balls in our time, I think, and chew hallucinogenic plants. The play of light and the smoke created an otherworldly illusion—'smoke and mirrors,' you might say. After a while, the prophecy would be handed to the supplicant written, as often as not, in myrrh ink. The important thing, Joe, is they represented the tools of their trade."

Joe stared at Blake slack jawed.

"You see what happened? There was only one king in that room—a baby named Jesus. They laid the symbols of their power at the feet of a baby. He received the tokens of their power. That means the forces that frighten you are under submission to God. They cannot prevail. No, I do not worry about Harry Potter. Some persons may become enthralled by what he represents and lose their way, some may actually practice dark arts and lose their souls, but for the rest of us, Harry Potter and his gang are no more threatening than the unlikely gang from *Star Trek.*

"So to answer your question, I am concerned about our children. If you want me to sign a petition to do something about child pornography, child abuse, or homeless children, by all means, bring it around, but this one—no."

Pinned in behind the table, Sam had no choice but to listen. She did so with considerable admiration. Without realizing it, she'd worked her way through a half dozen cookies as her gaze shifted from one man to the other. Her appreciation of Blake had previously been attached only to his sermons, which she usually enjoyed. Otherwise, positioned at the front of the church, costumed in a white alb and stole, and backlit by candles, he seemed a remote and foreign presence. She had not seen this determined side. And at that moment, she began to realize that her drift from the church was occasioned as much by a perceived lack of intellectual challenge, as by its archaic forms and substance. Karl or no Karl, she decided she would stick with this church business for a while longer. As she left, she glanced back at Blake and for a fleeting moment wished he were a few inches taller.

Chapter Forty-one

Karl Hedrick sat in his section chief's outer office for an hour past his appointment time. He supposed the psychology ploy was meant to intimidate him. He found himself growing angry instead. At eight-thirty he stood to leave.

"Tell Bullock I will be in my cubicle when he's ready."

"Mr. Hedrick, he's expecting you to wait. I'm sure he'll only be a minute more."

"Frances, I will not get on your case, because you are only doing your job, but I know, and you know, there is no one in there with him. He is playing head games and I am not willing to participate."

Just then the door swung open. Frances must have depressed the talk switch and Bullock heard what he'd said.

"Inside, Hedrick," he said, and lumbered back in his office. Frances gave Karl a weak smile and shrugged.

The next forty-five minutes consisted mostly of Bullock haranguing Karl, who listened as patiently as he could for as long as he could. Then, when Bullock came up for air, Karl recited the list of mistakes, misconceptions, and plain errors that had marked the operation to date. He reminded Bullock that it had been the Picketsville police who had saved his bacon in the past. He pointed out that going into the town and interviewing possible victims in the open invited their man to skip town, and then rounded on the idiocy of employing an incompetent answering service.

Bullock's jaw dropped. His face turned cerise. Finally he sputtered that Karl would be on probation starting immediately and that he, Bullock, would recommend his termination. In the meantime, Karl would be well advised to rethink his words and perhaps his career choice. Karl knew there was a process and he could not be fired in anything less than ten working days unless he posed a clear threat to the Bureau. He thanked his boss and left the building. He didn't feel like clearing out his desk just yet, if ever. The possibility existed that this last set of errors might catch up with Bullock long before the process to terminate began. He found his car, having packed it earlier, and drove southwest to Picketsville. He had a job to do.

◇◇◇

T.J. arrived at precisely three o'clock. If Sam had been watching, she would have noticed that he also arrived at two forty-five, two fifty, and two fifty-seven. She had picked the hour when she would go off shift and could spend the time without a conflict. Ike had okayed the use of a cruiser.

Sam met T.J. at the door. "Are you ready?" He smiled and nodded. "Okay, then let's roll."

"Let's roll," he repeated.

They crossed the parking lot to the black and white. T.J. climbed in the passenger side. Sam settled behind the wheel and snapped her laptop into its docking station on the dash. They drove onto Main Street and toward the Covington Road.

"We'll just cruise to the edge of town, make a loop to the north and hit the interstate. We have a limited jurisdiction there, but it's easy riding."

"Can we make the siren go?"

"No, sorry about that, but unless we are in hot pursuit or want to alert someone, the siren stays off." T.J. looked disappointed. When they'd driven west a few miles, Sam called in their location and Essie, whom she'd primed before they'd left, answered with a stream of official-sounding directives. T.J. sat up, eyes bright. He turned and pointed to the computer.

"What does that do?" he asked.

"It's a computer on a wireless network. It talks to the ones in the office and the state's database." T.J. had a blank look on his face. "Okay, say we are following a car and it is doing something suspicious, like weaving back and forth. I can type in the license number and the computer will tell me all about the car, its owner, and anything else I might need. Watch." She typed in the number of an old Honda Civic in front of them. In a moment the data flashed on the screen. "Can you read that?" T.J. squinted and studied the words.

"It says Honda Civic and has a man's name. There is a year here, too. Is that the year of the car or of the man driving it?"

"Which line?" T.J. pointed to the screen. "That one is the year of the car. This one," she pointed to another line, "should be the DOB of the owner."

"DOB?"

"Date of birth—the year the owner was born."

They drove up an access ramp and headed north on I-81. T.J. alternately looked forward and then at the equipment in the car. Sam explained each switch and variation on the dash from the cars he'd driven. Finally he sat back in his seat to enjoy the ride. As they pulled up behind a silver sedan, T.J. asked if he could work the computer. Sam smiled and nodded. He carefully tapped in the license number. The data shifted to this new parameter. Sam glanced at the screen.

"See? There you go. That's the license number and the description of the car."

T.J. studied the information he'd created. He frowned and looked up at Sam.

"Deputy Sam, that's the wrong car. It's supposed to be a Ford Crown Victoria and that's a Mercury Grand Marquis." Sam looked more closely at the screen. T.J. was right. The two vehicles appeared essentially the same, and easy to confuse. The license number did not belong to that car.

"Okay, T.J., now you can use the siren but—wait a second— first, throw that switch there. That will turn on our lights. Now, for the siren, just turn it on for a second and then off again. We don't want to make too big a deal out of this."

T.J. did as he was told and the siren growled. The car in front slowed and pulled to the side of the road. Sam called in her location and the 10-37, suspicious vehicle she had stopped, on the cruiser's radio.

"You wait here, T.J., and watch. If anything looks funny you pick up the transmitter—that's this thing—push the send button—like this—and say 10-31. You understand?"

"Ten thirty-one. Yes."

Sam stepped out of the car and approached the driver's side. As she did so, she unsnapped her holster strap and freed her Glock. The window on the Sable slid down. Sam stepped up and looked in.

"Mrs. Morse, is that you?"

"My word, Samantha, don't you look smart in that uniform. I heard you left the college but now I see it's true what they said—you're a deputy sheriff."

"Yes ma'am, I am." Estelle Morse worked in the personnel office at Callend College. "We have a little problem here."

"I wasn't going too fast, I'm sure of that and—"

"It's not speeding, Mrs. Morse. You have someone else's plates on your car."

"Excuse me?"

"It appears someone switched license plates with you."

"Oh dear, is that serious?"

"Maybe. Stay right here." Sam walked back to the police car. "T.J., what's the owner's name on the Ford?"

"That license belongs on a car belonging to someone named Enterprise."

"It's a rental. Okay. Essie, 10-63. I have a car out here belonging to Estelle Morse from up at the college wearing plates from an Enterprise rental. See if they are missing a car. It's probably already at the chop shop, but give them a buzz. I'll send Mrs. Morse to you for a set of temp tags and you can explain to her what she needs to do next. Handle the stolen plates with gloves at the edges just in case the mope who took the car was stupid and left us some prints."

"Ten-four."

Sam returned to Mrs. Morse and told her what she must do next. She also assured her several times that she was not in trouble and that everything would be fine. When she slid back in the cruiser, she saw that T.J. had been looking through the material on her clipboard.

"Good job, T.J., I might have missed that."

"I was reading your papers."

"They're just the latest things we're working on and some forms," she said.

"There are pictures here."

"Yes, they are pictures of people we want to talk to."

"Why do you want to talk to Donald and Hollis?"

Chapter Forty-two

Ike didn't expect to hear again from Bolt. He'd spooked him back into the mountains or wherever he had found sanctuary and nothing short of a major upheaval would pry him loose. No matter. He called his opposite number in Floyd County, who said he'd keep an eye out for Bolt and ask his people to keep their eyes open as well. At that moment, Bolt and Kamarov were at the bottom of Ike's list. The person he wanted, and wanted badly, was the owner of the pickup that had been involved in Whaite's death. He wanted to know if he should be looking at a hit and run or a murder, and if the latter, what had Whaite done, or said, that had triggered it. Either way, his top deputy was gone and he was angry. Jurisdiction belonged to Floyd County and he feared Whaite's death might not rate the sort of effort he wanted. Jurisdiction or no, he aimed to find a way in. He just hadn't figured out how.

"Well, well, looky what the cat dragged in. What do you want around here, backstabber?"

In all the years he'd known her, Ike had never heard Essie speak rudely to anyone. She remained the one cheery voice among a crowd of variously grumpy ones. Except for a rare brush with PMS, Essie could be counted on to have something upbeat to say to anyone walking through the door—from known felons to the town gossip. Ike stood up to get a better look at the object of this amazing outburst. Karl Hedrick stood frozen in place, mouth open, and hand on the knob of the still open door.

"Shut the door before you give us all pneumonia," Essie added, "preferably from the outside." Ike made a mental note to never have Essie angry at him.

"Karl," he said and waved him into his office, "you're a little off base, aren't you, or did your boss finally figure out we had his man, in a manner of speaking—oh, and in the same state as the last time you barged in here."

Karl let the door fall to and stared first at Essie, then at Ike.

"I don't know what either of you are talking about. Maybe I should go out and check the address. I could have sworn this was the Picketsville Sheriff's Office. I must have made a mistake."

"You made a mistake, all right," Essie said. If she'd been authorized to carry a gun, she looked like she might have used it.

"Hey there, Karl," Billy Sutherlin said. "How you been?"

"Don't you talk to him, Billy, he's an enemy."

"We need to talk," Ike said and waved at him again. "In here."

Karl, looking perplexed, walked in and at Ike's gestured invitation, sat down. Ike closed the door.

"Cutthroat," he said.

"What?"

"We know you are with Cutthroat and we know you've been tracking Kamarov. You must have cross-checked John Does and figured out that we have him."

Karl stared at Ike as if he wanted to find some part of the speech he could respond to and had failed.

"You got me, Ike. Except for 'John Doe,' I don't have a clue."

"Karl, you know Sam is our wizard of cyberspace. She just finished in a dead heat with the gurus up at Langley for snooping. She found Cutthroat before they did and she found you. You want to fill me in. If you do, I might be able to keep her from using her sidearm on you when she gets back."

"Wow. That is a load. I can't help you, Ike, because I don't have a clue what you're talking about. I just drove down here from a session with my section chief, Bullock—you remember him? And he reamed me out pretty good, but he could take a lesson from you guys. What do you think...no, how about this?

I tell you what I have been doing and why I am here and then you can tell me what I've done wrong."

"You really don't know?" Karl shook his head. "Okay, talk, but be quick. I expect Sam back within the hour."

Karl explained he'd been in Picketsville Thursday and Friday of the previous week and then was called back to DC to meet with Bullock that morning. He described his cross assignment to the fraud squad, how they'd been tracking Brent Wilcox and since he, Karl, knew the territory, he'd been sent in.

"We're investigating a Ponzi operation. He'd been selling shares in a Public Lands Access program and promised huge returns to his investors. He says he has an inside track on the natural resources reclamation in several national parks and trust lands. It all sounded legal. He quoted statutes that allow it and so on. The trouble is, he's not filed a single application to access the lands, and he's collected huge sums. You with me so far?"

"A Ponzi scheme?"

"When I realized that you were out of the loop, a deliberate move on our part, by the way, I complained. That's when I moved into Bullock's crosshairs. He's still angry about the other thing." The other thing referred to a murder investigation earlier that Ike had worked and that made the FBI look bad. Ike sat back and smiled. He loved it when he guessed and got it right.

"I know Wilcox. You should have told me you were coming. He's not stupid and I could have helped. In fact, there is nothing I'd have liked better."

"Yeah, I pointed all that out to the boys in DC and they suggested I consider a career change. I'm on probation pending a hearing to terminate."

"You weren't involved in Cutthroat?"

"Never heard of it, and I am just pissed enough to blow the cover of anybody in the Bureau right now. Sorry. What or who is Cutthroat?"

"It's a long story, Karl, and since you remain in the bosom of J. Edgardom at the moment, I can't tell you. Right now, I need to figure a way to keep Sam steady while we sort this out. See, she found your name in a personnel list for what we believe is a black program out of the FBI. You said you'd been reassigned and there you were. That upset her, but not sufficiently to want you sent to the moon. It was the woman in your apartment who answered your phone that finished her."

"Oh, man, I don't believe this. Ike, there wasn't any woman in my apartment. It was an answering service Bullock hired. He got it into his head that answering machines posed a security threat or something. He shut down our machines and then, to make the whole operation a complete FUBAR, he ordered us to cut off all communications to anyone and especially you all. I told you, he's a pretty dim bulb."

"No other woman?"

"No, and I've been trying to reach Sam for days and either get her voice mail, dropped, or, lately, a recording saying the number is out of service."

"Two problems—she can't use the phone when she's driving—new town ordinance and her phone died anyway. She has a new one complete with new number. She didn't want to keep the old one."

"This is so bogus. I'm being hammered from both sides because my boss is an idiot. Worse—I have to go to hearings in the next week or so to keep my job...so I can still work for him."

"You have my sympathy. Offhand, Karl, do you know if the Bureau has any other special agents named Hedrick?"

"No, but I can find out. Can I use Sam's computer?" He said Sam's computer. Everyone did, as though it had nothing to do with Ike's operation. Ike let it pass. The truth? Without Sam, he probably wouldn't have anything going in that area at all.

"Make it quick."

Karl hustled around the corner to Sam's space, ignoring the dirty look sent his way by an outraged Essie Falco.

The door burst open and Sam entered with T.J. Harkins in tow. Ike held up his hand to silence Essie, who looked like a volcano ready to explode.

"Ike—you have to hear this. Tell him about the pictures, T.J."

Chapter Forty-three

"In here," Ike said and stole a glance at Sam's office door.

"In a minute, Ike, I need to get copies of the rest of the pictures for T.J. to look at."

"That can wait. In my office—now."

The outside door opened again and Colonel Robert Twelvetrees came in, his hand on the booking counter to make sure of his footing. "Where's my driver? Sergeant, where are you?"

"I've got him, Colonel. He has some information for me. As soon as we're done, he's yours. You can have a seat at that empty desk. Essie, help the Colonel."

He had Karl in one room, Sam in another, and Essie playing avenging angel.

"This is looking more and more like a Restoration farce," he muttered, "and this is Act One."

Once Colonel Bob was settled, Ike took Essie aside. "Ditch the bad attitude, Essie, we have some serious work to do here and I don't think Karl is the bad guy. In fact, I think at the end of the day, you are going to owe me my jelly-filled back. Now go in Sam's office and tell Karl to sit tight. If he finds the answer to my question, show him how to call me in my office."

"But—"

"An order, Essie. Now go."

"Ike," Sam called through the door, "it will only take me a minute—"

"Sam, first things first. T.J., what can you tell me about these pictures?" Ike closed the door. Sam and T.J. sat with their backs to it and did not see Essie head for Sam's office, or return.

"Well, Sheriff Ike, they are pictures of Donald and Hollis."

"You know these two, then."

"Yes, sir, I do."

"How?"

"Donald lives in a house that is behind mine. He used to be my friend, but not any more."

"Where exactly do you live?"

T.J. frowned, turning *exactly* over in his mind. "I live in Willis now but not next week."

"You are moving?"

"Yes. My mom and me are moving to my Aunt Rose and Aunt Minnie's apartment. We have to leave our house."

"Donald is your neighbor. How about this Hollis person. How do you know him?"

"He is Donald's friend. He hurt his leg one afternoon at Donald's house."

"He told you that?"

"No, sir, I saw him fall down the steps and then Donald came out and they drove away. And that night they came back and Hollis had crutches and a big bandage on his leg."

"Okay, T.J., that's very useful. Thank you. Is there anything else you can think of that might help?"

"No, sir. But I saw the license plate."

"He helped me turn up another bit of crime," Sam said.

"Really? That wouldn't be Mrs. Morse and her stolen tags, would it?"

"T.J. was the one who spotted them."

"Well, good job." Ike's phone rang. When he picked up, Sam made a move to rise. He waved her back down.

Karl started talking. "I found him, Ike. There is a Kevin Hedrick in the Bureau, Special Agent Kevin Hedrick. He is listed as on special assignment to Andover Crisp. No details."

"Kevin? Okay. I'm going to relay that information to a certain person in a minute, and then send her to you. Is that agreeable?"

"You bet."

"Who's what's his name, Crisp?"

"Not much of a book on him. They call him Darth Vader."

"Got it." Cutthroat, the Dark Side of the Force.

Ike told Sam what he could remember of Karl's story and mentioned that Kevin Hedrick was the Hedrick she'd found in her hacking—Hedrick, K. She looked doubtful and then her face softened. It was enough that she wanted to believe. He sent her to her office.

"T.J., the colonel's waiting for you. I guess it's time to go. Thank you for making those IDs."

"Would it be all right if I used the bathroom?"

"Certainly." Ike pointed T.J. in the right direction and stepped out of the office.

"Sorry to hear about your deputy," Colonel Bob said. "How'd it happen?"

"Ran into a tree on a slippery road. Maybe an accident, maybe not. We're checking. We have a witness who thinks he might have been run off the road, but…"

"Not reliable?"

"Well, she's old, can't see too well, is hard of hearing, and her cat knocked over her teacup at the wrong time."

"Leave out the cat and I've been there, done that. Don't much cotton to cats. Now you take a dog…sorry, you were saying?"

"Anyway, she thought she saw a truck hit Whaite's car. So I'm looking for a pickup with a mashed-in passenger side fender and some red paint on the door. That's it. So, Colonel, I hear T.J. drives for you. How's that working out?"

"Best thing that has happened to me in the last decade, Sheriff."

"What I don't understand is how he managed to get a driver's license in the first place. I mean, he's nice, but—"

"Don't sell that boy short. He's slow, but not stupid. He can read and, therefore, with some coaching, he managed to memorize all the answers in the driver's ed book. He still knows them, by the way, every danged one of them, and he drives to them. If any of your people need a brush-up on traffic law, just call the boy."

"Still, it has to be hard—"

"Sheriff, you need to rearrange your thinking. You are too young to know everything, and one of the things you don't know is what the world looks like to someone like the Thomas Harkins of this world. He manages just fine. He can work things out. It just takes him more time. Concepts are a struggle for him, but I daresay, over half the senior class at Picketsville High has the same problem. Only theirs stems from plain laziness, T.J.'s from a shortage of gray cells in the right place." Ike sat on the edge of the desk and started to say something, then thought better of it.

"Look, in my day, oh…maybe not mine exactly, close…but, anyway, say one hundred or so years ago, most youngsters raised in the country, and what we now delicately refer to as the inner city, never finished high school. As soon as they were able to help put bread on the table, they went to work. If things were bad at home, they didn't get counseling or a visit from social services, they hopped a freight train and headed west. In that world, in the world of a century, century and a half ago, T.J. wouldn't seem much different from any other kid. He could harness a team, plow a straight furrow, and work all day—better'n most—no distractions. He could get by as well as the next young man. He could dig ditches, shovel coal—in a non-technical world he could fit right in. When I was in the cavalry I had a horseshoer like T.J., big African-American named Sampson. Worked hard, raised a family, but slow. You see, people like T.J. might be taken advantage of, but they manage. What he wouldn't do is stand out as strange. He's loyal, honest, and never has a mean word for anybody. That counts for a lot in my book, and he's employable. Think about it. T.J. is just a four-cylinder engine in an eight-cylinder world." T.J. walked in the room. "Okay, T.J., let's saddle up."

"Sometimes Colonel Bob thinks he's still in the U.S. Cavalry., T.J. said with a grin. "He went to war with General Patton." T.J. steered Robert Twelvetrees to his car and drove away. Ike stared out the door at the car's taillights.

"Did you hear all that, Essie? That's why other cultures honor their older citizens instead of warehousing them in nursing homes. What you just heard was the voice of experience—the wisdom that only comes with age."

"Heard what?"

"Never mind. Break up the happy reunion in Sam's office. I need to talk to the two of them."

Everitt Barstow flung himself through the door.

"My God, this must be Act Two. Dr. Barstow, is there something we can do for you?"

"Arrest Brent Wilcox. He took my money." The phone rang.

"I'm putting the well-worn jelly-filled on this being either Ruth or Karl's boss. Any takers…Essie? No?" He picked up.

"Ike, what did you do to Brent Wilcox?" Ruth demanded. Ike began to laugh. "What's so funny?"

"I just won a bet with myself."

"Congratulations. Now, what happened between you two?"

"You have a source. You are calling at someone's behest. Let me guess. Agnes is upset. Her sometime beau, Brent Wilcox, has flown the coop."

"How'd you know? Never mind, Agnes says that Wilcox told her you threatened him last week. And then the FBI came around asking questions and now he's apparently left town."

"Ask Agnes if he was driving a rental car. A pretty big, fancy one?" A pause.

"She says she thinks so."

"Would it have been from Enterprise?" A shorter pause.

"She's not positive, but she thinks she remembers a green E on the bumper."

"Bingo."

"What? What has this to do with—?"

"Agnes' boyfriend has been running a Ponzi scheme in town. You know what a Ponzi is?"

"Enough. And you put the FBI on to him?"

"No, that was all their idea. I just refused to file assault charges against Flora Blevins for a very graphic suggestion she made to him in my presence."

"Agnes is not going to like this."

"So what else is new with Agnes? How much money did she invest?"

"I'll ask later." Ruth rang off and Ike turned back to Everitt Barstow.

"Dr. Barstow, you heard all that?"

"Yes, but…Wilcox was running a Ponzi?"

"That's about the size of it."

"Well, why didn't you arrest him sooner? He took my money."

"Perhaps if you and your friends had been a little more forthcoming with the FBI last week, he might have been. It was their investigation, by the way, not mine. Sorry."

Barstow opened his mouth to speak, stopped, and slouched out of the room just as Karl and Sam came in. Sam was flushed from the roots of her hair to where her collar covered what Ike suspected was bright red clear down to her knees. He decided not to ask.

"You two," he barked, "in my office, now."

Chapter Forty-four

Ike hustled the two into his office. They both unconsciously ducked coming through the door. A pair of giraffes, Ike thought.

"Ike…" Sam began.

Ike waved at her to wait and indicated they should sit.

"Karl, how badly do you want to be an FBI agent?"

Karl frowned. "Ever since I was a little kid, that's all I wanted to do. The other kids in the neighborhood all wanted the NBA or the NFL, but not me. I was going to be a G-man. I took a lot of heat for that, especially because of my size."

"Do you want to go back?"

"That's the problem. Bullock has essentially poisoned the well for me. If he has his way, I'll have a hearing on my competence soon. I could be sacked or not, but it would be desk duty for me for who knows how long."

Ike studied the young man. He certainly had the credentials and, Ike guessed, the smarts, courage, and instincts to be good at anything he put his mind to.

"Okay, I have something for you that might alter that—some information that could pull your boss' chestnuts out of the fire. If he bites, he wouldn't dare have you fired. You want it?"

Karl frowned and nodded. "Sure. But I don't understand."

"The Bureau's, shall we say, obvious, clumsy, inappropriate, unprofessional—you pick one or all of the above—presence in this town, and all that interviewing, at your chief's orders as we know, spooked your Ponzi operator. He's skipped town, gone, kaput. They may or may not track him down again anytime soon. I can give him to you today, and you can look like the Lone Ranger to your superiors. It may or may not save your boss' butt. I don't know and I don't care. That will depend on how perceptive his supervisors are. In any event, it ought to save yours."

"What have you got on Wilcox?"

"He's driving a Ford Taurus with stolen plates. Essie has the numbers. He should be easy to track. The Taurus has already been reported as stolen, by the way, so your guys had better move fast before some other country hick cop beats them to the punch again."

Karl's eyes lit up. "Can I use your phone?"

"You can use that empty desk. And I want to talk to your boss when you're done."

Sam, whose blush had faded in the previous few minutes, stood to leave with Karl. "Hold on, Sam. Sit."

Karl slipped into Whaite's old desk and picked up the phone. Ike turned back to Sam. "I reworked the duty roster this morning and you are off tomorrow. You might want to use the time to help Karl."

"Help? Oh, help, right, I got that end covered, Ike, thank you. You say you changed the schedule this morning?"

"Just anticipating. You never know how these things will work out." He walked to his office door. "Essie," he yelled, "you owe me a jelly-filled."

"No, I don't. Now, this here is a fix-up. The bust-up was real and for the reasons I said."

"We'll talk about that later." The phone rang again. "And this has got to be Act Three. Hello? Tom? What does the mayor of Picketsville want with his 'ought to remember who your friends are, Sheriff' today?" Ike listened, smiled, and sat back in his chair. It didn't squeal. Somebody had finally responded to a work order.

"Calm down, Tom, the FBI is on it right now and should have your man in custody by nightfall. I wouldn't be too hopeful about recovering your money, though. He was working a Ponzi and by the time all this is sorted out, there won't be much left. What? I'm sorry about that…next time check out anybody who wants your money but says you have to keep what you're up to a secret. It's a tip-off."

Karl wigwagged that he was finished with his call. Ike stepped into the main office and took the phone from Karl.

"Special Agent Bullock? How are you-all this fine day?"

Everyone in the room stopped talking and stared at Ike. Never in all the years he'd lived in, worked in, or simply occupied space in Picketsville had he ever spoken with an accent. But today his mouth seemed filled with corn pone.

"Yessir, well, Special Agent, this here is Sheriff Ike Schwartz down at Picketsville…you remember? Well, that's mighty fine. See, here's the thing, your ole boy jest pulled that'n off something fine." Karl flinched at *boy.*

"He's what? Suspended from duty? Well dog my cats if that ain't sumpin' else. Well, now I sure am sad to here that, yessir. Well now, here's what I'm wonderin'. We have us a federal offense in the act, you could say, and I'm just, as I say, just wonderin" iffen I can borry your boy so he could help us tomorra? Big case—interstate bank fraud. Shore could use some—he can? As long as I like? You'll do what? Assign him to us on a interagency loan. Well that's mighty nice of you, Special Agent Bullock. Yessir, mighty nice, and thank yew."

Ike hung up and turned to the group. "What?"

"What was that all about?" Sam said.

"Dog my cats?" Essie added.

"Needed to get that bonehead thinking he was doing us a favor. He has to be angry at Karl even with the tip on Wilcox. He was set to fry him and now he can't. I figured he couldn't resist cashing in on one of our operations, especially since he would be dealing with good ole Sheriff Hamhocks. Anyway, Karl, you're going to score some more points with your people before we're done here. Hell, we might even get you a promotion."

The phone rang. "There isn't supposed to be any Act Four in these plays. Who can this be?"

"Sheriff?" Colonel Twelvetrees sounded serious. "You have a minute?"

"Got the rest of the day, Colonel. What have you got?"

"I found your truck. No, that's not quite right. T.J. found it. See, we are a team. I am nearly blind—can't see things worth a hoot, but I can grasp their significance. T.J., on the other hand, can see the things clear as day, but not see the significance, you follow? I told him you were looking for a truck with a crushed passenger side and some red paint. He knew where one was. I asked 'where?' and he said 'at the house of the man Sheriff Ike asked him the questions about.' He said you should go see Donald. That work for you?"

"Tell T.J. it works beautifully."

"I'll tell him. Now you understand what I was saying to you earlier? It's a matter of fitting him in the right slot, not setting him apart."

Ike hung up. "We may have our truck. Donald, that's T.J.'s neighbor, has one, it is banged up on the passenger side and has red paint on the door. Oh, and he's one of the people we have on the pictures from the ATM cameras. That will help us get a warrant. Can you two be back here tomorrow by two? I could use some help."

"We're going for Oldham?"

"He's the one with the credit and bank cards—that's your department, Karl—and the suspicious truck—that's ours."

"Why two in the afternoon?"

"It will be one o'clock tomorrow afternoon before I can clear warrants in Floyd County. We're crossing jurisdictions and I need them, and I have some calls to make. We can use probable cause on account of the credit cards to search the house and property. That will get us the truck. We'll give it a going over, too. We can sweat Oldham a little and who knows where that might lead? Maybe he's the guy, maybe not. Red paint is red paint."

"Not this time," Sam said. "If his is the truck, we have him cold."

Chapter Forty-five

Most of the snow in the valley had melted or turned to slush, except out in the country. There a thin sheet remained, part snow, part ice, covering fields left fallow for the winter or struggling to produce a crop of winter wheat. In the moonlight, you couldn't tell anything about the snow except it sparkled and gleamed like an old-fashioned Christmas card. Ruth edged toward Ike. The car's center console prevented any thoughts she might have had to snuggle. She smiled and wondered when she'd last thought of snuggling. She'd have been in her teens, probably.

"It really is beautiful, isn't it?" Ike nodded, and swung the car into his parents' driveway.

"Is there anything I need to know about the celebration? I mean, I am not used to Christmas, much less Chanukah. And even then, the commercial version of Christmas is the only one I know."

"This is nothing like either. We are not orthodox. Rabbi Schusterman told Abe as far as he was concerned we might as well go to the Episcopal church for all the piety he saw. He said Blake Fisher had a better sense of Judaism than either of us. He's probably right. He called us 'bacon Jews.'"

"Bacon Jews?"

"Very, very unkosher."

She sat back and watched the scenery slide by. The Schwartz farmhouse stood a half mile from the road. The row of trees on either side of the driveway flashed by, creating a changing panorama like a film strip. Ike pulled up to the front porch.

"Hop out. I'll park the car over by the barn. There will be others coming and I want to give them room."

Ruth stepped gingerly from the car onto crusted snow and climbed the steps to the front door. She hesitated. Should she knock or just let herself in? She did not know what her relationship with Ike entitled her to. Before she could decide, the door swung open and Abe Schwartz, wearing a bright red flannel shirt, held out his hand.

"Come on in, Miz Harris."

"It's Ruth, Abe, not Ms. Harris. Please?"

"Well, thank you for that, Ruth. Now you get on in here and have you some punch and eats. Where's Ike?"

"Parking the car."

She stepped into the hallway and shed her coat. Abe took it and hung it on an old-fashioned oak coatrack. The house was warm and filled with the aroma of country cooking. A blast of cold air signaled Ike's arrival. He hung up his coat next to hers and led her into the front parlor. It had been decorated with an evergreen tree festooned with what appeared to be odd-shaped balls. There were garlands of pine and ivy strung around the room, and a menorah had been placed on the mantle.

"Except for the menorah, this could be any Christian holiday home," she said.

"How so?"

"Well, you have a Christmas tree, and it's decorated and…is that mistletoe?"

"It is, and Abe is headed this way, so if you don't want the old coot to buss you, step away."

"Who says I don't want your dad to give me a kiss? Look, I'm moving right under it, so there." Abe smiled and obliged.

"Merry Christmas," he said.

"And a…what? Happy, merry, joyful…Chanukah."

"Any and all will do. Let me get you a dish." Abe wheeled and headed for the dining room, where he proceeded to heap food on a plate.

"Good Lord, he isn't going to eat all that, is he?"

"Actually, he's filling it for you. Abe eats like a bird."

"One of you two Schwartzes will be the death of me. Wow, thank you, Abe. Can I get a doggie bag?"

"She's a card, Ike, you keep her close. You ain't getting any younger and you ain't much of a catch either."

"He really loves me. He just says those things to keep me humble."

"Somebody has to. Anyway, it's all very…um, ecumenical."

"You think? Actually it's primarily Jewish."

"That's a what, a Chanukah tree, then? Come on."

"The trees, evergreen, even the mistletoe, have nothing to do with the Christian holiday. They are pagan symbols co-opted by Christians somewhere along the way. It is their genius. The menorah on the mantle is Jewish, and so are the dreidels on the tree."

"The whats?"

"Tops. Chanukah toys for children."

"No Christian symbols here at all?"

"Just the one."

"Where?"

"We put a star on the top of the tree."

"The only Christmas I know is trees, Santa Claus, and somebody singing 'White Christmas.'"

"That's an American shopping mall Christmas—sorry, holiday celebration. The courts have pretty much removed most of the Christian symbolism from public places."

"And Jesus is…?"

"The Holiday Infant. Not even my time, but I think that's pathetic. Sorry. Now I'm waiting for the ACLU to take them to court on the rest of it as well. Separation of church and state and all that. Paganism is a religion. In fact, the Supreme Court has said so. Satanism, Wicca, they all come under the designation of religion."

"And?"

"And, I reckon that means we'll be taking Halloween out of the schools next. No more witches and devils. The pity is, we pride ourselves on our pluralistic society, and now we are tearing it down in the name of not offending anyone."

"You're on a rant, aren't you?"

"Just a little one—in honor of the season. See, it's as though you have a box of precious stones and you crush the red ones because they offend the green ones. And then they are crushed because the blue ones have issues and pretty soon you have…?"

"I give up—what?"

"Sand. We are homogenizing our society and losing our brilliance."

"Oh, really—"

"You know the problems Old Europe has? They used to be homogeneous. Now they are faced with an influx of Turks, Africans, and Arabs, and they don't like it. They are being forced to become pluralistic. We are going the other way, and it worries me, that's all. Soon the level playing field of homogeneity will be attained, and even the vestiges of your pagan ancestors will have disappeared."

"But not *your* pagan ancestors?"

"No, our story begins at the beginning and does not include pagans in any of it, except for an occasional drop-in."

"Like my namesake?"

"Precisely. They are important to the story but only—"

"No 'but only,' Ike. Face it—no Ruth, no King David, end of story."

"Well, we might assume that the Lord could have managed a David some other way."

"I know little or nothing about theology and less about Judaism, but I will bet you a night of sweaty bed wrestling your scholars would not agree. If I understand the book your mother gave me right, it's that story or no story."

"You're probably right. And that leads you to what conclusion?"

"That your more-or-less Christian mom is a better Jew than either you or your dad is now, or ever will be. She is on to something."

"What?"

"It's not for me to say, but I need to talk to her and soon."

Other guests began to arrive and Ike and Ruth were distracted for the moment. Leon Weitz cornered Abe, who smiled and began one of his anecdotes about politics in the Commonwealth. Blake Fisher came in looking much too young and alive and escorting a beautiful young woman, who, he claimed, played the organ. To Ruth's chagrin, he confirmed Ike's description of the decorations. Several other couples arrived, people she did not know but assumed were family or friends. Ike greeted them and brought most over to her to be introduced. Had she been raised in Virginia, she would have recognized most of the names as belonging to former governors, senators, and the upper echelon of Commonwealth politics. She smiled and tried to recall the memory tricks she'd been taught to retain names. She failed.

From time to time, individuals and small groups disappeared down the hall. They returned within minutes. She looked at one group and raised one eyebrow to Ike.

"They are wishing my mother the best for the holiday—saying hello, maybe a disguised goodbye."

"Can I...?"

"She'll call you, Ruth. She's saving you for later. Eat your food."

"I did. I ate more than I ever do and I didn't make a dent in this pile of cholesterol-enhancing...didn't anyone ever teach you about salad?"

"It's not the season for salad. From Thanksgiving to the first of January, we eat 'til it hurts. You are not participating. You need to get into the program."

"So arrest me, Sheriff. You'll never take me alive, copper—at least not with this in my system."

Ruth spent the next hour mingling with the guests. She put her still-heaping plate down only to have Abe hand her a new one. She stuck to the punch, which she assumed was nonalcoholic. It wasn't. She lost track of Ike. She scanned the crowd in the parlor and the dining room without success. She put her plate down again. No Abe, no threat of a third. Finally she caught sight of the two of them in the hallway.

"She would like to see you, Ruth," Abe said. "She's pretty worn out with all the coming and going but she said to send you in."

"I won't stay long." She made her way down the hall toward the rear of the house. The door stood ajar. She tapped lightly, paused, and went in. Ike's mother seemed much as she remembered from her last visit—paler maybe, but that could be the effect of the candles flickering on the mantle.

"Happy Chanukah and Merry Christmas, too," Ruth said. She took a seat next to the bed.

"How are you, Ruth?"

"Very well, thank you."

"They think I don't know about moving the party up. They think I might not make it for another week. Men!"

Ruth smiled and took her hand. "Ike said you wanted to see me, especially."

"I do. He's a good man, isn't he, my Isaac?"

"Yes, he is. A little unruly at times and annoyingly independent."

"He's like his father. More than either will admit. They go at each other…oh my, the arguments they get into. I think they take the other side just to be perverse. You ever notice that with Isaac?"

"Does it snow in Maine?"

"What? I guess it must but—"

"I'm sorry, figure of speech. Your son can be the most contrary man I ever met. Yes, he will deliberately bait me. If I say black, he'll say white. Sometimes I could—"

"He must care for you very much. He only does that with people he loves."

"Well, I—"

"It's all right. Now tell me, what about my story? Did you read it?"

"Yes, it and several others. It's history but it's more than that, isn't it?"

"Yes, a whole lot more. And?"

Ruth thought for a long moment. Was she really ready for this? She looked into the luminous questioning eyes of the dying woman opposite her. She blinked back a tear.

"David is a fine name for a boy," she murmured.

"Yes, isn't it? Thank you, Ruth."

Chapter Forty-six

Ike cradled the phone and frowned. Steve Bolt had sounded like a drowning man, first because he was obviously frightened and second because a weak cell phone connection made him sound like he was speaking underwater. He wanted to know if Ike knew anything. Ike repeated the things he'd said before. He listened to Bolt's retelling of the plan to rob Kamarov. He wanted to know what his chances were; if he told everything, could he get immunity. Ike wasn't certain what sort of immunity he wanted but agreed as long as whatever he had to confess didn't involve grand theft or murder in any of its prosecutorial forms he had a chance. He had to explain the differences between manslaughter and first degree. Bolt apparently remembered enough of the same information from an old *Law and Order* episode and agreed.

"Is there anything else? Anything you forgot to tell me?"

"Well, there was the license plate on the car."

"The one you were kidnapped in?"

"Yeah."

"What about it?"

"I got it."

Ike wrote the number on a scrap of paper and said he might need Bolt to testify in court at some time in the future, and Bolt said that he'd have to find him first and hung up. Apparently he didn't know that cell phones could be traced, and while pinpointing the exact location might be difficult, they could get close enough. More importantly, Ike had also learned enough from Leon Weitz to know that once the right people were told about Whaite's killing and that Bolt might be implicated, mountain justice would kick in. Whaite's extended family would find Bolt's hiding place and spit him out like a watermelon pit.

◇◇◇

At one forty-five the search warrants from Floyd County arrived. Since the credit cards would have been stolen and the hit and run occurred in their jurisdiction, the county sheriff promised help as needed. Ike had nothing else to do until Sam and Karl arrived. Two o'clock, he'd said. He looked at his watch. Three minutes to go.

The door opened and Sam and Karl blew in with a gust of cold air.

"I assume you had to turn in your service piece with your suspension. I can loan you one or—"

"I have one, backup, no problem."

"We'll go in plainclothes, I think. Stick your gun in your belt, purse, whatever, and let's go."

◇◇◇

Hollis limped into the bar. He'd lost one of his crutches the night before. He didn't remember how or when. Hollis only drank beer and assumed that since it only had twelve percent alcohol, he could never get drunk. He, like many young and, in his case, stupid people, never connected their behavior with reality and went careening drunkenly through life or down highways, a threat to themselves and those around them. Donnie sat in the corner looking smug. Hollis wasn't sure if he wanted to sit with him or not. He'd heard rumors.

"You hear about the fire police?" he said, and sat down.

"How many times I got to tell you, they aren't called fire police?"

"What did he want with you?"

"Nothing I couldn't handle, and I guess they'll be some respect for me around here from now on."

"Why?"

"You don't think that police's car just happened to hit that tree, do you?"

"Jeeze, what did you do, Donnie?"

"I ain't saying, but nobody messes with my stuff."

The Creator, for reasons known only to him, had wired Hollis' brain differently than the rest of humankind. Those who knew him realized he could read and did so, voluminously. He had a native intelligence in there somewhere that often popped out in the most unlikely places and times, but at the same time they said he didn't have the brains of a hop toad. Even so, in the confused circuitry of his central nervous system, he heard Donnie's unspoken message and intuitively knew he needed to put some distance between himself and his friend.

"Gotta go," he said, stood, and winced as he put weight on his bad leg.

"Sit down, you just got here." Donnie pulled him back into the booth by his shirttail. "Beer," he shouted to the barkeep.

"Come and get it, Mr. Mountain Man." Several of the regulars laughed. Donnie's face turned red.

"You'd better watch it or—"

"Or what? You going to pull that little pop gun of yours and—"

The door swung open and three people sauntered in. Two were abnormally tall—a black guy and a redheaded woman. The third, tall enough, looked hard, like he could be trouble. Nobody needed to see badges to be told they were police. Nobody except Donnie and Hollis.

"I gotta go," Hollis repeated and stood well out of Donnie's reach this time.

"That's them," the tall woman said. "That's both of them."

Hollis swallowed and looked behind him, hoping that she meant someone else. He thought about running but the three of them stood between him and the door and, besides, he had enough trouble walking. Running was out of the question. Out of the corner of his eye he saw Donnie's hand move toward his pocket—the pocket where he usually kept his pistol.

"Don't even think about it, Oldham," the middle guy said. He flipped open his parka and flashed a badge. Hollis saw the butt of the Magnum in the guy's belt. The wind went out of him and he collapsed back in the booth.

"Donald Oldham, I have a warrant for your arrest for grand theft larceny. Stolen credit cards," the middle guy said and added, "And you, too, son. You're Hollis somebody, aren't you? What's your full name, Hollis?"

Hollis might have answered had he not fainted dead away.

Chapter Forty-seven

Ike stared at Oldham's hand. If it didn't stop moving toward his pocket, he'd have to draw down on the kid and he didn't want that. One more inch and he'd do it. His fingers closed over the butt of his pistol and tensed. At the moment he would have drawn, Karl took two long strides to Oldham and pinioned his arms at his sides. He then flipped him bodily out of the booth and face down on the table, knocking over a half-filled glass of beer. Oldham flailed about but Karl caught each wrist in turn and cuffed him. He rummaged in his pockets and withdrew an old colt .38 Police Special, a knife, a wallet, and four credit cards. Hollis slid off the bench and into a rumpled heap on the floor. Four men in the bar stood and applauded.

◇◇◇

The Floyd County Sheriff's Department provided an interview room and a holding cell. Hollis began blubbering his story the minute he came to. He had to be stopped until he had been Mirandized. Once done, he began again and spilled the whole story. Two deputies were sent to the middle school to pick up his brother, Dermont. Another search warrant arrived to allow a search of Hollis' house. Ike guessed the FBI would be the next group in if Sam found what he suspected on the father's hard drive. Hollis' parents arrived and were ushered into the Sheriff's office to wait. Ike let Donnie cool his heels in the holding cell. His gun was bagged and sent to the local lab for ballistics tests.

Ike and Karl, accompanied by a Floyd County deputy, drove to Donnie's house. Ike sent the deputy into the house to search while he and Karl lifted the tarp from the truck in the backyard. T.J. had been right. The passenger side door and front quarter panel were badly damaged and showed evidence of red paint. It looked as though Donnie had tried to wipe it away but failed.

"Well, well," Ike said. "If Sam is right, I guess we got our guy." He bent over the fender and flaked off a sample of the red paint into an envelope. "We'll need a tow truck to take this to the impound yard. In the meantime, I'll get the lab working on this sample."

Karl had climbed into the bed. He flashed his light into the corners and then lay flat and peered under the tool box. He reached in and grabbed something.

"I have a shoe," he said.

"Just one?"

"Yeah. It's been here a while, I think. It's wet and the heel is loose, must not have been nailed on tight enough. It's not scuffed, though."

"You have gloves on, right?" Karl held up a latex-sheathed hand and gave Ike a look. "Sorry, had to be sure. Hand me the shoe and I'll bag it."

Ike took the shoe and held it up at eye level. It was the mate to Kamarov's missing loafer. He turned his back to Karl and twisted the heel. The old-fashioned roll of microfilm dropped into his hand. He slipped the shoe, its heel restored, into a bag, and palmed the film.

"We'll let the Floyd people finish up here, Karl. We have everything we need to sweat Donnie Oldham."

"Too bad it's out of our jurisdiction. I know the folks in Picketsville would dearly love to put this guy away."

"Oh, we'll have our turn. Don't forget, for now, Kamarov is ours."

"This guy did the Russian?"

"Yep."

◇◇◇

Donnie sat in the interview room with his arms folded across his chest. Ike sat opposite and stared at him for a full minute. Donnie squirmed and finally could not endure the silence.

"You got nothing on me," he said.

Ike shrugged. "You've been read your Miranda rights?"

"Yeah, yeah. Big deal."

"So why did you force Deputy Billingsly off the road?"

"Who says I did?"

"I say you did. There is red paint on the damaged side of your truck. We have a witness who will testify it was not there the day before the crash. You slammed into him that night and forced him into a tree. You killed him just as surely as if you'd shot him with your pistol."

"You can't prove it. I scraped against some red-painted buffers at the Exxon station."

"No, that won't work. See, you'd have to identify the station and then there'd be witnesses who would say you were never there and, from where you are sitting, just figuring out which gas station to pick might pose a problem."

"It don't matter. Red paint is red paint."

"Not this time. The man whose car you smacked into spent hours restoring it. It is, or was, a collector's car, a show car, and he painted it himself."

"So what?"

"When he went to buy paint, he got a deal, a bargain. He painted it with paint from a Harley-Davidson motorcycle supply house. You want to calculate the odds of another car being in your area that night painted with red motorcycle paint? See, the formulas for paints are fairly specific. Now, if he'd been driving a Ford, you might argue the paint could have come from any of the cars in the line—Lincoln, Mercury…But a motorcycle red Chevy Chevelle? No, you're cooked, Oldham. The best you can do is plead out—an accident, slippery roads, all that."

Donnie looked stricken. "Motorcycle—"

"Paint. Right. You will be remanded for that here in Floyd County. As soon as the lab work comes back on the paint, you can expect to be rearrested on at least three charges relating to Deputy Billingsly's death."

"Well, does that mean I can go now?"

"Oh my, no. Is that what you thought I said? No, there's still the credit card theft. We've spoken to your friend Bolt, and though he would rather not, he will testify you knew about the cards."

"I don't know what you're talking about."

"Hollis talked. His brother practically wet his pants when the police hauled him in. He talked, too. We have surveillance camera photos of you at several banks using them. Since you went over the state line to do so, and since bank robbery is technically a federal offense, you will spend some time with the FBI soon. Special Agent Hedrick is on the phone with them now. He's having a good week, as it turns out, but that's not your concern. The FBI will want you to stay put, so no, you aren't going anywhere."

"Federal? Hey, it was all Hollis' idea."

"I don't think so. No, that seems very unlikely. No one will believe Hollis came up with that idea. It seems so unfair, doesn't it? Who'd have thought a couple of credit cards would get you in so much trouble."

Donnie Oldham was never very big, but at that moment he seemed to shrink down to the size of a ten-year-old.

"How did you come by the cards?"

"I found them. I figured, finders keepers."

"Wrong answer. Here's what I think happened. You worked out the deal with Bolt to break in and take the cards after Harris left for Richmond, but you got greedy. You decided to rob Harris one day early, only you didn't figure on him being a problem because he looked old and out of shape."

Oldham ran his fingers through his thin hair and started to speak.

"Not yet, kid. So, you figure you'll wait until he gets his cash and then you'll rob him, only instead of handing you his wallet, he moves in on you. I knew him, he would have. So, what happened? Nothing to say…?

"Okay. What next…? He grabs your gun and in the struggle, it goes off. Naturally, you panic and pump four more rounds into him. You put the body in your truck and haul him out to the country. Am I close? Never mind, it doesn't matter. The problem is—you dumped the body of the man you knew as Randall Harris in my backyard. Very stupid of you. If you'd dropped him anywhere else, another six feet farther west, even, you might have gotten away with it. But I recognized the man, see? His real name was Alexei Kamarov and he was, shall we say, connected. You wouldn't believe all the people and agencies that have been looking for him."

"You don't know what you're—"

"Spare me the tough guy crap. We dug bullets out of him and we have your pistol at ballistics. They will match. Then we have the shoe."

"Shoe?"

"The dead man's shoe. It must have been dark when you dumped the body. When we found him, he was missing a shoe. It wasn't on the path from the road to the spot where you dumped him, so it had to be somewhere else. Guess what we found in your truck? Deputy Billingsly must have seen it that night. That's what he was doing in your truck, but you couldn't know that. You probably thought he was after you for the credit cards."

"I thought he was a fire investigator. He had that red car—"

"He must have seen the shoe and would have asked for a warrant to search your truck the next day. The shoe puts Kamarov in your vehicle.

"The shoe, the ballistics, and Bolt will put you away forever, Oldham, and since murder, even murder two, outranks both bank robbery and hit and run on the big crime hit parade, I get to keep you."

Epilogue

Charlie Garland had his feet up on the desk when Ike arrived.

"How'd you get here so fast?" Ike said.

"You called. I came—*veni, vidi, vici,* or something—Julius Caesar."

"I know. You didn't answer my question, and how about removing your size eleven triple E penny loafers from my desk."

"Helicopter."

"News Channel 4?"

"No, government issue. They had a delivery to make in Roanoke anyway, and I hitched a ride. They will be back for me in thirty minutes. Can you tell me what I need to know in that time or will you have to fly back to Langley with me?"

"There's not much to tell, Charlie. I called you down here to give you a present and close the file on the Russians."

"What have you got?"

"Well, they were definitely the men who snatched Bolt. I ran the license plate he gave me. It turns out to be a vehicle leased to their embassy. Not diplomatic plates. Just a car they used for odd jobs, you might say. I'm guessing they were the same ones who torched Bolt's house and popped the guy in DC. You can check that bit up there. There is nothing either of us can do about that."

"Right. You said you had a present for me. Couldn't you have just sent it? Do you know how cold it is in a government-issue helicopter?"

"I didn't want the Agency mail room to have a shot at it without your seeing it first."

"Okay…what have you got for me?"

Ike slipped the roll of microfilm from its envelope and laid it on the desk. Charlie let his feet drop to the floor with a crash. He bent over the films. He pushed his glasses up on his forehead and looked some more.

Ike pulled open a desk drawer. "There's a magnifying glass in here."

"Thanks. Do I dare ask where these came from?"

"Let's just say they are a gift from our late friend."

Charlie lurched back and nearly tipped over the chair. "You may have saved the Agency's rear end, Ike."

"Oh well, I could have done worse. Here's the rest. There is a Bureau man you should call named Andover Crisp. He's the guy who is, or was, running the black program. You should tell him that the game is up and that Kamarov will be buried down here. You should also tell him that whatever Kamarov promised is gone forever."

"You could tell him, Ike. After all, you're the policeman with an interest."

"I am in enough hot water with the FBI as it is. You do it."

"That's it?"

"Just about."

Charlie stood and grinned. "You know, Ike, a while back I thought we should bring you back in. We could make that happen, you know. Now I see you're going to be much more useful to us on the outside." He strode to the door, shrugged on his coat, and left. Ike listened to the thwocka, thwocka, thwocka of chopper blades and shook his head.

◇◇◇

"How many times have you asked me to go away with you for a weekend?" Ruth fixed Ike with an unblinking stare. This had to be important.

"I don't know. Let's see, maybe once a week for six months, so that would be—"

"A lot, and I've always turned you down, right? Okay, I have a conference to go to in Toronto the second week in January. We can go a few days early and stay over the weekend. You put somebody in charge of your—"

"I just lost my only really experienced deputy. I'm not sure if I can—"

"You find somebody, Schwartz. You are going to the CASE Conference with me next month. That's it."

"I...okay. Give me the dates and, wait a minute, Toronto in January? That's like in Canada, Ruth. They have snow and ice and cold. Can't you find a conference in someplace warm, like the Bahamas or Maui?"

"I'm giving a speech or I wouldn't be going at all. So, this is the one I am going to with you and," her voice softened, "we need time and we need to talk, Ike. Important talk and we'll never do it if either of us is within fifty miles of our offices. You understand?"

He read the concern in her eyes and there was more—something new.

"I'll have to buy a suitcase, a necktie and...should I...? Oh my God."

"What is it? You have a funny look. If it's about not going—"

"No, no, I just thought of something."

"What?"

"When all this started—the Kamarov business—Whaite called and asked if I wanted him to shove the body over the state line and let them handle it. It was a funny thing to say at the time." Ike closed his eyes and shook his head. "It just hit me, everything that went down after that—Whaite's death, Sam, Karl, even this trip—none of it would have happened if I had just said yes instead of no."

To receive a free catalog of Poisoned Pen Press titles, please contact us in one of the following ways:

Phone: 1-800-421-3976
Facsimile: 1-480-949-1707
Email: info@poisonedpenpress.com
Website: www.poisonedpenpress.com

Poisoned Pen Press
6962 E. First Ave. Ste. 103
Scottsdale, AZ 85251